FRIENDS
OF ACPL

3 1833 05817 8036

D0966718

MISS JACOBSON'S JOURNEY

MISS JACOBSON'S JOURNEY

CAROLA DUNN

THORNDIKE
CHIVERS

This Large Print edition is published by Thorndike Press, Waterville, Maine, USA and by BBC Audiobooks Ltd, Bath, England.

Thorndike Press, a part of Gale, Cengage Learning.

Copyright © 1992 by Carola Dunn.

The moral right of the author has been asserted.

ALL RIGHTS RESERVED

All of the characters and events portrayed in this work are fictitious.

The text of this Large Print edition is unabridged.

Other aspects of the book may vary from the original edition.

Set in 16 pt. Plantin.

Printed on permanent paper.

LIBRARY OF CONGRESS CATALOGING-IN-PUBLICATION DATA

Dunn, Carola.
  Miss Jacobson's journey / by Carola Dunn.
    p. cm. — (Thorndike Press large print gentle romance)
  ISBN-13: 978-1-4104-2114-2 (alk. paper)
  ISBN-10: 1-4104-2114-7 (alk. paper)
  1. Large type books. I. Title.
PR6054.U537M58 2009
823'.914—dc22   2009030314

BRITISH LIBRARY CATALOGUING-IN-PUBLICATION DATA AVAILABLE

Published in 2009 in the U.S. by arrangement with Carola Dunn.
Published in 2010 in the U.K. by arrangement with the author.

U.K. Hardcover: 978 1 408 47716 8 (Chivers Large Print)
U.K. Softcover: 978 1 408 47717 5 (Camden Large Print)

Printed in the United States of America
1 2 3 4 5 6 7 13 12 11 10 09

MISS JACOBSON'S JOURNEY

CHAPTER 1

London 1802

"But I don't want to get married!" Miriam scowled mutinously at the gilt-framed mirror, where dark red ringlets were taking shape under the skillful hands of her abigail. "At least, not yet. It's less than two months since I finished school. I want to see the world. I want to dance and have fun."

"God willing, there'll be dancing aplenty at your wedding, Miss Miriam."

"Oh Hannah, I want to go to balls and assemblies. I told you, several of my schoolfriends have promised to invite me when the Little Season begins."

"Hold still now, child. It's fated that all men should be fools but a girl needs a husband and how are you to find one at your balls and assemblies, tell me? You'll meet none but *goyim,* for sure."

"Perhaps I shall marry a Gentile." Miriam remembered her best friend's brother, who once came to visit the Seminary for Young Ladies where she had been educated. Tall, blond, with twinkling blue eyes, he had driven up to the door in a dashing curricle and taken the two girls out to tea. She had dreamed for weeks of those broad shoulders, fashionably clad in wrinkle-less blue super-fine. Even now the memory of his teasing grin made her feel weak at the knees.

Hannah's horrified exclamation banished the vision. "Marry a Gentile! God forbid. You'd never be able to bring up your children in the faith of their forefathers."

"I haven't precisely been brought up as a good Jew."

"More shame to them I won't name, sending you off to that goy school where they don't observe the Sabbath, let alone the Holy Days."

"They didn't make me go to church on Sunday."

"Nor to the synagogue on Saturday, more's the pity. It's my belief the master's repented of such ungodliness, and that's why he's so pleased with the young fellow the matchmaker's found for you. A real scholar he is, I've heard, studying to be a rabbi. Speaks Hebrew and knows the Torah by heart. And rich as King Solomon besides, for he's the only son of a moneylender in the City."

"So Mama told me." Sighing, Miriam wondered whether any of her schoolfellows, after their chatter of marquises and earls, would have to settle for a parson. Yet perhaps being a rabbi's wife wouldn't be too dreadfully dull, if the man her father had chosen turned out to be handsome and amusing and not too bound by tradition.

"You should be thanking God that he's a young man, not a greybeard. There now." With a last twirl of the hairbrush, Hannah stepped back to admire her handiwork.

"Thank you, Hannah dear." Miriam stood up and smoothed the skirts of her pale green mull-muslin morning gown. The finest Mechlin lace trimmed the demure high neckline and the cuffs of the long sleeves; bodice and hem were embroidered with darker green vine leaves, while a matching satin ribbon encircled the high waist and tied in a bow behind. Her stylish elegance gave her confidence.

"Pretty as the Queen of Sheba," the abigail observed with satisfaction. "To think the baby I rocked in her cradle is ready for a husband! Your bridegroom will fall in love with you at first sight, Miss Miriam, God willing. Just the jade earrings, now, and you'd best be off to show the mistress."

The delicately carved jade fastened at her ears, Miriam crossed the hall to her mother's dressing room, knocked, and entered.

"I am ready, Mama."

Mrs. Jacobson, seated at her dressing table in a lilac silk wrap, turned to inspect her daughter. The wife of a wealthy importer of furs, she was generally much occupied in entertaining her husband's associates and in charity work, to the detriment of her relationship with her only child. Miriam felt she hardly knew her, and was relieved when she nodded approval.

"Excellent. Only you are a trifle pale, my dear. Perhaps the tiniest dab of rouge — no, we must not forget that your suitor is a Talmudic scholar. Pinch your cheeks a little."

Miriam complied, but pointed out, "My complexion is naturally pale, Mama. I doubt it will leave any lasting effect."

"Then you must do it again just before the matchmaker arrives," said her mother sharply. "You have been instructed how to behave, Miriam, and I trust you will not use this occasion for a display of wilful temperament."

Bowing her head with apparent meekness, she listened in rebellious silence as the instructions were repeated, with a stress on

10

the necessity for a modest, compliant demeanour.

"You are most fortunate," Mrs. Jacobson concluded, "that your father has gone to the trouble of finding you so excellent a match. You must strive to deserve his kindness, and to earn a like benevolence from your husband. Pray go down now and remind your uncle that he is to sit in the drawing room today. The rest of the family will arrive shortly. I must dress."

Miriam curtsied and withdrew. A lecture from her mother on female submissiveness was less than convincing, she decided as she made her way downstairs. The absence of the slightest speck of dust on the elaborate tracery of the wrought iron balusters bore witness to Mrs. Jacobson's absolute rule over her household. And though she verbally upheld her husband's authority and did not meddle in his business, he almost always deferred to her judgement in other matters. She even aspired to control her brother, though his gentle disregard of her suggestions frequently defeated her.

Thinking of Uncle Amos, Miriam smiled. She had grown fond of the kind, if absent-minded, Doctor Bloom since her return from school had coincided with his unexpected arrival from the Continent. He had left England when she was a small child, to study medicine in Germany. Since then, occasional letters made their way through the turmoil of revolution and war in Europe to announce his receipt of his diploma, his marriage, his extensive travels. The sketchy accounts of his journeys in pursuit of medical research fascinated his young niece.

The Peace of Amiens and the death of the beloved wife who had sheltered him from the practical side of life had combined to bring him back to England. Since his homecoming, his more detailed accounts of his sojourns in far-off lands had whetted Miriam's appetite for adventure.

She grimaced as she opened the library door. No doubt marriage was going to put a stop to all hope of adventure.

As she expected, Uncle Amos was seated at the long table surrounded by sheaves of paper and open books. His patriarchal grey beard and gold-rimmed spectacles made him look older than his forty-odd years. Absorbed in his work, he seemed not to notice her entrance.

"Uncle, I beg your pardon for interrupting, but Mama asked me to remind you that she requests your presence in the drawing room."

Taking off his spectacles, he smiled at her

vaguely. "I have not enough data to draw credible conclusions. I must go back to Russia, but how can I manage without my Shirah? If I have to make arrangements for transportation and food and lodging, as well as treating the sick, I shall have little time for collecting and collating information."

"Perhaps you ought to seek another wife, uncle."

He closed his eyes and pinched the bridge of his nose, a deep sorrow crossing his face. "No, I shall never remarry. Perhaps you are too young to understand, my dear, but it would be disloyal to her memory. Now, what were you saying about the drawing room?"

"The matchmaker is bringing my suitor today."

"Ah yes, I remember. *Mazal tov,* Miriam. May you share as much happiness as I did with Shirah."

"Thank you, Uncle. It seems tradition dictates that all the family should gather to approve him — and to add to my embarrassment."

"If you prefer it, I shall stay here."

"Oh no, please come. It is my other uncles and aunts and cousins I could well do without, but you will be a support to me."

Smiling at her, he pushed back his chair,

came round the table and kissed her cheek. "I wish you happiness," he said again, "and I shall do my best to support you."

They went through to the drawing room, a long, high-ceilinged room with tall windows overlooking the garden. Not for the first time, Miriam wished her mother had not chosen to decorate it in crimson and ivory. She was sure the rich reds of the curtains, the Turkey carpet, and the brocade-covered chairs made her hair look insipid brown, or worse, clashed with it. Her cheeks seemed the paler in contrast, too. Surreptitiously she pinched them. How dreadful if, instead of falling in love with her, her suitor took a dislike to her on sight!

Annoyed with herself, she recognized an unaccustomed nervousness. Where was the calm common sense her teachers had so often praised, even as they castigated her stubborn determination to go her own way? Her palms were damp and her mouth was dry.

She turned resolutely to Uncle Amos, catching him in the act of opening the book he had brought with him. "What information is it you need in Poland?" she asked.

"I told you, I believe, that I am investigating the incidence of diabetes in Jews? I have much data for Germany and Poland, and it seems clear that in those countries Jews are more prone than Gentiles to develop the disease. But when I was in Russia I failed to obtain the relevant numbers for Gentiles." He sighed. "I should have liked, also, to compare the Ashkenazim with the Sephardic Jews of Spain and the Mediterranean area."

"There are both Ashkenazim and Sephardim in England, are there not? Can you not work right here at home?"

"The lines are too intermingled here. You see, the various comparisons are necessary to determine whether the high incidence is due to diet or to inherited factors. And there are other illnesses to be studied, such as the one that cripples and kills the children of Jews but rarely strikes Gentiles." He sighed. "So much work to be done!"

Miriam's father came in just then. A heavyset, good-humoured man with a bald patch and shaved chin balanced by luxuriant side whiskers, he kissed his curtsying daughter then took both her hands and looked her up and down.

"A beauty, just as your mother was. I hope this young man she has found is worthy of you, my love."

"I thought he was your choice, Papa." She should have guessed that her mother was responsible.

"No, no, it was all settled between your mother and the matchmaker, except for the financial side, of course. I've not even met your bridegroom, only his father. The settlements are most satisfactory, and you cannot do better than to wed a man with a true understanding and respect for the Torah and the Talmud. I have been remiss in my duties, I fear."

The tip of Miriam's tongue quivered with a tart and most unfilial question as to whether the sudden discovery of religion was his idea or her mother's. She managed to bite it back. Her parents' generation, she realized, busy with the worldly opportunities newly opening as society grew more tolerant, had let the religious observances of their forefathers lapse without much consideration. Perhaps her own generation would succeed in reconciling the demands of the modern world with the claims of the faith of Abraham and Moses.

Once again, she wondered whether her chosen husband was a strict follower or a liberal interpreter of all the endless rules and rituals. Perhaps he would utterly disapprove of her. The nervous agitation she had succeeded in banishing began to reappear.

It turned to irritation when, a few minutes

after her mother's arrival, the butler ushered in a dozen relatives. Her unmarried female cousins flocked about her, giggling and offering envious congratulations. Their sparrowlike twittering almost drowned the butler's next announcement.

"Mrs. Weiss and Mr. Cohen."

Miriam scarcely noticed the matchmaker's vivid purple pelisse and the fruitbowl of matching grapes on her extraordinary bonnet. Of her words she heard only the excited, self-congratulatory tone. She was staring in horror at the black-clad apparition that sidled into the room after the woman.

In only one respect did he match her dreams: he was tall, or would have been if not for his stooped shoulders. He was also thin as a rake, pallidly sallow, with weak, lackluster, slightly red-rimmed eyes and dangling sidecurls. A wispy attempt at a beard adorned his chin, bearing out the impression that he was no more than two or three years older than Miriam — a mere youth, not a man.

Her father took her hand and began to lead her forward. She jerked away. "No! I will not." Looking round wildly, she saw Uncle Amos and rushed to his side in a swirl of skirts. She turned to face with defiance her aghast family, the flabbergasted matchmaker, and the gawky boy they wanted her to wed. "You cannot expect me to . . . I'm going to go to Europe with Uncle Amos, to look after him. His work is far more important than marriage."

As her furious mother bore down upon her, she saw the boy's face flush a painful red. For a moment her heart misgave her — how thoughtlessly cruel she had been to humiliate him so! — but then the expostulating crowd surrounded her, hiding him from her sight. Her attention turned to defending herself.

No one else was taking any notice of him, either. By the time Miriam had been persuaded at least to make his acquaintance, he was long gone.

One chilly morning towards the end of September, the crimson drawing room was the scene of a subdued farewell. After four weeks, Mrs. Jacobson still had not quite forgiven her errant daughter, but at the last moment she softened and folded Miriam in a warm embrace.

Miriam kissed her rose-perfumed cheek. "Don't worry, Mama. I shall take care of Uncle Amos and Hannah will take care of me. And this time next year," she couldn't resist adding, "when I come home, we shall

set about looking for a bridegroom together."

Her mother sighed and at last reluctantly
admitted, "You are very much as I was at
your age. God preserve and bless you, my
child."

Her father escorted her out to the luxurious travelling carriage he had provided,
which was to go with them on the packet to
Calais. Aaron Jacobson had a low opinion
of French carriage-builders.

Handing her in, he leaned forward to tuck
a fur rug around her knees and a heavy
purse into her hand. "For fripperies," he
whispered. "Your uncle has plenty for expenses."

He withdrew as Hannah climbed in on
the opposite side and handed Miriam her
huge grey muff of rare chinchilla furs from
South America. Uncle Amos joined them,
carrying a book, with his gloved finger
marking his place. The carriage started moving.

Miriam looked back, waving to her father
until they turned the corner of the street.
Then she settled back on the bottle-green
velvet squabs, straightened her chinchilla-
trimmed pelerine, and beamed at her uncle.

"At last," she said, her brown eyes sparkling, "on the way to adventure!"

"God willing," said Hannah.

CHAPTER 2

France 1811

The diligence from Lyon lurched and jolted at a snail's pace through the outskirts of Paris. The younger of two shabbily dressed women turned from the grimy, rattling carriage window and addressed her grey-haired companion in a foreign language. Their weary fellow-passengers took no notice; Napoleon's empire brought all sorts of strangers to his capital city.

"Do you remember the first time we drove into Paris, in my father's carriage?" Miriam said in Yiddish. "How comfortable it was!"

"And a nice price it brought when you managed to persuade your uncle to sell it. Ah, all men are fools but Amos Bloom was a sainted fool, may his name be a blessing."

Hannah spoke Yiddish with a strong English accent, but her French and German were even worse. It was not safe to speak English. The resumption of the

French war with England in 1803 had prevented their planned return home, and Napoleon's subsequent conquest of most of Europe had made their mother-tongue a private luxury.

"I miss him so." Miriam sniffed unhappily.

Hannah patted her hand in its darned woollen mitten. "As well you may, child, for what we are to do without him only God knows."

"I want to go home." She fell silent, her mind ranging back over the memorable years of travel. She had seen most of the continent, and she didn't regret a moment, but that was over now. Scarce a month had passed since Uncle Amos, always careless of his own health, had succumbed to an inflammation of the lungs. Losing him changed everything. Now Miriam longed to settle down, to marry and bring up a family.

England's blockade and Napoleon's Continental System were porous, she knew. Now and then on arriving in a new city they had found money awaiting them, credited to her father for Canadian beaver or South American chinchilla furs smuggled across the Channel. Yet she had no idea how to go about contacting smugglers. Her only hope was that Monsieur Benjamin would be able to advise her.

At last the diligence turned into the rue du Bouloi and thence into the coach yard. The door opened, the step was let down. Miriam descended and turned to help Hannah, who moved stiffly after six days on the road. Their boxes were unloaded, and Miriam, in fluent French, arranged for them to be kept until she sent for them.

Only an hour or two remained of the chilly March day. What she would do if the Benjamins were away from home she didn't dare to think.

The narrow streets of Paris were as filthy as she remembered them. The central gutters stank, and pedestrians huddled to the walls to avoid being trampled by horses' hooves, only to find themselves dodging piles of garbage outside every door. Piles of rubble still showed where the abandoned hôtels of the *ancien régime* had been demolished a dozen years ago, and wide areas of the town had been razed to make room for new splendours. Yet everywhere the new public buildings and monuments stood shrouded in rusting scaffolding, work at a halt as the Emperor's attention focussed on conquest.

By the time Miriam and her faithful

servant reached the rue du Mont-Blanc, their shoes and hems were black with glutinous mud. Here at least some attempt had been made to provide a pavement down each side of the street.

"This is the place, isn't it? It seems familiar." Miriam paused outside a milliner's shop, gazing with envious eyes at the elegant creations in the window. "Yes, 'Chez Fleury'. Look at that bonnet, Hannah, the one with the striped ribbons."

"No use pining for what you can't have. There's the door, Miss Miriam, squeezed in before the next shop."

The narrow passage was dark and dingy, shared by the rich on the first floor, the paupers in the garrets, and everyone in between. Two flights of steep stairs brought them to their destination. Miriam knocked and then held her breath, straining to hear the sound of approaching footsteps.

The door swung open, and there was fat Berthe in her black dress and spotless white apron.

"Mam'selle Jacobson! And Hannah!" She bustled them into the spacious vestibule, closing the door firmly on the squalid landing. "But where is the good doctor? *Ah, que madame sera ravie de vous revoir, mademoiselle.*"

"Monsieur and madame are at home, Berthe?"

"They are walking in the Luxembourg gardens. Monsieur has felt himself very well since Doctor Bloom adjusted his diet. The uncle follows you closely, mademoiselle?"

Berthe was overcome by the news of Doctor Bloom's death. Her double chins quivered and she wiped her eyes with her apron. When they came home, the elderly Monsieur and Madame Benjamin were no less distressed. Monsieur promised to recite Kaddish, the mourners' prayer, at the synagogue next Sabbath.

In her renewed grief, Miriam found comfort in the thought of God's praises and prayers for peace being said in her uncle's name. In Milan, too, where he had died, and in Lyon, where she and Hannah had stayed a few days with friends, Kaddish would be spoken for him. Amos Bloom had made himself loved wherever he went.

"Mais, la vie continue," said Madame at last. "What are your plans now, *ma chère?"*

Miriam explained that all she wanted was to go home to England. Monsieur promised, doubtfully, to make enquiries. Though retired, he had many contacts with merchants of all sorts, including importers and exporters, but he would have to be careful.

By then, Miriam was too tired to worry. After a hot bath — a real luxury in a city without a proper water supply — and a superb meal, she sank into the soft embrace of a feather bed and instantly fell asleep.

The reverberating boom of a cannon woke her next morning. Snuggling beneath the warm covers she counted the reports, hoping they didn't signify a victory over the English army in the Peninsula: one, two, three . . . twenty, twenty-one, twenty-two . . . From the street outside came shouts and cheering. Twenty-three, twenty-four . . . Miriam lost count.

Berthe came in, beaming, with a tray of hot chocolate and rolls. "I was sure the noise must have wakened mam'selle." She set the tray on a bedside table and drew the curtains at the window, admitting the sounds of rejoicing as the cannon's thunder at last came to an end.

"What is it?" Miriam sat up. "What has happened?"

"Twenty-one for a girl, a hundred and one for a boy. The Empress has borne a son. At last we have an heir to the throne, mam'selle. Today there will be *grande fête* in the streets. See, already the shops are closing, the crowds are dancing."

Slipping out of bed, Miriam went to join

26

the corpulent maid at the window. Apprentices were putting up shutters on the shops on the other side of the rue du Mont-Blanc, while from the upper windows people leaned, shouting and waving. In the street, some enterprising person had produced a banner painted with bees, Bonaparte's symbol, and the words, *"Vive le roi de Rome!"* Someone else sang:

"Et bon, bon, bon,
C'est un garçon,
Vive Napoléon!"

In no time the chant was taken up by the swirling crowds and the walls echoed to the sound.

Miriam was torn by conflicting feelings. The Emperor Napoleon had opened ghettos and emancipated the Jews as he marched across Europe, but he had brought death and destruction, too, and he was her country's bitter enemy. She watched in silence, until Berthe glanced down at her bare feet and exclaimed in horror.

"You will catch a cold, mam'selle. Return to bed this instant!"

To Miriam's disappointment, Madame advised against an expedition to see the celebrations. Fountains running with wine, she pointed out, were scarcely calculated to lead to decorous behaviour among the lower classes, and even at the best of times the soldiers quartered in Paris were a rowdy lot. Miriam was unpersuaded, but Hannah's refusal to set foot out of doors settled the matter.

Instead, while Hannah unpacked, cleaned and mended their scanty wardrobes, Miriam opened the scuffed red leather box containing her uncle's papers.

One day, she had promised him, she would set them in order and do her best to get them published. For the moment, she simply wanted to reduce the quantity as much as possible. Though she had helped Uncle Amos with his work and knew which documents could be spared, she hated to throw anything out, but she and Hannah might have to leave in a hurry and travel light.

She smiled as the little portraits she had drawn in the margins reminded her of old friends and patients. Uncle Amos had a tendency to forget names, but he never forgot a face.

For several days the labour of love kept her from dwelling on their difficult situation. The Benjamins, kind hosts, provided every comfort and showed no impatience to see them gone. Nonetheless, as time passed and Monsieur had no luck with his enquiries, Miriam began to think of seeking employment.

They had been in Paris for a week when Monsieur came home looking smug and announced, "At last, a possibility. There is a young man recently arrived here from Frankfurt, a Monsieur Jakob Rothschild, who, I have heard, is in close touch with his brother in London."

"In touch?" Miriam asked dubiously. "Do you mean he might be able to transfer some money from my father?"

"Better than that." He lowered his voice and glanced over his shoulder. "Monsieur Rothschild, *on dit,* occupies himself with bringing gold from London to Paris. Our Minister of Finance has reported to the Emperor that the British government fears being weakened by the outflow of bullion, so Monsieur le Ministre will not attempt to stop it."

"And you believe that where gold crosses the Channel in one direction, people may cross in the opposite direction?"

"*Précisément.* I have arranged that you will call on Monsieur Rothschild at 5, rue Napoléon, tomorrow morning. I shall send for a fiacre to pick you up at ten o'clock. All

I ask, ma chère Miriam, is that you are discreet."

"I shall not mention your name, monsieur, I assure you." Miriam went on to express her deep and sincere gratitude for his efforts in her behalf, but secretly she was disturbed. The thought of begging favours from those who were bleeding England of gold repelled her.

Later that evening, she mentioned her disquiet to Hannah.

"Now, Miss Miriam, you're not going to spoil everything!" said her abigail in alarm. "God forbid you should help England's enemies, but letting them help you's nothing to carp at."

"No, I suppose you are right. Wait, I have it! If they do send us by the same way the gold is coming here, I shall keep my eyes open and when we reach home I'll report all I see. Papa knows people in the government. Perhaps we'll be instrumental in stopping the wretches."

"Just don't you let on how you feel about them, or it's us'll be stopped in our tracks," groused Hannah, but she knew her mistress too well to try to dissuade her.

On the morrow, Miriam had Hannah arrange her hair in ringlets, instead of the practical coiled braids she usually wore. She dressed in her best morning gown, an aging periwinkle-blue silk she had had made in a small town in Germany that was never less than three years behind the Parisian modes. A grey woollen cloak completed the depressing ensemble. Hannah, in serviceable brown, clomped after her down the stairs to the fiacre.

Stepping into the dirty, dilapidated vehicle, Miriam wrinkled her nose, wishing her old-fashioned host had ordered one of the new, open cabriolets she had seen dashing about the town. However, she had more important matters on her mind. As they rattled through the streets, she rehearsed her carefully prepared appeal.

"If only I knew more about Jakob Rothschild," she said. "Monsieur Benjamin described him as a young man, but that might mean anything up to forty, I daresay."

"You're not thinking of flirting with him to get him to do your bidding!" Hannah scolded.

"Of course I shall, if necessary. We certainly don't have enough money to tempt him, so I must use the only weapon I have."

"One of these days you'll land yourself in trouble, that you will."

"Come now, you know I never go beyond

the line of what would be acceptable in the drawing room of the fiercest dowager. My schooling taught me that, at least. How long ago it seems, and how differently my life has turned out from anything I ever expected." She laughed. "Much more interesting!"

A few minutes later they reached the rue Napoléon. For a nerve-racking quarter of an hour they waited in a luxurious marble-floored vestibule, until Monsieur Rothschild's secretary came to ask their business.

"I wish to speak privately with monsieur," Miriam said as haughtily as her shabby attire permitted.

"Monsieur speaks only German and Yiddish, mademoiselle. You may tell me . . ."

"I speak both languages. My business with Herr Rothschild is private," she insisted.

With a slight bow he departed, returning a moment later to usher them into an elegantly appointed drawing room.

"Monsieur will join you shortly, mademoiselle."

Glancing round at the elaborately ornate Louis XV furniture, the delightful Fragonard hanging over the rococo mantelpiece, Miriam felt shabbier than ever. Herr Rothschild would laugh at the pittance in her reticule. She must rely on her feminine wiles.

She pinched her cheeks and went to warm her hands at the fire. Hannah stayed by the door.

It opened and in came a short, slim, red-haired youth, clad in the latest Parisian fashion — the English swallow-tail coat as influenced by French military uniforms. He bowed gracefully.

Miriam stared in dismay as she curtsied. He was far too young for her to flirt with, no more than eighteen or nineteen, with a boyish spring to his step and an air of scarce-suppressed energy. Surely this was not the man she had come to beg for passage to England!

But it was. He introduced himself in excellent Hessian German: "Jakob Rothschild, at your service, Fräulein."

Abandoning her prepared opening, she said bluntly, "I understand that you have connections in London, Herr Rothschild. I am anxious to travel to England, and I hoped you might be able to help me."

"You are Engish?" he enquired, suddenly intent. "You speak German well. *Bitte, setzen Sie sich, Fräulein Jacobson.*"

She took a seat on a gilt and brocade chair by the fireplace. "I spent the last several years traveling around Europe with my uncle. I speak several languages."

"French, of course." He stood opposite her, leaning against the mantel with a natural elegance. "Spanish?"

"A little, and some Italian."

The latter he brushed aside as of no account. "You know the south of France? The Pyrenees?"

"My uncle and I spent some time among the Jews of that region," she admitted with some caution, beginning to wonder at his interest. "I have crossed the Pyrenees more than once." Twice, actually; once in each direction.

He gazed at her consideringly. "But you are an Englishwoman. You would like to help your country?"

"Miss Miriam!" Hannah stepped forward, an urgent warning on her lips.

"It's all right, Hannah. Mein Herr, at present my only wish is to return to my country."

To her surprise, the young Rothschild laughed. "So, you have heard that I and my brother Nathan are smuggling gold from England against the wishes of the government. I believe I must trust you with the truth, Fräulein, for you appear to be the very person I need."

"The truth?" she asked, bewildered. "You need me?"

"The truth is that Nathan, who is a naturalized Englishman, has been commissioned by the British government to convey a very large sum of money to General Wellington in Portugal. I have received the gold here in Paris and now it must be transported through France and across the Pyrenees."

"I'm delighted to hear that you are working for the British government, but what has it to do with me?"

"You have asked a favour of me, now I shall ask a favour of you. I need a guide to assist in this venture. You speak French and Spanish, you know the country. Help me in this and I shall see that you reach England safely."

"Surely you can hire someone!"

"For this task, I cannot trust anyone I might hire in France."

"I suppose not," Miriam unwillingly agreed.

"You see, Fräulein, your government sent a guardian with the shipment, an English goy to make sure that we Jews do not cheat. But this *gentleman*," he said the word in English, "Lord Felix Roworth, knows nothing of France. There is also Nathan's agent, who must accompany the gold so that he can take Wellington's receipts back to my brother. He too is unfamiliar with the route. What am I to do?"

In the pause that followed this plaintive question, the fall of a log in the grate sounded loud. Her unseeing gaze on the rush of sparks up the chimney, Miriam recalled that one of the reasons she had insisted on accompanying Uncle Amos on his travels was a desire for adventure. The years had been interesting, she felt she had been useful to him, but there had not, really, been any adventure worth mentioning. A bubble of excitement swelled within her.

Hannah read her mind. "Miss Miriam, you wouldn't . . ."

"Your patriotic duty," Jakob Rothschild interrupted. "General Wellington is in desperate need of funds to pay the British Army."

"You will send us home as soon as we return to Paris?"

"From Bordeaux, if you wish it, Fräulein." Suddenly he was all business. "You brought your luggage with you?"

"No, but we packed in case we needed to leave quickly."

"Give me the direction and I shall send for it. You leave today."

"But I have not taken proper leave of my

hosts," Miriam protested, "and I am not dressed for travelling."

"You may change your clothes when your boxes arrive, and write to your hosts in the meantime. I shall see your letter delivered. There are writing materials in my office. Come this way, please. You must make the acquaintance of your travelling companions while I complete the arrangements."

He led the way through a connecting door into a large room furnished with a desk, a huge iron safe, a number of straight wooden chairs and three or four plain leather-covered armchairs. Two of the latter were occupied. The occupants rose to their feet and bowed as Miriam entered.

"Lord Felix Roworth." Jakob Rothschild indicated the tall, broad-shouldered gentleman with golden hair and blue eyes. Immaculate in a coat of snuff-brown superfine, elegantly simple cravat, dove-grey waistcoat, skintight buckskins and white-topped boots, he appeared to be in his late twenties. "Isaac Cohen," Herr Rothschild continued the introductions. "Mees Jacobson."

Miriam glanced at the second man and nodded, but she scarcely saw him. Her gaze swung back at once to Lord Felix. He was the very embodiment of her schoolgirl dreams.

CHAPTER 3

"Here are pens and ink for your letter, Fräulein." Herr Rothschild crossed to the desk and took some sheets of paper from a drawer. "Cohen, the lady goes with you." He spoke in Yiddish now. "I must make final arrangements. I shall return shortly."

Miriam was distantly aware that Mr. Cohen uttered an unheeded protest. She was all too aware of Lord Felix's rude appraisal, swiftly followed by sneering dismissal.

"What did he say, Cohen?" his lordship enquired in English in a haughty tone.

"Miss Jacobson goes with us," said the other curtly. The air between them crackled with animosity.

As she moved to the desk she turned her attention to Isaac Cohen. Nathan Rothschild's agent, a year or two older than his lordship and a trifle taller, but more slenderly built, was dressed in a fashion less elegant than businesslike. His hair was dark, crisply springing from a broad brow, and his dark eyes stared at her with undisguised hostility.

He looked vaguely familiar. Seating herself at the desk, Miriam wondered momentarily whether she had met him before. Surely she would have remembered him; he was really rather good-looking in his own way, though not to be compared with the arrogant Lord Felix.

Dipping a quill pen, she began to write to the Benjamins, but already she had half a mind to back out of her agreement with Jakob. Neither of her prospective travelling companions had exactly greeted her advent with delight. In fact, while she wrote she listened with mingled amusement and indignation as they grudgingly united in opposition to taking her with them. They appeared to dislike that idea even more than they disliked each other.

Hannah, who had come to stand behind her, bent down and whispered, "God forbid we should stay where we're not wanted, Miss Miriam."

"It doesn't look promising, does it?" She signed the note, blotted and folded it, though far from certain it would be needed. "Only, what if we can't find anyone else to help us cross the Channel?"

"There'll be others, God willing, as won't send you to Spain afore they'll send you to England."

"I'd like to help that English general — but you are right. To travel so far with two gentlemen who resent our presence would be foolish. Herr Rothschild will find someone else. I hate to continue to impose upon the Benjamins, though."

"They're glad to have us, for your uncle's sake. Let's be off."

"No, I cannot just walk out on Herr Rothschild. We shall wait until he returns."

An uncomfortable silence enveloped the room's occupants. Lord Felix stood at the window, looking out, his fingers tapping impatiently on the sill. Mr. Cohen strode up and down the room, frowning. His lithe pacing reminded Miriam of a black panther she had once seen at the Tower of London zoo.

Neither of them so much as glanced at her, and she realized that neither had spoken a word directly to her. The situation was impossible.

Taking another sheet of paper, she drew a swift sketch of a lion and a panther snarling at each other. In one corner two female figures fled shrieking, while in another a troop of French grenadiers took aim at the

bellicose cats. She was adding Jakob Rothschild, in the form of a fox, to the drawing,
when he himself came in.

"All arrangements are made," he announced.

Miriam jumped to her feet and sped
towards him. She and the two others converged on him, all talking at once though
Lord Felix must have known his English
would not be understood.

Young Jakob was unruffled. Somehow
Miriam found herself being escorted to a
chamber where her and Hannah's belongings were piled. Hannah had stayed behind
in the office. In her place, a thin, severe-
looking Frenchwoman, all in black, with
urgent, irresistible determination helped her
to change into a dark blue woollen dress.
Her protests were brushed off like an ir-
ritating fly, and while she combed out her
ringlets and swiftly braided her hair, the
boxes were removed.

The secretary took her back to the office.
Hannah rushed to her side, but the others
took no notice of her reappearance. Lord
Felix, a caped greatcoat of drab cloth now
concealing his elegance, watched in angry
puzzlement as Herr Rothschild showed an
impassive Mr. Cohen some papers.

"These are your passports," he explained

in Yiddish. "You are Swiss admirers of Napoleon, traveling for pleasure to see the country. You and the Fräulein are brother and sister, and milord is your cousin."

With a mocking grin, Mr. Cohen glanced at Lord Felix.

"What is it?" demanded his lordship. "What is the wretched little Yid up to now?"

"According to our passports, you have joined our family."

"The devil I have! Do I look like a bloody Jew?"

"Jews come in all shapes and sizes." He shrugged. "You have a different surname — we'll be Cohens but you'll be Rauschberg — so perhaps your father was a goy."

"Rauschberg? Why not my own name?"

"Roworth is too English by half, unpronounceable in any other tongue. I trust you are not going to expect to be addressed as 'my lord'?" The last words were a sneer.

"As relatives," Miriam pointed out, "we ought doubtless to address each other by our first names."

They both turned to glare at her.

"I can't see why I must be related at all!" Lord Felix objected furiously.

"To make it plausible that we should be traveling together. If you insist on accompanying our shipment all the way, then

42

you will have to accept Herr Rothschild's arrangements."

"*Genug shoin!*" said the red-haired youth adamantly. "No more arguments. Come, the carriage is ready." With unshaken calm he walked out.

And Miriam followed, her protests once again ignored. She was beginning to see Jakob Rothschild as Fate personified.

"If it's fated we go," Hannah muttered behind her, "then it's no use fighting it."

Their boxes had already been tied onto the back of the vehicle that awaited them in the courtyard. It was a large berline, its undistinguished black paint somewhat the worse for wear. A boy held the reins of the team of four ill-matched but strong-looking horses.

"I must see the gold," said Lord Felix abruptly in an undertone.

Jakob obviously caught the word "gold". He knocked on the side of the carriage and Isaac translated his words.

"There are secret compartments in the walls, which are too complicated to show you, but you can inspect what is under the seats and floor."

Isaac stayed outside with Miriam, ignoring her, while the other two men climbed into the berline. She couldn't see what they were doing, but apparently his lordship was satisfied for they soon stepped out again.

"Where is our coachman?" Isaac asked, casting an annoyed glance at the empty box. "If he doesn't come soon, it will scarcely be worth leaving today."

"The man who drove you from the coast is needed elsewhere," said Jakob blandly, "and I have no one else available who is trustworthy. It is well known that all English gentlemen can drive coaches."

"But I am not a gentleman." Isaac's laugh was ironic. He turned to Lord Felix and said in English, "It seems we are expected to drive ourselves."

"Drive this?" A scowl distorted his lordship's handsome features. "I am accustomed to tooling a four-in-hand sporting curricle, not a shabby travelling carriage weighted down with bullion! I wager it's as heavy as a fully loaded stage coach."

"I thought all young bucks made a practice of bribing the stagecoachmen to take a turn at the reins," said Isaac sarcastically, "but if you can't do it, there's no more to be said."

"Of course I could do it!"

"I see, it's simply beneath your dignity. Then alas, poor Lord Wellington will have to whistle for his gold."

"Why don't you drive?"

"Because I don't know how."

To Miriam's amusement, this confession wiped the scowl from Lord Felix's face and replaced it with smug superiority. She was beginning to think that, though probably uncomfortable, the journey might prove entertaining.

"Felix, you had best teach Isaac so that he can spell you on the box," she said.

Once again they united to glare at her, but after a moment his lordship gave a reluctant nod. "We shall travel faster in the end if we can take turns," he acknowledged. "We'll give it a try once we're past the city traffic." He turned towards the horses then swung back. "But I've not the least notion how to get out of Paris."

Jakob had foreseen the difficulty. The boy holding the horses was to show the way to the Orléans road. He scampered up onto the box and Lord Felix climbed up beside him. Isaac, more gentlemanly than the noble English gentleman, handed Miriam and Hannah into the carriage.

Seating herself facing the horses, Miriam smiled and thanked him. His lips tightened and without answering he turned away to exchange a last word with his employer's brother.

Disconcerted by his obvious resentment

— it was unfair of him to blame her when her presence was entirely Jakob's fault! — Miriam cast a questioning glance at Hannah, seated beside her. The abigail was about to speak when Isaac joined them. A moment later the berline jerked into motion and they rolled out of the yard.

Despite its unprepossessing exterior, the carriage was well-sprung. Inside, there was less space than Miriam had expected, no doubt because of the hollow walls, but the cushions, though worn, were surprisingly comfortable. She leaned back against the squabs. They felt all the softer when she recalled the deplorable seats in the diligence that had brought them to Paris.

She had not expected to leave the city by the Orléans gate, on a dangerous journey to Spain, with two strangers who made no bones about their dislike of her and each other. And all of them with Swiss passports!

"Isaac, how did Herr Rothschild obtain Swiss passports?" she asked.

"Anything can be bought if you can pay the price," he told her curtly.

"He must have had them ready and added our names at the last minute. I suppose the papers are in order for leaving Paris? They will be checked at the gate."

"I have a pass signed by both the Finance

Minister and Savary, the Minister of Police."

"The Rothschilds bought the minister and the police chief, too?" Miriam was sceptical.

"I believe not, though the police prefect of Calais was handsomely bribed to turn a blind eye. No, these papers were obtained through the Minister of Finance, who is delighted to encourage the flow of gold from England to France. The Rothschilds are very thorough, Miss Jacobson."

"And very hard to resist! But you must call me Miriam, since we are supposed to be brother and sister."

"Not by my choice, I assure you!"

His vehemence reawakened her curiosity. Surely there was more to his resentment than mere annoyance that she was to travel as his guide. She studied his averted face, racking her brains to think where she might have seen him before. How could she have forgotten so unlikely an event as having deeply offended an attractive young man?

Enlightenment failed to come. "Have we met before, sir?" she ventured to enquire. Hannah, looking dismayed, laid a cautionary hand on her arm.

Isaac turned from the window, his expression compounded of bitterness and incredulity. "You don't remember?"

"I'm sorry, I'm afraid I don't."

"It is not for me to remind you," he said stiffly.

She would have pressed him, despite Hannah's warning, but just then there came a shout of "Halte là, citoyen!" The berline stopped. The boy who had showed the way scampered past on one side and a moment later a uniformed figure in a cockaded shako appeared at the opposite door.

Miriam clutched Hannah's hand. Perhaps their passes were in order, but suppose the man decided to search the coach? The Benjamins had mentioned that the police were always on the look-out for smugglers, though she thought goods were usually smuggled into the city, to avoid the city taxes.

Isaac let down the window.

"Monsieur, 'dame, vos papiers, s'il vous plaît." The soldier took the package Isaac handed him, studied the papers, and looked suspiciously around the interior of the vehicle.

"Je suis Cohen. Voici ma soeur et sa bonne," Isaac said in passable French with a strong accent, "and our cousin Rauschberg is driving. We are not rich aristos, you understand, to hire a coachman."

The man stepped back to examine Lord

Felix on the box, sighed, and shrugged his shoulders. *"Vous êtes suisses?* Then that explains itself. *Passez, messieurs."*

The carriage rolled onward, across the hundred-yard space of demolished buildings intended to prevent smugglers tunneling into the city. Miriam let out her breath in a long sigh.

"God be praised," said Hannah.

They continued in silence for a few minutes, then Isaac asked irritably, "What did he mean, *'Ça s'explique'?"*

"Our being Swiss explains our peculiarities, especially where language is concerned. It was very clever of Herr Rothschild to provide Swiss passports. Every valley in Switzerland has its own dialect of French or German, often mutually incomprehensible, so no one will wonder if we speak Yiddish, or French with a peculiar accent." At once she wished she hadn't criticized his accent, however indirectly, but he didn't seem to notice.

"Jakob told us you speak good French and know France and Spain. I suppose you are well acquainted with Switzerland also?" He sounded disbelieving.

"As a matter of fact, I am." She would have continued, pleased that at least he was showing some interest, but the carriage suddenly halted again. With a gasp, she swung round to peer out of the open window, fearing to see troops galloping after them.

"Cohen, come up here!" came a shout from the box.

Miriam shuddered. "For pity's sake, tell him not to use English in public, and to call you Isaac."

Not deigning to reply, he stepped out.

As the berline started off once more, Miriam turned to Hannah. "So I have met him before, and you recall the occasion?"

"Child, child, he is the young man the matchmaker brought to your father's house."

Miriam stared at her, aghast. "Oh no! He can't be!"

"How could you forget him?"

"I was a mere girl. That was nine years ago and I have seen so much, met so many people, since then. But are you sure? Isaac Cohen is not an uncommon name. That boy was a fright, weedy and stooped and colourless, and this man is . . . well, quite different."

"After all, he's had nine years to grow up, too."

"It cannot be him. He was a Talmudic scholar, studying to be a rabbi, and excessively wealthy besides. Why should he be

50

working for Nathan Rothschild?"

"It's all in the hands of God, Miss Miriam. If it's fated, it'll come to pass. But rich or poor, it's the same fellow, for sure."

"He did seem familiar, right from the first." She laughed ruefully. "If he had been as good-looking then as he is now, I might have had second thoughts about running off with Uncle Amos. I was positively odious to him, was I not? No wonder he loathes me. I don't suppose he will ever forgive me."

CHAPTER 4

So the girl didn't even recall having insulted him before her entire family! Isaac's anger at the memory of his humiliation grew and he was relieved to escape her presence, however temporarily. His long legs making short work of the climb up to the berline's box, he settled at Roworth's left side on the hard wooden seat.

"How could you be so crackbrained as to shout out in English?" he rebuked his lordship. "You'll get us all arrested. And since we are now cousins you'd best accustom yourself to using first names."

"I made sure no one was near before I called you." Roworth's voice was as cold as his aristocratic face. "Now, if I am to attempt to teach you to drive, you'll start by observing carefully." With the slightest flick of the reins he set the horses in motion.

Isaac observed. Barely taut reins in the left hand, whip in the right, guiding the team looked not much more difficult than riding. Wielding the whip was doubtless an acquired skill, but Roworth seemed not to use it.

Ahead the road stretched straight into the distance between poplars just coming into leaf. Though they were still close to Paris, the only traffic was a carrier's wagon coming towards them. It had rained in the night, just enough to damp down the dust, but now the midday sun shone in a cloudless sky. The fields on either side, still cultivated in the ancient strips long abandoned in England, formed a precise, rectangular patchwork of green and brown.

The scene, even the lack of vehicles so close to the capital, was very unEnglish. However objectionable his travelling companions, Isaac was glad of the opportunity to see more of a foreign land.

The rear of another slow-moving, heavy-laden cart loomed ahead. "Watch," said Roworth sharply. "Not the horses, my hands."

His whip hand assisting with the reins, he directed the team around the cart. Isaac quelled a grudging admiration for the neat way he accomplished the manoeuvre. After all it was not much of a feat, since they were moving at not more than eight miles an hour and the cart crawled along at less than a walking pace.

Roworth embarked on a patronizing explanation of draught reins and coupling reins, tugs, traces, buckles and bits and curb chains.

"Unless you have a competent groom with you, you must always supervise the harnessing of your cattle. A badly harnessed team will pull unevenly and soon wear itself out, besides being difficult to control. I always see to the harness myself before a curricle race," he went on with some enthusiasm, then paused and added bitterly, "that is, I used to."

No doubt he lost his curricle to a wager, Isaac guessed contemptuously. A typical spoiled scion of the nobility with no consideration as to who paid for his extravagance.

"Shall I take the reins now?" he asked.

"No. Stopping again will just waste time, you'll have to wait until we reach the first stage. In the meantime, repeat what I've told you about the harness, if you can remember."

Isaac was word perfect, but he suspected that actually dealing with the tangle of straps and rings would be another matter altogether.

His thoughts drifted back to the infuriating female inside the berline. Wealthy, beautiful — he could still feel the shock of delight that had overwhelmed him at his first sight of his prospective bride — Miss Miriam Jacobson ought to have easily found another husband after brutally rejecting him. Instead, it seemed, she had been wandering across Europe, shabbily dressed, with none but her maid to accompany her.

The Jacobsons were still pillars of London Jewry, and Isaac couldn't believe they had cast off their only daughter, their only child. Miriam was still beautiful; her mahogany-red hair, glimpsed under her bonnet, unfaded; her pale complexion translucent as fine porcelain. Despite the years and the dowdy clothes, her loveliness had once again made his heart jump, before he realized who she was. She should be married and raising a family, not guiding an expedition fraught with danger across an enemy country.

He wondered how Jakob Rothschild had persuaded her to set off on a long journey with a man who detested her and another who despised all Jews.

In fact, Isaac himself was strongly tempted to walk back to Paris and quit the Rothschilds' service without further ado. He foresaw nothing but trouble. However, persistent by nature, he was unwilling to give up on a job he had undertaken. Besides,

Nathan Rothschild had been good to him and deserved his loyalty, and last but not least, delivering the gold to Viscount Wellington would strike a blow for England. Roworth might make it plain that he didn't consider a Jew to be a true Englishman, but Isaac was as patriotic as any man born and bred in Britain.

Whatever her faults, England was his country. Change must come from within, not be imposed from without by a bloody-handed tyrant like the Emperor Napoleon.

"Bloody hell!" swore Roworth as the berline's wheel dropped into a pothole and jolted out again. "You'd think the Emperor of most of Europe would spend some of his ill-gotten gains on repairing his roads."

Inside the carriage, Miriam groaned. "The road has been amazingly good so far. I knew it couldn't last."

"It's not so bad in a decently sprung carriage," Hannah consoled her. "Just be glad we're not in the diligence again, praise God."

"How right you are. And we shall be able to get out and stretch our limbs at the posting houses. We've been traveling at least two hours, at a reasonable pace compared to the diligence. Surely we must be near the end of a stage by now." She leaned forward to look out of the window. "Yes, I believe I see an inn ahead. I trust that toplofty lord has the sense to stop there."

The toplofty lord did indeed have sufficient sense to pull into the yard of the Auberge du Chapeau-rouge, a low, whitewashed building that appeared to be deserted. As Miriam opened the carriage door, Lord Felix swung down from the box and a vacuous-faced ostler slouched out of the stables, chewing a straw.

"Catter newvo chevalls," called his lordship.

The ostler gaped at him, the straw falling unnoticed from his gap-toothed mouth.

Light dawned on Miriam. "Four new horses — *quatre nouveaux chevaux!* I must go and interpret for him."

"Nay, child, let the men work it out for themselves, God willing. They're fools, to be sure, but best indulge them unless they're in such a pickle they can't find their own way out."

In fact, Isaac had joined Felix and in his painstaking, accented French was instructing the ostler to provide a fresh team. Felix was obviously disgruntled by his intervention, especially when it proved successful.

The man nodded and said wisely, "Ah, you'll be foreigners, without doubt."

"Swiss," Isaac confirmed.

"But why did monsieur expect me to understand German?" He shrugged and, not waiting for an answer, turned away to call another ostler to help.

Miriam could tell that Isaac was trying to suppress a grin. Hoping to preserve the peace she stepped forward, too late.

Isaac's grin escaped. "The fellow thought you were speaking German."

Felix cast him a furious glance and stalked off to watch the change of horses.

Chuckling, Miriam tugged Hannah round behind the carriage. "What a set-down for his lordship! But oh dear, how are we going to manage with one member of our party speaking schoolboy French, another who might as well not speak it at all, and the two of them at daggers drawn?"

"It's all in God's hands, Miss Miriam. If he wills it, all will go well."

"We could wait for the next diligence to take us back to Paris. I wish I had refused Herr Rothschild as soon as I heard his proposal. Once I had agreed, he made it impossible to change my mind."

"It's too late now. There's the whole British army waiting for their pay."

"And goodness knows what sort of bumble-broth those two would fall into without me. At least I can attempt to stop them slitting each other's throats," she said, resigned. "We'd better go back and see how they are getting on."

Isaac had disappeared. Felix, seething with frustration, had taken off his gloves and was feeling the foreleg of one of the horses the ostler had led out. He saw Miriam and hurried across to her.

"That horse is throwing out a splint. Tell them he'll be lame in a mile or two." The peremptory order made her look at him askance. "Please," he added grudgingly.

She obliged. After some argument, the ostler took the horse back into the stables. "There isn't much to choose from," Miriam explained. "The army takes all the best horses."

"I daresay he'll find something quick enough if you give him this." He took a coin from his coat pocket and handed it to her.

"An écu d'or! That is far too much."

His nostrils flared in disdain. "We'll never reach Wellington if you mean to haggle like a Jew over ha'pennies."

"We'll never reach Wellington if you mean to cause talk and raise suspicions by flinging gold about," she pointed out coldly.

He had the grace to look abashed. "How much?"

"Five sous will be plenty." Noting the strength of his square, well-kept hand, she selected a coin from the handful of change he held out to her and turned to follow the ostler.

"I'll come and pick the one I want," he said, falling into step beside her.

Miriam was annoyed to find herself very much aware of his muscular figure and vigorous stride. Stealing a glance at his handsome, arrogant profile, she wondered what he would look like if he smiled, and whether he ever did. It was the outside of enough to find herself condemned to weeks of intimacy with a Nonpareil who held her in contempt! At least she had already taught him that she was not easily intimidated.

An acceptable horse chosen, they returned to the carriage. Isaac had obtained some bread and cheese. He was giving a share to Hannah, laughing at something she said. His white teeth gleamed against the healthy glow of his olive skin and his eyes crinkled at the corners in the most attractive way.

Then he caught sight of Miriam and Felix. His face closed like a slammed door.

To the devil with both of them! Miriam thought, refusing to make use of the arm Isaac offered to help her into the carriage. For England's sake she would do what she could to smooth their path to Spain but she'd die before she tried to make friends with them.

Isaac, his amour-propre bolstered by his minor triumph over Roworth, had caught the momentary flash of hurt in her eyes. He felt a pang of remorse. For the first time he questioned whether it was fair to blame a woman of seven-and-twenty for the deeds of a heedless girl of eighteen. No doubt she had changed since that dreadful day in 1802. He certainly had.

It dawned on him that if she didn't realize who he was, she must be thoroughly puzzled by his antagonism.

His musing was interrupted by Roworth's sarcastic "Coming?" The last horse had been harnessed and it was time for him to try his hand at driving a team of four. He'd never noticed before how large the horses were.

The offside wheeler, a black-maned sorrel, rolled its eye at him with a derisive snort. He frowned at it sternly and moved to join Roworth on the box.

"Stop! Take the reins before you come up, so that you have control at all times, and mind you don't tug on them, or the team will start off without you. No, dammit, that's not how to hold them. Did you not observe how I do it? The first and second fingers of your left hand go between the reins, with the left rein lying over the knuckle of your forefinger."

The stream of scornful instructions continued until at last Isaac had the proper grasp. Gingerly he stepped up to the box, careful not to pull the reins taut, and sat down, his legs stretched out with his feet against the dashboard.

"You are sitting quite wrong. Your feet should be a little farther back than your knees. What the devil are you doing with the whip? Clutch it like that and you'll have to drop it when you need to use your right hand on the reins."

His left arm was positioned wrong, his wrist bent at the wrong angle. How he managed to drive out from the yard onto the highway he had no idea. He thanked God for a miracle.

Unfortunately the world seemed to have woken up from its noonday rest. Carts and wagons, private carriages, riders and pedestrians thronged the road. Well, Isaac had to admit that it wasn't exactly crowded, but there was a great deal too much traffic for his liking. He was glad that his mentor didn't appear to trust him to drive at a trot.

The reprieve was temporary. After a

quarter of a mile, Roworth said, "They are working together as a team now. You can pick up the pace, gradually."

Somewhat to Isaac's surprise, the horses obeyed his directions — even the insolent sorrel. Soon they were rolling along the road at a fine pace. He was beginning to feel almost competent when they rounded a bend and found themselves stuck behind a lumbering diligence.

The leaders and the near-side wheeler automatically slowed, but the sorrel decided to overtake. Isaac hadn't the least notion what to do.

"Good gad, do you want them stepping over the traces?" Roworth leaned across and pulled on one of the reins, looking smugly superior as the sorrel fell back into line. "We must overtake," he added impatiently. "We shall never reach Spain if we get stuck behind every slow-moving vehicle. I'd best take over."

"No, I can do it," said Isaac with grim determination. "We'll never reach Spain if you have to drive all the way. Just tell me what to do."

"For a start, wait until that carriage coming the other way is past."

His condescension was infuriating. Keeping a tight rein on his own temper, Isaac listened carefully to the instructions. When the road was clear, Roworth repeated each step at the appropriate moment. A dozen times during the manoeuvre Isaac wanted to close his eyes and pray but he resisted the temptation and drove on.

As the leaders drew up neck-and-neck with the diligence's team, he saw from the corner of his eye its driver saluting with his whip. He didn't dare respond. And then the diligence was falling behind, the sorrel's rump was level with the others' noses, they were past.

"Don't pull in too sharply," snapped Roworth.

Confused, Isaac overcorrected. The offside wheel came perilously close to the ditch before the berline was once more rolling smoothly down the highway.

Close behind him something clicked. He glanced round to see that a small panel in the front of the body had opened.

"Watch the road!" came Roworth's anguished cry.

As Isaac quickly turned his attention back to the road, he heard Miriam's dry voice, "Can we let go the straps and breathe again?"

"Until we come to the next obstacle," Roworth said forebodingly, but a few minutes later, when they reached a straight stretch, he had enough confidence to start munching on bread and cheese.

Tooling the coach along, Isaac was on the whole quite pleased with himself. At least his driving was better than his lordship's French.

For practice, he drove all but one stage until at dusk they decided to stop for the night in the next village. By the time he turned into the yard of a sizeable inn by the name of Le Grand Cerf, he was exhausted, his arms heavy as lead and his eyes burning from constant concentration. He blinked round in dismay at a half-dozen carriages already standing in the yard. He simply couldn't go any farther.

Miriam took one look at him as he stumbled down from the box and declared, "I shall make arrangements for our accommodation. Do you wait here while I make sure that there are chambers available."

She and her abigail went into the inn. Isaac slumped down onto the berline's step while Roworth waved away the ostlers and paced up and down for a minute or two. Then he came to lean against the carriage, gazing into the distance with his hands in his pockets.

After a moment, he said abruptly, "Even

the best of professional stagecoach drivers rarely drive more than three or four stages at a time. It's hard work." As if ashamed of this admission, he strolled away again before Isaac could react.

Miriam came out of the Grand Cerf and told the ostlers to unhitch the horses. An inn servant began to unload luggage from the berline. Felix returned.

"I have reserved two chambers," Miriam said in a lowered voice, switching to English. "The private parlours are all taken, though. They are busy with travellers going to Paris to pay their respects on the birth of the emperor's heir. We'll have to dine in the public *salle-à-manger,* and Felix will just have to hold his tongue all evening."

"I've no desire for conversation," his lordship grunted. "Nor have I any desire to share a chamber. Ask for a third."

She regarded him with a faint, mocking smile. "I fear all are occupied or reserved. Jewishness is not contagious, you know."

Roworth was disconcerted. Isaac grinned. Changed or no, Miss Miriam Jacobson was still outspoken to a fault.

"I have ordered dinner an hour from now," she continued, "and hot water to be taken up to our chambers at once. I trust you have no objection, Lord Felix?"

"Only to that mode of address, Miss Jacobson. I am the eldest son of an earl and my correct style is Lord Roworth."

"I beg your pardon, my lord," Miriam said ironically. "Herr Rothschild must have introduced you incorrectly."

His lips curled in scorn. "A Jewish moneychanger from Germany cannot be expected to understand English titles."

"Stop this nonsense," Isaac commanded. "While we are travelling among enemies, we are Miriam, Felix and Isaac. And Isaac, for one, will be glad of a meal and any place to sleep." He hoisted himself to his feet.

Miriam led the way into the inn. Pausing in the busy front hall, where waiters and barmaids scurried back and forth, she turned to address Isaac in Yiddish. "Pray remind Felix that he is now a Swiss bourgeois. If he comes down to dine in full evening dress everyone will stare. I shall see you both later; I'm going up to change now."

"Not, I trust, into full evening dress."

She shook her head with a rueful smile. "It is many years since I owned a gown that London Society would consider fit to wear to dinner. Come, Hannah."

Ascending the stairs, Miriam wondered whether Isaac was beginning to thaw towards her. No, more likely he was just grateful for an excuse to needle Felix, she decided regretfully. She weighed the miserably few coins in the purse in the pocket of her cloak. By the morning she must decide whether to continue to bear-lead this most unsatisfactory expedition. If she went any farther, she wouldn't be able to afford the diligence back to Paris.

She and Hannah would be utterly dependent on Felix, Lord Roworth, and Mr. Isaac Cohen.

CHAPTER 5

A chambermaid showed Miriam and her abigail to their chamber, a large but sparsely furnished room, and a few minutes later their boxes and hot water arrived.

While Miriam washed, Hannah unpacked her sole evening gown. Miriam herself had added the only ornament to the forest-green satin: amber silk embroidery on the bodice and around the hem, matching the amber ribbon around the high waistline. Whatever the weather, she always wore a shawl with it, carried low over her elbows to hide the worn seat. She still possessed one of the shawls she had brought from England, of pale green cashemire with a fringe.

After years of experience, Hannah was an expert packer, but inevitably the gown was somewhat creased.

"I'll just take it down and iron it," she announced. She had long since perfected the use of sign language to explain what she needed. "You'll be wanting to look your best tonight."

"Will I?"

"Of course you will, dining with two handsome gentlemen, even if they are in the sulks like a pair of schoolboys. I'll have to eat in the coffee room with you, Miss Miriam, being as how I'm your only chaperon, but I daresay they'll let me sit at a separate table."

"Fustian. I'm sure Isaac won't mind you joining us."

"But his lordship — God forbid I should take the liberty of sitting down to dinner with a lord."

"Just let Felix dare to object!"

Hannah shook her greying head in exasperated admiration. "You'll come to grief one of these days, acting so saucy, mark my words. That's not how they taught you to behave in that fancy goy school."

"No," Miriam agreed, laughing and hugging her maid, "and a fine life we'd have had of it if they had succeeded in turning me into a milk-and-water miss."

"Aye," Hannah muttered as she headed for the door, "a fine life, married and settled with your children about you." Her hand on the door handle she turned. "And I don't like you calling them by their given names, neither. It's not proper."

"But it's necessary. Neither of them is the least likely to consider it an invitation to improper advances!"

Hannah sighed and departed.

Miriam opened Hannah's box and dug out a much prized, therefore rarely worn, therefore still smart black bombazine dress. There were, after all, two gentlemen to impress. Unconsciously echoing Hannah's sigh, she acknowledged that her green satin was no more likely than the use of first names to invite improper advances, alas.

Not, of course, that she had any desire to attract such churlish gentlemen as Isaac and Felix, however handsome. What she longed for was a loving husband. Surely it wasn't too late to hope one day to be "married and settled with your children about you." *From your mouth to God's ears,* she thought, making use of one of Hannah's favourite phrases.

Unpinning her braids, she vigorously brushed her hair until it fell in a rippling russet cloak about her shoulders. Ringlets tonight? No, too much trouble for those odious, unappreciative wretches.

Just a few careless curls falling across her white brow and wisping about her ears.

Hannah returned with the green gown

and, after some persuasion, donned her black bombazine. Together they headed for the coffee room. Miriam had just set foot on the bottom step when she noticed a slight figure in a top hat entering the hall. He took off his hat, revealing hair as red as her own.

"Herr Rothschild!" Hannah exclaimed.

"Hush, he may not want his name known."

"What's he doing here? Something's gone wrong, I feel it in my bones. May God save us from misfortune!"

Jakob Rothschild had seen them. A look of vexation crossed his youthful face, so brief that Miriam wondered whether she had imagined it. He came to meet them, bowed, and said blandly, "Good evening, Fräulein."

"Good evening, sir. I did not expect to encounter you here. Is something amiss?" She gathered an impression that his mind was working swiftly.

"I hope not. I followed to make sure that all goes well."

"That depends on what you mean by well." Now was the moment to tell him she wanted nothing more to do with his scheme.

"I fear you were given little opportunity to consider. Perhaps the venture is too difficult, or you cannot reach an accord with your companions?"

Miriam guessed that he was deliberately challenging her. She was sure of it, yet she couldn't resist the challenge. "Do not trouble yourself, mein Herr. I am quite capable of accomplishing what you ask of me."

Hannah moaned.

Jakob inclined his head. "I am glad to have my judgement of you confirmed, gnädige Fräulein."

With a reckless feeling that she had burned her boats, Miriam asked gaily, "Will you dine with us?"

"Thank you, I have already dined. Do not let me keep you from your dinner. It remains only for me to wish you bon voyage, and my most hearty thanks." He bowed over her hand and stood aside.

Continuing towards the coffee room, Miriam suddenly frowned. How had he known that they would spend the night at the Grand Cerf? She glanced back, but he was talking to the innkeeper and it did not seem worthwhile to interrupt.

The coffee room was crowded and clamorous. A red-faced waiter rushed up and escorted them to a table in a far corner, where Felix already waited, his back to the wall. He was wearing a dark blue coat that, while displaying his broad shoulders to advantage, was loose enough to don without assistance. His shirtpoints were of moderate height, his neckcloth tied in a simple knot without a stickpin. Altogether, only his golden hair, ice-blue eyes, and powerful frame seemed likely to draw attention.

Miriam noted that several young ladies were eyeing him with appreciation. Their faces fell as she joined him.

He half rose and bowed slightly but made no effort to seat her. She took the chair opposite him, and Hannah diffidently sat down beside her. Felix raised supercilious eyebrows but said nothing.

The noise in the coffee room was more than loud enough to cover a quiet conversation. Miriam resolved to induce him to talk. If she mentioned Jakob Rothschild's arrival, he would make some unpleasant remark about devious Jewish moneylenders, and besides, what she really wanted was to smooth relations between him and Isaac. Perhaps they would never be friends, but they ought to stop sniping and learn to appreciate each other's good points.

"Isaac learned to drive very quickly, did he not?" she opened. "Of course, he was taught by an expert."

His eyes narrowed appraisingly, as if he expected a trap, and he rejected her compliment. "I daresay the English aristocracy has an inbred skill with horses, as do Jews with money-making."

"And with languages?"

His cheeks reddened. "I read French and understand a little. I've never had occasion to speak it." He returned to the attack. "If Isaac had been in a narrow lane, or driving a sporting rig with a team of blooded fifteen-mile-an-hour tits, he'd have gone off the road a dozen times."

"Only once, surely!" Her dry comment surprised him into what she chose to regard as the beginning of a smile, though it was in truth no more than the merest twitch of the lips. "It seems to me," she went on, "that no one would begin to learn to drive with a valuable, high-bred team. Indeed, how many who have never driven even a single horse start with four-in-hand?"

"He did well enough," Felix conceded curtly.

Satisfied for the moment, Miriam asked, "Is he coming down? I'm famished." Too late she recalled a precept from her schooldays: a lady never admits to anything so vulgar as an appetite. Once again, his lordship had an excuse to turn up his noble nose at her.

Amazingly, he seemed unaware of her faux pas. "I'm hungry too," he said, sounding almost human. "He may have fallen asleep. If he's not down in a few minutes I'll send someone to fetch him. In the meantime, will you be so good as to order a bottle of claret?"

Miriam graciously forebore to point out that she would also be the one who had to send someone after Isaac.

In fact, Isaac had already descended the stairs. Earlier, on entering the Grand Cerf, he had been too tired to notice the whereabouts of the coffee room, and now there was a sudden dearth of servants in the hall. He glanced around to find his bearings.

In a dark corner, scarcely lit by the oil lamps hanging on the walls, he saw two men, one short and slight, the other tending to plumpness. Jakob Rothschild and his brother Kalmann! As Nathan's courier Isaac had met Kalmann on several occasions in various French, Dutch and German ports. What the devil were those young schemers doing here?

Striding towards them, he saw Jakob pass a package to Kalmann, who hurriedly stowed it in the pocket of his greatcoat.

76

Then Jakob noticed Isaac's approach and laid his hand on his brother's arm.

"Has something gone wrong?" Isaac demanded. "Are we suspected?"

"I just came to make sure everything is running smoothly," Jakob assured him.

"And Kalmann?"

The brothers exchanged glances. "We've decided he is to ride ahead to Spain, to make arrangements to smuggle the gold past the French lines. You will meet him . . ." he looked questioningly at Kalmann.

"At Pamplona, just the other side of the Pyrenees." A thoughtful frown crossed Kalmann's youthful face with its long side-whiskers. "I shall wait for you by the cathedral at noon every day from the tenth of April — no, the ninth is the first day of Passover."

"You cannot waste eight days observing Passover!" said Jakob impatiently. "Even Father would agree that this business is too important." He turned to Isaac. "For a week from the tenth he will be in Pamplona. Can you be there by then?"

"I think so. I've learned to drive the coach," said Isaac with pardonable pride. "But it might be best to allow longer than a week."

"Kalmann will be needed elsewhere. He

will make arrangements for someone to contact you if you turn up after that."

"If," thought Isaac. After the seventeenth of April the Rothschilds would presume that their plan had gone awry. They would take their losses and concoct some other way to smuggle gold to Wellington. He had no doubt that they'd do their best to rescue their employee and his companions, but whether they would succeed was another matter. "I cannot believe it is right to take a woman with us on what may prove a dangerous journey," he exclaimed.

"I spoke to the Fräulein a few minutes ago, and she is willing."

"We don't need her. My French is good enough to get by."

"And your Spanish? No, the language is only a part of it. The presence of a woman in the party will help to divert suspicion. Standing here talking, on the other hand, can only draw suspicion. We must go."

Isaac looked round. Two waiters were carrying loaded trays from the kitchen down the hall to the coffee room, and the landlord was greeting some newly arrived guests. No one appeared to be taking any notice of the three men in the shadows. He turned back. Jakob and Kalmann had silently vanished.

A thousand doubts assailed him as he

made his way to the coffee room. Jakob's explanations had holes big enough to drive a coach and four through. His employers were known for the cunning complexity of their plans, and he was sure he was embroiled in a far more tangled intrigue than they had informed him of. Not that he could do anything about it. Having undertaken to deliver the gold to Wellington, he would endeavour to carry out his obligation.

He only hoped that the Rothschilds' machinations were up to their usual brilliant standards.

His qualms must be kept from the others, he decided. No purpose would be served by alarming them. There they were, at the far end of the crowded room, a bottle of wine on the table between them, talking to each other with apparent amity. Isaac frowned. They must be speaking English, foolhardy to say the least!

Starting across the room he changed his mind. Amid the clamour of voices and clatter of knives and forks, plates and glasses, anything less than a shout was indistinguishable from the general hubbub.

Felix caught sight of him and said something to Miriam. She turned and smiled at him. For the first time since that unforgettable day nine years ago, he saw her without a hat. The lamplight drew fiery gleams from her coronet of braids and teasing clusters of curls, and lent an air of mystery to her lustrous brown eyes. Her mouth was all too inviting.

He returned her smile. Let bygones be bygones, he advised himself.

That advice didn't apply to Felix, of course. Felix had never caused any specific injury for which he could be forgiven. He simply epitomized a type Isaac loathed.

As he sat down beside Felix, diagonally across from Miriam, Isaac addressed her in Yiddish. "I hope I have not kept you waiting. If you are as hungry as I am, you must be cursing me."

She laughed. "How did you guess? We were about to send for you."

"God forbid my mistress should utter a curse," said the abigail, shocked. "May you live long, sir, and in good health."

"I thank you for your good wishes, Miss . . . ?"

"Greenbaum, sir," she said coyly. "Hannah Greenbaum."

"Miss Greenbaum." He noticed that Miriam was pleased with his politeness to her maid. No doubt his high-and-mighty lordship had objected to her presence at their table.

A waiter dashed up and set before each of them an earthenware bowl of appetizingly fragrant onion soup topped with toasted cheese.

"Oh dear." Miriam also spoke in Yiddish. "I forgot about the cheese. The soup is certainly made with beef stock, so it is milk and meat in one dish. I did try to order dishes that are not too obviously *treif,* though the kitchens cannot possibly be kosher, of course. And then there was English taste to be taken into account, too."

"As far as I'm concerned, this smells like heaven," Isaac assured her, picking up his spoon. "I discovered long since that if I tried to eat only kosher food while traveling on business I'd starve." He tasted the soup. "Delicious."

She sighed in relief, but curiosity was uppermost in her voice when she asked, "Did you once strictly observe *kashrut?* I thought you were a puritanical follower of every last commandment of Halakah, not just the dietary laws."

So she had recalled that dreadful occasion! "I was — but you were swift to draw conclusions about me from a very brief glimpse," he said dryly.

She looked stricken, her pale cheeks flushing. "I . . . I'm sorry. I behaved unforgivably. I have learned not to judge by first impressions, I promise you."

"Not unforgivably, understandably. We were both too young to think of marriage, and we'd not have suited. Let us forget it."

Her suddenly elated expression made Felix, glumly consuming his soup in silence, raise his eyebrows again. Isaac didn't explain. He grinned at her, glad to feel the weight of his long-held resentment rolling off his shoulders.

And she really had done her best to avoid treif for his sake, he realized, as the rest of the meal was served. She couldn't have guessed that one of the roasted chickens would arrive stuffed with oysters, the other with pork sausage. Delicious, both of them.

CHAPTER 6

"Drat," said Miriam, settling onto the berline's comfortable seat, "I was looking forward to this morning. I was hoping that with a bit of encouragement Felix would turn out to be human after all."

"It's just as well his lordship's going to sit up there on the box for a bit," Hannah disagreed. "I wouldn't be surprised but what Mr. Cohen's forgot how to drive, tired as he was last night. 'Sides, I daresay they'll both be taking a turn inside for it looks like rain to me."

"It does, doesn't it?" Unlike the weather, Miriam brightened. "And I'm sure Isaac will soon be capable of driving by himself. That will give Felix one reason the less for counting himself so superior."

"He don't think himself superior when you and Mr. Cohen's chattering away in French or Yiddish. I been watching his face, and if you ask me the poor lad feels like a child as is left out of a game."

"Oh dear, yes, he must feel sadly isolated. I know, I have a famous idea! I shall teach him to speak French as we go along. He claims to have some knowledge already."

"That'd be right kindly of you, Miss Miriam, and God will bless you for it."

"You praise me too highly. I was thinking that it may well come in very useful for all of us sooner or later if he can speak something other than English, and teaching him will help to pass the time. I do hope it rains."

The heavens obliged. Before they reached Orléans a light drizzle began to fall, and when they stopped there to change horses Felix appeared at the carriage door.

"May I join you? There is no sense in both of us getting wet."

"Of course," said Miriam with a smile, ignoring his moroseness. "I take it Isaac has passed the test?"

"I wouldn't trust him in a country lane, or city traffic, but Orléans appears to be little larger than an English village."

"A little larger! Did you see the cathedral?"

"I'd not have thought you would be interested in a Christian cathedral."

"We worship the same God," she said gently, "and I imagine even a free-thinker might value beauty created in His service. You are not so partial, I'm sure, that you would refuse to admire a magnificent building because it belongs to the Roman church and you are an Anglican."

Felix looked decidedly taken aback. "True," he conceded. "Yes, I saw the cathedral and to my mind it does not compare with, say, Winchester or Wells."

Miriam chuckled. "A pardonable prejudice."

As the berline rolled out of the inn yard, she lowered the misted window a little to look out. Leaving the town behind, they drove along the green, fertile Loire valley, the grey, rain-dimpled river now close, now a distant prospect or hidden by trees. A gust of wind drove a shower of drops into her face. She laughed and shook her head, struggling with the strap to raise the window again.

Felix came to her aid. Sitting back, she turned to him. "I trust you are not so set against all things French that you will refuse to — er — improve your grasp of the spoken language?"

"Considering our situation, I should be a veritable mooncalf to do so."

"Then suppose you tell me something you wish to be able to say, and I shall tell you how to say it in French."

"I'll pay well for four good horses," he said promptly.

She translated, and he repeated the words several times after her, with an earnest determination she found endearing. They moved on to other phrases related to hiring horses, until Miriam was floundering among a tangle of harness parts.

"I've not the least notion what you are talking about, let alone what the French equivalents are," she expostulated.

"I don't suppose you have," he admitted, grinning. His face was transformed. If he had been handsome before, he was irresistible now, and Miriam found herself smiling idiotically in response. "Not one female in a thousand would know what a curb chain is," he went on. "How does one say, 'What's that called?' "

"Comment est-ce qu'on appelle ça?"

"Commong tess con a pell sah?"

"Not bad. Try again."

"You say it again first."

"Comment appelle-t-on cela?"

"That's not the same."

"Oh no, sorry. There are several ways of saying the same thing, just as in English you might say 'What's that called' or 'What do you call that' or 'What is the word for that'."

"I thought 'what' was 'coy'."

"Coy? Oh, *quoi!*" She chuckled.

Felix looked affronted by her mirth, but then, reluctantly, he laughed. "Coy — kwah. No wonder that ostler decided I was speaking German. But 'four' is also spelled q-u-, yet you said it is pronouced 'katra', did you not?"

"Yes, sort of." Miriam frowned in thought. "Of course, the 'w' sound doesn't come from the q-u- but from -o-i, like *toi et moi.*"

"I'm not ready yet for twah ay mwah," he said in haste. "Where did you learn French?"

"Où est-ce que vous avez appris le français?"

"No, I mean where did you learn it?"

"At school. At the Cheltenham Seminary for Young Ladies."

"They accept Jews?" His evident incredulity made her look at him askance, and he added stiffly, "I beg your pardon, Miss . . . Miriam. I don't doubt your word."

She nodded acceptance of his apology and continued, her tone dry, "I emerged from that less than exclusive establishment speaking not much better than you, but I've spent a year and more in France since then. My uncle spoke Yiddish, and good German, and some Polish and Russian, but he'd had no occasion for French before I joined him. As I already had a foundation in the language he relied on me to interpret for him. I may not know about harnesses, but I have a superior vocabulary of medical terms."

"Your uncle was a doctor?"

Whether his interest was genuine or by way of a peace offering, Miriam was not sure. Either motive was acceptable, she decided, and regaled him with a history of her travels.

By the time they reached the next inn he was definitely interested, even somewhat admiring. If he was also somewhat disapproving, it only went to show that he was beginning to think of her as a gently-bred lady, not merely a Jewess, or so she hoped. Admittedly her life with Uncle Amos had not conformed to the highest standards of propriety.

Tact — and the continuing drizzle — dictated that she stay in the berline while the horses were changed. She watched, though, and heard Felix say grandly, *"Je paierai bien quatre bons chevaux."*

Once again Miriam winced at his accent, which seemed to her appallingly English, but the ostler simply gave him an odd look and moved to obey.

Felix grinned in triumph at Isaac, descending from the box. Isaac said something, inaudible to Miriam, that wiped the grin from his lordship's face, replacing it with a scowl. Sighing, she sat back against the cushions.

"I wonder why those two are at daggers drawn."

"Jew and Gentile's like oil and water," said Hannah philosophically.

"There's more to it than that, I vow. Now that they are both on speaking terms with me, perhaps I'll be able to find out why they loathe each other so."

"Let sleeping dogs lie, Miss Miriam."

"But they're not sleeping. They snap and growl at each other constantly."

"Like that picture you drew at Mr. Rothschild's house."

"Did you see it? The lion and the panther?"

"I've got it right here in my reticule." She patted the capacious drawstring bag of faded tapestry-work. "God forbid I should have left it lying there for anyone else to see."

"You're right, it was careless of me. What should I do without you, Hannah?"

"I'm sure I can't imagine," snapped her faithful servant, "for all we'd not be on the road to Spain if you ever heeded a word of my advice."

"It's fated," Miriam reminded her, depositing a fond kiss on her lined cheek before turning to peer out of the rain-spotted window. "Where has our panther got to? I haven't had a chance yet to tell him about seeing Jakob Rothschild last night."

"That fox was meant for Mr. Rothschild, wasn't it? He's a cunning one, sure enough."

At that moment the carriage door opened and Isaac stuck his head in. "May I join you, ladies?"

"Of course. Are you very wet?"

"Not too bad." Shrugging off his top-coat of dark brown drab with its modest single cape, he spread it over half the unoccupied seat, perched his hat on top of it, and sat down. "How did you persuade his lordship to let you teach him French?" he enquired, pushing back a damp lock of black hair from his broad brow.

"It was no more difficult than persuading you to let him teach you to drive. You both have sufficient sense to see the need."

"Enough, at least, to accept the need once you had suggested it. I begin to think Jakob was right to send you with us."

"Is that intended for a compliment? I thank you, kind sir." She fluttered her eyelashes at him and he smiled, his sensitive, rather serious face lightening. He really was almost as handsome as Felix when he smiled. Miriam's heart gave a strange little quiver and she hurried on: "Did you know Jakob was at the inn last night?"

"Yes. I didn't realize you had seen him." Isaac frowned now, but in puzzlement, she thought, not annoyance. "Kalmann was there, too."

"Kalmann?"

"The next youngest brother. He's to meet us in Spain."

"Next youngest? I was surprised at Jakob's youth."

"Kalmann is three or four and twenty, I suppose. The Rothschilds begin young. Nathan was scarce twenty years of age when he arrived in England in 1797."

"Who are they? My parents used to entertain all the leading Jews in London but I don't recall ever hearing mention of the name Rothschild."

"There are five brothers. Old Mayer, the father, rose from curio dealer in the Frankfurt ghetto to banker for the Prince of Hesse and virtual director of the finances of Denmark. Nathan was sent to Manchester to buy cotton, before the family decided to trade only in money. He didn't move to London until 1805."

"We left England in 1802," Hannah put in.

"And now Nathan is shipping gold by the hundredweight for the British Government," Miriam marvelled. "I suppose it really is bound for General Wellington? You seemed surprised that Jakob and Kalmann appeared at the Grand Cerf, and I don't see how they knew we were there."

"I'm not sure what they are up to, but you can depend upon it that Wellington will receive the gold as promised. Nathan believes that dishonesty defeats its own purpose. A bank is built on trust; lose that and you're in the suds."

"That makes sense. But why smuggle the gold through France?"

"Even with the English blockade the sea lanes are precarious, and the Rothschilds already have many lines of communication all over Europe. They persuaded the French Minister of Finance to support this venture by convincing him that the British Government opposes it. Besides, they are taking advantage of Napoleon's current preoccupation with his new Austrian wife, and now his heir. By the time the Emperor turns around to look, the flow will be well established, the necessary officials bribed."

"This is the first shipment, then?"

"It is, and thus the most dangerous. It was unconscionable of Jakob to involve you."

"I daresay I could have refused if I had tried," Miriam admitted, "but he was very persuasive and he promised to get us to England afterwards."

"So you wish to return to England? Surely you could have done so years ago."

"If it had been easy, I daresay I might have. But Napoleon was preparing to invade England, Uncle Amos had no desire to go, and I enjoyed seeing the world."

Miriam found herself once again recounting the story of her travels and Uncle Amos's death. Isaac was a more sympathetic, less disapproving audience than Felix. Nonetheless, by the time they reached the Coq d'Or at Blois she decided it was ridiculous that she had now told her life history twice while she still knew next to nothing about the others.

"It will be their turn to talk this afternoon," she said to Hannah as they tidied themselves before rejoining the gentlemen for refreshments. "I'm beginning to like both of them, and I'm determined to see them on better terms with each other."

"Tread carefully, Miss Miriam," advised the maid. "God forbid you should offend them when you've just got them half way tamed."

"I shall have the lion and the panther eating out of my hand yet," Miriam vowed.

When they went down to the dining room, she discovered that whatever Felix ate out of her hand it wouldn't be *saucisson à l'ail.* That the Coq d'Or's sausage was exceptionally garlicky she had to admit. Its rich aroma met her as she entered the room. It made her mouth water and a number of other patrons were downing their shares with evident gusto, but Felix stared at the delicacy with glum disgust, his nostrils quivering.

She sat down beside him.

"I cannot," he said, raising his napkin to his nose. He even looked a trifle green about the gills.

"And I ought not," said Isaac. He looked relieved to have an excuse for not tasting the pungent sausage.

Miriam hesitated. She had acquired a taste for garlic on her travels, and she refused to let considerations of kosher and non-kosher rule her. But on the other hand garlic had a nasty way of lingering on the breath. Shut up in the berline with non-garlic-eaters, she'd be afraid to open her mouth.

"And I shall not," she said, sighing. "I asked for cold meat." She signalled to a waiter who removed the offending dish, returning shortly with a plate of cold chicken and a cheese board.

Oddly enough, neither Felix nor Isaac wrinkled their noses at the emanations from a ripe Camembert. A pair of crisp-crusted loaves rapidly disappeared, and the level in the carafe of vin rouge du pays had sunk to a bare half inch when Miriam saw two men in scarlet uniforms and white-plumed shakos enter the dining room.

Two others stood outside, blocking the door.

She felt the blood drain from her face. Felix dropped his napkin and began to rise.

"Soldiers!" he hissed.

"May God preserve us," gasped Hannah, as Isaac reached across to lay a hand on Felix's arm.

"Sit down. You'll only draw attention to us. Perhaps they have come for a meal."

Miriam shook her head. A swift glance had shown a glimpse of scarlet at every window and at the swinging door to the kitchen. "They're searching for something . . ."

The gold-braided, black-mustached officer rapped on the nearest table with his cane. Abruptly the hum of conversation ceased.

"Vos papiers, citoyens!"

Her voice trembling, Miriam completed her sentence in a whisper. ". . . Or someone."

CHAPTER 7

With outward calm, Isaac took the package of papers from the inside pocket of his coat and laid it on the table. Seeing the sheen of sweat on Felix's forehead, he was proud of the steadiness of his hands, his self-control in not swinging round to look at the soldiers. Or would it be more natural to look? Miriam, an artificial expression of mild interest on her face, was watching their every move.

He ventured to turn his head. The scarlet coats were startlingly bright against a background of smoke-stained walls and the sober apparel of travellers and citizens of Blois.

The officer made his way slowly from table to table. He waved away the papers of women and elderly men and checked the rest against a list carried by his subaltern. A short, round-faced young man, he seemed to take a malicious delight in lingering over names as dissimilar as Dutoit and Dufours while his victims squirmed.

At the tables he had passed, a subdued murmur of conversation arose again, but even there sidelong looks followed the soldiers' progress. Isaac felt his nerves stretching towards breaking point. If only the officer had chosen to circle the room in the opposite direction, by now they would know the worst. If only there was something he could do other than sit and wait like a rabbit mesmerized by the stare of a snake.

He glanced at his companions. Miriam gave him a pale, strained smile; the only other sign of her tension was her clenched fist on the table top. Catching his eye she lowered her hand to her lap. His admiration for her composure redoubled his anger at Jakob for embroiling her in this adventure.

Felix reached for the carafe and poured the last drop of dark red wine into his glass. His taut posture, the very woodenness of his motions in one accustomed to move with vigour, bespoke his uneasiness. He raised the glass to his lips, then suddenly set it down and pushed it across the table towards Miriam's maidservant.

Isaac saw that Hannah was shaking with fright, her terrified eyes fixed on her beloved mistress as she muttered over and over in English, "May God spare her, my dove, may

God spare her."

He put his arm round her shoulders and picked up Felix's glass. "Drink," he commanded in Yiddish, authoritative yet gentle.

She gulped convulsively, spluttered and coughed as the wine caught the back of her throat. Tears rose to her eyes and her colorless cheeks turned crimson. Miriam jumped up and sped round the table to dab at her face with a napkin, while Isaac patted her on the back.

His expression sardonic, Felix watched them fuss over the abigail. He appeared relaxed, and Isaac realized that the incident spurred by his unexpectedly kind gesture had lessened the tension.

It had also drawn the officer's notice. The little man strutted towards them, his bearing so expressive of pomposity that Isaac would have laughed had he not held their fate in his pudgy hands. Twirling the waxed end of his mustache, he bowed to Miriam, who stood straight and tall with one warning, comforting hand on Hannah's shoulder.

"Vos papiers, s'il vous plaît, messieurs."

Isaac handed him the package. He leafed through the passports with agonizing slowness, paused to peruse every word of the letter signed by the Minister of Police. Then he folded them and dropped them on the table with a nod to Isaac. Isaac began to breathe again.

"Continuez," the officer ordered his heavy-set sergeant with a wave. Taking off his shako and smoothing his thinning black hair, he turned to Miriam with a gleam of admiration in his sharp little eyes. "So mademoiselle is Swiss. A beautiful country, and a people of independent spirit."

She smiled at him. "Under the protection of the Emperor, monsieur. May one enquire as to what a captain of the Emperor's army is searching for here?"

"For deserters, mademoiselle. Alas, not all Frenchmen are willing to put their duty to the Emperor and to France above their personal concerns."

"I am shocked to hear such a thing. The more honour to those who serve willingly." Miriam batted her eyelashes in a coquettish way that made Isaac fume, but he didn't dare intervene.

Leering, the repellent little man preened his mustache. "I thank mademoiselle for her good opinion."

"No doubt your vigilance deters many deserters, monsieur?"

"Would that it were so! You know, perhaps, that conscripts are chosen by means of a lottery? You will not credit it, mademoiselle, but as many as three quarters of the eligible young men do not put in an appearance on lottery days. Then there are those who pay another to take their place, those who riot when the names are called, even those who cut off a finger or blind themselves to evade service."

"Disgraceful!" Despite the censure in her tone, Miriam looked a trifle sick at this last revelation, Isaac thought.

"And of those who join the army, fully one in ten later deserts. Last year alone sixteen thousand runaways were caught, convicted, and fined."

"You must be proud to be entrusted with work of such importance to the Empire, monsieur."

His chest swelled, but he said modestly, "I do my duty, mademoiselle." Swinging round, he addressed Felix and Isaac. "And you, messieurs — the Grand Army has no prejudice against foreigners, not even against Jews. Do you not yearn to fight for our glorious Emperor?"

"Oh, monsieur!" Her eyes wide with unfeigned distress, Miriam neatly recaptured his attention. "Pray do not tempt my brother and my cousin to abandon me unprotected."

"I should count it a pleasure to offer mademoiselle my protection," he assured her, gallantly lascivious.

She produced a convincing simper. "You are kind, but our families await us at home. Besides, there is a great deal of your magnificent country we have yet to see."

"You are travelling to admire the glories of France? I trust you are enjoying your stay in Blois, my home town."

"We have only just arrived, monsieur."

"Ah, then there is much pleasure in store for you. You are aware, I am sure, that it was here Jeanne d'Arc raised her standard against the accursed English pigs."

Felix's face darkened, nostrils flared, chin rising aggressively. He must have understood the captain's words. Isaac glared at him and after a moment fraught with danger he subsided, his shoulders slumping. Oblivious, the captain continued to expound upon the splendours of Blois until the stolid sergeant appeared at his elbow to announce that everyone present had been checked.

With a low bow, the captain pronounced himself delighted to have made mademoiselle's acquaintance, desolated to have no excuse for lingering. He kissed her hand with unnecessary fervour, saluted Isaac and Felix, and departed.

Miriam sank into her chair, her smile wry.

"How fortunate that it has stopped raining," she said softly in English. "I'm afraid we're going to have to tour Blois."

The gentlemen groaned in unison.

"Why did you let him draw you into conversation?" Felix snapped.

"A female cannot have too many admirers," she teased. "No, actually I thought it would serve to divert any suspicion he might have felt. Surely he would not expect fugitives to chat with him."

"Let alone to flirt," muttered Isaac, too low for her to hear.

He paid the reckoning and they went out. Despite Felix's disparaging comparisons with English towns, castles, and cathedrals, Isaac enjoyed strolling about the steep streets of Blois. The Loire sparkled in the sun and the air, though fresh and clean after the rain, yet bore tantalizing traces of foreign odours.

When they returned to the Coq d'Or, it was his turn to drive. A new team was hitched. Taking the reins from the ostler, who rushed off to serve another patron, he mounted to the box whistling.

Felix, about to hand Miriam into the carriage, turned and scowled at him. "Not 'Sweet Lass of Richmond Hill,' you numskull," he hissed. "You're lucky the ostler did not hear you."

Isaac scowled back. Admittedly he had not realized what he was whistling, but he considered it most unlikely that a French ostler would recognize the tune as English.

"Try 'For he's a jolly good fellow,' " Miriam suggested. "It is the same tune as 'Malbrouk s'en va-t-en guerre,' a most patriotic, if inaccurate, French song."

But Isaac had lost the urge to whistle. Damn the man for an arrogant, condescending bigot! At least, prejudiced as he was against Jews, Felix would not take advantage of his proximity to Miriam in the berline, even if she had not Hannah to guard her. Isaac grinned sourly.

Inside the carriage, Felix requested an explanation of "patriotic, if inaccurate."

" 'Malbrouk' is a French version of Marlborough," Miriam said. "The song is about the Duke of Marlborough going off to the wars, and it boasts that he will never return."

"But of course he did. In fact he was created duke as a reward for defeating the French!"

"I daresay they prefer to forget that."

"I daresay." He laughed. "Teach me the verse."

So Miriam found herself once more embroiled in a French lesson. Whenever she tried to steer the conversation to more personal matters, Felix determinedly ignored her hints. Hannah gave her an anxious look that said as clearly as words, "Don't set his back up."

So she abandoned — temporarily — her attempt to delve into his past and concentrated on teaching pronunciation.

A couple of hours later, the berline pulled up in a village street, in front of a building with an indecipherable inn sign hanging over the door. Felix reached for his hat.

"Thank you, Miriam."

It was the first time he had addressed her by name. She felt an infuriating flush of pleasure rising in her cheeks.

"You are a rewarding pupil, Felix."

"I doubt anyone will take me for a born Frenchman."

"Perhaps not, but how you would dislike it if they did! You try hard, and what more can a teacher ask?"

"I never imagined a lesson could be so enjoyable. You are an excellent teacher. I find it difficult to believe that you are Jewish."

"I am, I assure you," she said firmly, not sure whether to be annoyed, amused, or pleased. At least he was beginning to exempt her from his deplorable prejudices, to see her as a person, not just as a Jewess.

"Of course, there are exceptions to every rule," he added, and stepped down from the carriage before she could voice an exasperated protest.

"Drat the man!" she exclaimed.

"He's not a bad-hearted lad," Hannah said unexpectedly. "God willing, given a chance he'll learn not to judge people he doesn't know."

"Why, never say you have fallen for his pretty blue eyes, Hannah. He is a handsome fellow, is he not?"

"Handsome is as handsome does, Miss Miriam. You'll do well to remember he's a goy, and too young for you into the bargain."

"Too young? I put him at just about my age."

"And it's an older man you need, as can control your starts. But if I'm not mistaken his lordship's no more than four or five and twenty, though he looks older when he's on his high ropes."

"I bow to your judgment. His lordship is a mere stripling, young enough to learn the error of his ways."

A waiter appeared at that moment with a tray of coffee and biscuits, ordered presumably by Isaac since his youthful lordship's command of French did not as yet extend so far. Miriam realized it was a long time since their nerve-racking luncheon in Blois. Gratefully she gulped down the milky brew and nibbled on a biscuit.

"What I wouldn't give for a cup of tea," sighed Hannah, sipping her coffee. "I do believe it's what I've missed most all these years. How I wish we were home safe already."

"It has been an exhausting, alarming day, my poor Hannah. I daresay we shall not go farther than one more stage today, which will take us to Tours. Seeing the sights in Blois delayed us."

"Will we stay at an inn in Tours? I vow I'll never feel safe at an inn again."

"Where else should we . . . Oh, you are thinking of Monsieur and Madame Lévi. They would certainly find room for you and me, but I hesitate to ask them to put up the men. Their house is small and they are far from well off."

"Let the men go to an inn without us."

"A poor time they would have of it, speaking French as they do. It is not a bad idea, though. Let us see what Isaac thinks of it."

The waiter came to retrieve the tray, and then Isaac joined them. As they continued along the banks of the Loire, Miriam laid the proposal before him. "After the soldiers at the Coq d'Or, I doubt I should sleep a wink at an inn," she explained.

He shook his head in smiling disbelief. "That's odd, I'd not have guessed you to be of so nervous a disposition."

"It's me, sir," Hannah confessed. "Made me quake in my shoes, they did."

"Perfectly understandable, Miss Greenbaum," he said sympathetically. "I was a trifle worried myself!"

"And that nasty little man making up to Miss Miriam and her not able to give him a set-down for fear of him taking against us. You never know who you'll meet in a public inn. But I wouldn't want to put anyone out, sir."

"A night spent with friends in Tours will give you an opportunity to recover from the fright. I'll tell Felix to drive straight to their house when we reach the town."

"I'll tell him," Miriam said quickly. "I can give him directions. Besides, sparks are bound to fly if you presume to instruct him."

He acknowledged the truth with a rueful grin.

Moving across to the seat beside him, she reached up to open the little panel in the front of the carriage. Her arm brushed against his shoulder. His eyes met hers and for an endless moment sparks flew between them — not sparks of anger and distrust but a tingling excitement that raced through Miriam's veins.

She tore her gaze away. Her voice was a trifle breathless as she explained the plan to Felix.

He grunted his qualified assent, "As you will, so long as I'm not expected to stay with your Jewish friends."

"I cannot imagine that they would want you," she responded tartly, slamming the panel closed.

Careful not to touch Isaac, she returned to her seat, only to find that he was laughing at her. "And you were afraid he and I might come to cuffs?" he teased.

"Well, I did not ruffle his feathers, he ruffled mine. He can be utterly infuriating! But sometimes he is companionable, even charming. Why do you dislike him so?"

The quizzical smile vanished. "His kind ruined my life. Born with a silver spoon in his mouth, brought up to consider the world his oyster, and when he finds the pearl is missing, borrows with no thought of how he is to repay."

"Ruined your life?"

"Did you know that peers cannot be imprisoned for debt? That if a minor lies about his age to borrow money, the contract is unenforceable and the lender cannot recover a penny? My father lent vast sums to some of the bluest blooded families in England. He was bankrupted by noble spendthrifts unable or unwilling to pay their debts to the Jew moneylender. He died in poverty."

"I'm so sorry." Leaning forward, Miriam held out her hand in earnest commiseration and he clasped it briefly. "So that is why you are working for Nathan Rothschild."

"His wife is my cousin. He took me into his business, but of course I had to abandon my studies."

"That must have been a fearful blow."

To her surprise, he looked a trifle discomposed but he said only, "It was a great disappointment, and my father was much grieved." He changed the subject. "Tell me about Monsieur and Madame Lévi. How do you come to know them?"

Even as she described how Uncle Amos had saved all five Lévi children from the evil consequences of the measles, Miriam wondered at Isaac's odd reaction to her comment. Was it connected with his abandonment of so many of the observances of Halakah? Her own mixed feelings about the lack of religion in her upbringing made her long to discuss the matter with him, but he was clearly reluctant.

At least she had learned the source of his antipathy for Felix. Now she must discover Felix's side of the story, and then she'd be able to attempt a reconciliation.

Dusk was falling when they reached Tours. Miriam watched through the window as Felix negotiated the city streets. He remembered her directions perfectly. Nonetheless she was relieved, and pleased with herself, when she recognized the house he stopped at, for it was over a year since their last visit. The signboard over the small shop on the ground floor read *"Lévi, tailleur, soierie."*

"You wait here, Miss Miriam," Hannah commanded. "I'll go see what's what."

Her rat-a-tat on the door of the tall, narrow, slightly shabby town house was answered by a youthful maid in a white cap and apron. Miriam was glad she had stayed in the carriage when Hannah was left standing on the step while the girl ran upstairs to make enquiries.

Returning, she invited Hannah to step in. Not two minutes later the door burst open and out rushed the entire Lévi family. Madame's round, beaming face appeared at the carriage window, her tailor-cum-silk-merchant husband grinning over her shoulder, all five excited children clustered about them.

"Miriam, ma chère, come in, come in. And bring these gentlemen with you. How could we let your friends stay at an inn? We shall make room somehow, never fear."

It was impossible to tell them that one of the gentlemen they welcomed despised Jews. Fortunately, Felix found it equally impossible to be so ungentlemanly as to rudely reject their hospitality. His face reflected his quandary as he allowed Monsieur Lévi to usher him into that den of iniquity, a Jewish home.

Miriam exchanged a mirthful glance with Isaac and bit her lip to suppress a giggle.

CHAPTER 8

"I believe you captured little Leah's heart," Miriam teased Felix as Isaac drove the berline out of Tours the next morning. "I am sadly jealous. She has been a favourite of mine since I nursed her through the croup after all the children had the measles."

"She reminded me of my youngest sister," he said defensively. "Vickie is just such a playful chatterbox."

"Like Leah, never waiting for you to answer?"

"Most fortunate that she did not, for I understood no more than one word in five. What was she saying when . . ."

"How old is your sister?" Miriam interrupted. She had no intention of allowing so promising an opening to degenerate into another French lesson.

"Victoria? She must be Leah's age, or thereabouts."

"Six or seven? And your other sisters, how

many have you?"

"Three more. Augusta is married, with two infants, Constantia is eighteen, and Lucy twelve. Connie ought to be in London right now, dancing through her first Season, instead of languishing at Westwood." His bitterness was unmistakable.

"She is not ill, I hope?"

"No, unless with disappointment. Thanks to Isaac Cohen's father, my father is deep in debt and cannot afford to present his daughter to Society."

"But Isaac's father is dead."

"I'm glad to hear it. I trust his demise will save some other unfortunate family from impoverishment. Yes, that is excellent news."

Hannah was shocked out of her usual deference. "It's not right to talk like that of the dead," she rebuked him, "may they rest in peace. God forbid we should any of us claim to be perfect."

Felix looked a trifle shamefaced.

"The earl borrowed money from Mr. Cohen, I collect," Miriam probed, "and failed to repay it?"

"On the contrary," he said coldly, "he paid every penny. In order to do so, he sold two small estates and mortgaged Westwood to the hilt. Instead of purchasing a commission in the army, I was forced to go to work at the Treasury."

In essence, his story was not so very different from Isaac's. To hold each other responsible for their respective difficulties was just plain muttonheaded. Miriam was sure now that she could effect a reconciliation, but she needed time to consider how to go about it.

In the meantime, what she really wanted to know was what the earl had done with the borrowed money. In all likelihood, given the predilections of the upper classes, he had gambled it away and had no one to blame but himself for his family's relative impoverishment.

It seemed less than tactful to enquire of his dutiful son and heir. Miriam restrained her curiosity. "You wanted to be a soldier?" she said instead.

"I wanted to fight Boney. England was expecting an invasion at any moment. Lord, the tales that flew about! The Corsican Ogre was digging a tunnel under the Channel, or building a fleet of hot air balloons to float above it. He ate babies for breakfast and dined on the heads of his enemies."

"May God preserve us!" Hannah moaned.

"Ugh!" said Miriam. "But none of those tales was true."

"Somewhat exaggerated," he acknowledged, smiling. "Nonetheless, I wish I were fighting Napoleon now, or at least Marshal Massena, in the Peninsula with Viscount Wellington. To my mind he is the greatest British general since the Duke of Marlborough."

"Tell me about him," Miriam invited. "For all I have agreed to deliver his gold, I know nothing of him beyond the fact that he needs the gold to pay his army."

"That alone tells you a great deal. Wellesley — Lord Wellington — expects his soldiers to pay the peasants for the food and horses they requisition, whereas the French simply loot what they need." Felix continued his fervent paean to the hero of Talavera and Bussaco.

Miriam was thinking how absurdly boyish his enthusiasm made him seem, when the carriage jolted to a sudden halt. At once his arrogant mask descended.

"What the deuce is that nodcock doing now?" He beat Miriam to the window and leaned out. "Oh, there's some sort of accident ahead."

Swinging the door open, he jumped down. Miriam followed. A few yards beyond the berline's reined-in team, she saw to her dismay a cluster of uniforms, dark green with white facings. In their midst the gleam-

116

ing steel barrel of an artillery gun pointed futilely at the grey sky.

She hurried after Felix.

The group parted as they reached it. One wheel of the gun carriage had slid into the ditch alongside the muddy road. Five of the six huge Percherons pulling it had kept their footing. They stood stolidly, heads hanging, but the left wheeler was struggling in scummy, hock-deep water. The harness tangled about its head and shoulders pulled it sideways, preventing it from rising.

Producing a pocket-knife, Felix pushed in grim silence through the arguing, gesticulating soldiers and began to cut the horse loose. Two of the Frenchmen joined him, one to help, one to berate them both.

Her attention elsewhere, Miriam left him to deal with them. On the grassy bank beyond the ditch, a soldier slumped with his bloody head clasped in his hands. An officer stood over him, his black boots crushing a clump of primroses.

"*Sot! Buvard!* See what you have done, *fils de putaine!*" he shouted.

Miriam eyed the ditch with distaste. It was too wide to jump, but then she spotted a plank bridge over it, back near the berline, where a gate led into a field. As she sped towards it, Isaac sprang down from the box, holding the reins.

"There's a man hurt," she called in Yiddish. "Tell Hannah to bring linen."

He nodded and was turning towards the carriage when an unearthly shriek made them both swing round. Miriam's gaze flew to the injured soldier. He and the officer were both staring at something farther along the road but after a moment they returned to their respective poses of sullen submission and acrimonious reproof. Where were those dreadful screams coming from?

In the field on the other side of the gate, a peasant was ploughing, neither he nor his horse taking the least notice of the commotion out on the highroad.

Miriam crossed the crude bridge and picked her way as quickly as she could along the bank. The ghastly noise was coming from the Percheron, she realized. Felix turned away from it, and called to her.

"The horse has a broken leg." He waved at the officer. "Tell him it will have to be shot."

Miriam translated. The officer looked curiously at Felix and shrugged.

"Go and take that horse," he ordered the soldiers who had followed Felix. He pointed at the plough horse in the field and watched the men obey, ignoring Felix.

White with anger, Felix jumped the ditch, pulled a pistol from the officer's holster, and strode back to the doomed Percheron. Frozen in disbelief, the Frenchman gaped after him. The crack of a single shot split the air. The screaming cut off abruptly as the horse sank onto its side against the bank.

Red with anger, the officer jumped the ditch. Miriam made no attempt to intervene. Half sickened, half relieved, she turned to the injured soldier.

Hannah arrived with clean linen torn in strips and one of the other soldiers passed them a canteen of water. The women concentrated on cleaning and binding the broken head of the gun-carriage driver, who had also hurt his ankle. He explained how he had come by his injuries, but since he spoke a near incomprehensible patois, Miriam was not much the wiser.

Pulling up his eyelid to inspect his pupil, Miriam decided he was not concussed despite the purpling bruise and horrid gash in his forehead. The smell of his stocking-less foot, when they managed to remove his boot, nearly made her faint. Her inspection of his swelling ankle to make sure it was sprained, not broken, was cursory. Hannah, in this instance made of stronger stuff, produced from the depths of her reticule a small vial of witch hazel, soaked a strip of linen, and wrapped it around the ankle.

She was engaged in this operation when the soldiers sent after the plough horse returned, leading the shaggy beast. The peasant, a wizened old man, scurried beside them, pulling on the sleeve of the nearest.

"At least pay me," he pleaded. "My only horse! How am I to feed my family if I cannot plough the field?"

"Va-t-en, mon vieux," said the soldier, not unkindly. "It is for the Emperor. You should be honoured."

The peasant fell back, wringing his hands. Miriam had no leisure to consider his plight for the officer was striding towards her, his face now hard with suspicion.

"Your companion spoke to you in English," he accused, gesturing with his discharged pistol at Felix, who followed him. "Now he won't speak at all."

"In English? *Mais non, monsieur.* We are Swiss. I speak French but my cousin speaks only SvitzerDütsch — Swiss-German."

"That's right," the injured soldier confirmed. "I had a Swiss *copain* once, a good friend, talked just like that."

"Ferme-toi la bouche, imbécile!" the officer snarled.

Miriam took advantage of the momentary

distraction to call to Isaac in Yiddish, "Come here, quick. He thinks we are English."

Isaac dropped the reins and started forward, reaching into his pocket for their papers. As she had hoped, Felix promptly rushed to hold the horses. With him out of the way, she explained the situation to Isaac, still in Yiddish. The language sounded sufficiently like German, and unlike English, to make the officer wonder whether he had misheard Felix in the heat of the moment — unless he was fluent in English.

He looked at them doubtfully. Surely he had sufficient problems on his hands with the ditched gun not to arrest them if he was uncertain, even though Felix had enraged him.

"Nos papiers, monsieur," Isaac said calmly, holding out the papers to him. "We have a pass from the Minister of Police."

For a moment he hesitated. "Pah!" he spat out, "I am no policeman." He turned on his heel and marched off, yelling at his men.

Miriam's patient winked at her. She smiled at him, took Hannah's arm, and urged the maid back to the bridge, where the old peasant stood hunched, gazing hopelessly after his conscripted plough horse.

"They stole his only horse," Miriam told Isaac. "Felix was just telling me that the French army seizes what it wants without compensation, but I thought he meant in foreign countries, not from their own people."

"What do you think the creature is worth? This is not exactly the sort of emergency Jakob had in mind, but how can one pass by with a full purse?"

"Give him a couple of napoléons d'or," she said with a look of approval. "They will at least ease the pain of being robbed in the name of Napoleon."

The peasant called down blessings on their heads and scurried off across the field, clutching the coins. Approaching the berline, Miriam saw that Felix was watching them with a strange expression on his face. The act of charity he had witnessed, she realized with satisfaction, fitted his concept of the miserly Jew no better than had last night's hospitality. He was confused.

"I'll drive until we are past the obstruction," he offered gruffly.

"I am perfectly capable of passing a stationary obstacle," Isaac flared up. "I only stopped to see if they needed help."

Sighing, Miriam left them to battle it out and reentered the berline. She was too drained to try to make peace. Hannah sat down beside her.

"I'm getting quite used to them French soldiers, Miss Miriam," she said proudly, smoothing her skirts. "Didn't turn a hair, I didn't."

"Well, I did. Felix's concern for that poor horse was admirable, but how could he speak English before a French officer like that!"

She said no more, for he joined them. They sat in tense silence as the berline began to move. When Isaac pulled out to pass the stranded gun, Miriam saw the officer standing with his back resolutely turned, determined to ignore them. On the other hand, several soldiers, including her patient, waved. She couldn't resist waving back.

A hundred yards farther on they drove past three more guns, drawn in to the side of the road. The teams stood patiently; the crews chatted or smoked their clay pipes, uninterested in the passing carriage.

"I wish I could blow them all up," said Felix passionately. "To think that they will soon be aimed at our men!"

"I daresay the absence of the gold we carry would do General Wellington more harm than the presence of a few more guns."

He looked disconcerted. "I daresay," he

conceded with obvious reluctance. "That soldier you bandaged, was he a Jew?"

"I doubt it. Should I reserve my healing abilities for Jews?"

"He was an enemy."

"He was in pain. Like the horse you shot."

"That officer was a brute." He paused, then went on stiffly, "I must beg your pardon, ma'am, for endangering you, and our mission, by my rash behaviour."

"I quite understand that you could not bear to leave the horse to suffer, and no one else cared enough to put it out of its misery. It was a pity you forgot the French words in the heat of the moment but all's well that ends well."

He did not appear to take much comfort from her sympathy. Finding himself so clearly in the wrong was a blow to his self-esteem. Miriam decided it would be wise to wait until he showed signs of recovery before she attempted a discussion of personal matters. She turned to Hannah, and they talked about the Lévi children until the carriage stopped at the next posting house.

Felix stepped out at once. The change of horses was quickly accomplished, Isaac took his place, and they were on their way again.

"Did you rake Felix over the coals?" Miriam wanted to know. "He apologized for imperiling the expedition."

"I should bloody well hope so! Of all the chuckleheaded things to do. No, I'd have liked to comb his hair with a joint stool but surrounded by French soldiers as we were it hardly seemed the right moment. Just wait till I get him somewhere private!"

"Since he is penitent, it will serve no purpose to reproach him now. Let it go, Isaac."

"You are too forgiving. If that officer had been more confident of his recognition of English, we'd all be under arrest right now."

"But we are not. Treating him like an errant schoolboy will only hurt his pride."

"He needs taking down a peg or two."

"Please?"

"Very well, I'll consider it." He still looked angry. "I don't know why you are so concerned for the feelings of a Jew-hater." He took a book from his pocket.

Obviously, it was the wrong time to try to persuade him that Felix was an agreeable young man. In fact, Miriam thought sadly, the breach between her companions seemed wider than ever.

CHAPTER 9

Luncheon was a sombre meal. Felix brooded and Isaac, though he held his tongue, had not forgiven him for his dangerous blunder. Miriam was glad to return to the carriage. She was almost beginning to think of it as home.

The road ran along the Vienne, a pretty river flowing between fields of sprouting grain and vineyards greening with new leaves. Before Miriam tired of watching the scenery, Felix tired of his solitary reflections and requested a French lesson. His ear for the language was improving steadily. She told him so as the berline rolled into Châtellerault and he flushed with pleasure.

He took his seat on the box, and Isaac replaced him inside the carriage.

"It's like a country dance where one is constantly changing partners," Miriam observed, laughing.

"You enjoy dancing?" Isaac asked.

"I hardly know. The lessons we had at school were fun, but of course we were all females. The girl chosen to partner the dancing master was an object of envy, though he was five foot two, the shape of a pear, and had bad breath. I was looking forward to the balls my friends promised to invite me to when they made their come-outs in Society — but I went off with Uncle Amos instead."

"I'm sorry for any part I had in depriving you of the pleasure."

She dismissed his wry apology with a wave. "My own choice. I am not too aged, I hope, to tread a measure when I reach England again! Do you like to dance?"

"I've never had any opportunity to find out."

"You don't disapprove? The Hasidic Jews in Poland dance, though they are the most hemmed about with restrictions of any community I know. Of course, they dance men with men and women with women."

"They make women shave their heads when they marry, and wear wigs," Hannah disclosed in accents of horror. "Did you ever hear the like? Now where's the sense in that, I ask you. God forbid Miss Miriam should cut off her beautiful hair."

"God forbid," he echoed, with such fervour that Miriam blushed.

She rushed into speech. "The Hasidim live in another world, a medieval world. Actually, so do most of the Gentiles of Poland and Russia. The peasants who work the land are still the property of the land-owners as they were in medieval times in England. Nothing has changed there for centuries."

"But we live in a changing world. Our ancestors adapted to changing circum-stances — the ways of life and worship of Abraham, the herdsman, evolved into those of the city-dwellers who built the Temple, and those were later adapted to the needs of the Diaspora. The history of Judaism is not static."

"I know so little!" Miriam exclaimed in frustration.

Hannah patted her hand. "There's an old saying, that a man who teaches the Torah to his daughter spreads heresy."

"But why shouldn't women learn too, whether it's the Torah or Latin and Natural Philosophy? I would have liked to be a doc-tor, like Uncle Amos. Both Jews and Gen-tiles shut women out of full participation in life," she challenged Isaac.

He took the wind out of her sails. "I agree. If you are not acquainted with the laws and their background, how can you decide which were more appropriate to another age and place, and which remain meaningful to you in today's world? I eat non-kosher food, and to wash my hands after meals and say a blessing aloud in Hebrew would draw unwanted attention, but I never fail to say it silently to myself."

"You do?"

"It's important to me. Yet in the end, all that's important is to love God and to love your neighbour as yourself. That is the foundation of our faith."

His declaration made Miriam feel more Jewish, and more proud to be Jewish, than any amount of Sabbath observance. She saw that tears stood in Hannah's eyes. For a few minutes they were all enveloped in their own thoughts.

Miriam broke the silence, her mind returning to a more immediate concern. "Then you don't really mind having to give up the life of a Talmudic scholar?"

Isaac hesitated, then said in a surprised voice, "To tell the truth, no. My father pushed me into religious studies. I believe he hoped his son's piety would atone for his worldliness. Once set on that course, I threw myself into it heart and soul, persuaded myself it was my choice. I even persuaded myself I resented having to quit it."

"But you are not truly distressed?"

"I suspect I was never really suited to a life devoted to book-learning."

"I'm glad." She was thinking of his transformation from stooped, weak-eyed boy to attractive, vital man, but his look of quizzical enquiry drew a different explanation from her: "I mean, I'm glad that you are not still grieving over your abandoned books."

"I would not have you think I now avoid books altogether. I brought Maimonides Guide to the Perplexed with me, since it's in Hebrew and will not raise suspicions." He patted his pocket. "And at home I have been reading English translations of the works of Moses Mendelssohn, the German philosopher who advocated dispensing with practices that keep Jews apart from society at large."

"Uncle Amos credited his ideas with making it possible for a Jew to study modern medicine without converting to Christianity."

Miriam was pleased to note that Isaac was impressed by her recognition of Mendelssohn's name and awareness of the significance of his teachings. Putting together Uncle Amos's occasional comments and snippets recalled from her distant schooldays, she managed to ask an intelligent question about the influence of the Enlightenment on Judaism.

The subsequent discussion lasted until the berline rumbled into Poitiers. Returning Isaac's smile as she took his helping hand to descend in the inn yard, Miriam realized she was happier than she had been since Uncle Amos's last illness.

Isaac's agreeable company and stimulating conversation delighted her. If only he would acknowledge Felix's good points the rest of the journey might prove unexpectedly enjoyable.

Recovered from his megrims, Felix climbed down from the box with an air of complacency. Miriam wondered why he was so pleased with himself. He started to say something, but three ostlers converged on the carriage, forcing him to hold his tongue. Though the inn he had chosen, the Tête-de-Boeuf, was an imposing brick building facing the town square, there were few carriages in the yard. The landlord himself came out to greet them.

Isaac requested a private parlour and four bedchambers, only to be firmly contradicted by Hannah, who understood enough French to know when she disapproved.

"I'll sleep in Miss Miriam's room," she insisted in Yiddish, adding darkly, "The place looks respectable enough, but you never can tell." Her concern was all for propriety. Inquisitive soldiers had already become a commonplace in her mind.

Promising three comfortable chambers, an elegant dining parlour, and a superb meal, the solicitous innkeeper ushered them into the Tête-de-Boeuf and summoned his servants to attend them. While Miriam ordered dinner, Felix and Isaac went upstairs, cheerful at the prospect of not having to share a bed as they had for the last two nights.

A chambermaid bearing cans of hot water led Miriam and Hannah to a spacious room furnished with a huge featherbed. She assured them that their luggage would be carried up at once.

"Both Felix and Isaac are in a good humour," Miriam said, taking off her grey cloak as the maid departed, "and likely to remain so if their chambers are as comfortable as this, and dinner as good as the landlord promised. As we have a private parlour, Felix will be able to speak freely. Perhaps tonight I shall be able to persuade them to cry friends."

"Better be quick about it, then, afore they

realize they're rivals."

"Rivals? What do you mean?"

"I've got eyes in my head, Miss Miriam. I've seen what I've seen. All men are fools, and if there's one thing they're more foolish about than others it's a pretty girl."

"Me?" Miriam laughed, but uneasily. "Nonsense. I'm not a girl any longer and my clothes are anything but smart. Besides, neither of them wanted me to go with them."

"Changed their minds, haven't they."

"Well, I have proved useful to them. I only hope they will change their minds about each other, for I like them both." She was glad when a knock at the door interrupted the disturbing conversation. A wheezing old man brought in their boxes and Hannah's attention turned to unpacking.

Once again clad in forest-green satin, Miriam regarded herself in the mirror. Her figure was still good, her pale skin flawless, her red hair thick and shiny, but no one could have taken her for an eligible damsel fresh from the schoolroom, she thought wistfully. Handsome young men like Isaac and Felix surely had their pick of the prettiest girls. If they found her attractive, it was because she was at present the only female other than Hannah with whom they were safe.

When she reached home, she would probably have to be satisfied with a widower for a husband. That wouldn't be so bad, she told herself, if he was kind and loving.

She picked up her shawl and Hannah helped her drape it to hide the worn patch.

"Do you reckon you'll need a chaperon?" said the abigail. "Being as how it's a private room and there'll be two gentlemen present." She managed to convey without quite saying it that she wouldn't trust either gentleman alone with her mistress.

"I need you as a chaperon, but still more, I need you with me as my friend. You can help me encourage them to be friends. Come on, I'm hungry."

The private room was as elegant as the bedchamber was comfortable. Miriam felt out of place in her plain, shabby gown amidst Louis XV furniture and gilt mirrors she suspected must have been looted from some château during the revolution. In fact only Felix seemed entirely at ease, though he had conscientiously not dressed in full evening finery.

The food, however, was so delicious as to banish discomfort. Felix regarded the ubiquitous sauces with some suspicion, but in the end he had two helpings of everything and three of the trout à la Provençale. He pronounced the wines, chosen by mine host, superb and consumed a considerable proportion of each bottle.

Conversation languished until the waiters withdrew, leaving dried figs and raisins, nuts, pots de crème, and a selection of cheeses, along with coffee and brandy.

"What a splendid meal," sighed Isaac, cracking a walnut. "No one can deny that the French excel in the kitchen."

"And the cellar," Felix said with a grin, warming a glass of cognac in his hand, "if in nothing else. Do you realize where we are?"

A vague memory stirred at the back of Miriam's mind. "Wasn't there a battle here?"

"Poitiers?" Isaac sounded blank.

"Don't you know your history?" Felix asked impatiently. "Poitiers is where the English under the Black Prince trounced the French and took their king prisoner. We'll do the same for Boney yet."

"When was that?"

"1356." Miriam recaptured memorized details of a lesson on the Hundred Years War. She could have cited the number of troops on each side at the Battle of Poitiers.

"Not our history then," said Isaac in an even, noncommittal voice. "The Jews were expelled from England in 1290. We didn't return till Elizabeth's reign, and we were not welcome until Cromwell and the Commonwealth."

Felix stared at him with a sneer. "I always doubted that a Jew could be a loyal Englishman." He set down his glass, pushed back his chair, and rose. "Pray excuse me, ma'am." He strode from the room.

Miriam gazed after him in dismay. What an ending to an evening she had expected to be a time of reconciliation! Isaac, his face a little pale, continued to pick the nutmeat from the shell. Hannah shook her head with a reproachful expression, as she had when Miriam was naughty as a child.

Isaac smiled penitently at the maid, then turned to Miriam. "I beg your pardon, I need not have said that."

"Well, I think it's a pity you did, but he was inexcusably rude."

"His lordship's tongue is liable to run away with him," observed Hannah. "Like that business with the horse. I doubt he means all he says. It's my belief the poor lad embarrasses himself more than anything."

"You are generous, Miss Greenbaum."

" 'Love your neighbour,' sir."

"Felix is only saying what he has been taught," Miriam put in. "It's up to us to teach him differently. And I believe he was disappointed that we didn't share his relish in the English victory over the French."

"How determined you are to defend him!" The flash of anger in Isaac's dark eyes made her think of Hannah's talk of rivalry. Was it possible he was jealous? The notion at once alarmed and thrilled her.

She needed an impersonal reason for peacemaking. "We have a long way to go," she pointed out, "and we have to rely on each other."

"True, alas. I shall endeavour to ignore his lordship's indiscreet outbursts. Is there any coffee left in the pot, Miriam? These French cups are ridiculously small."

Refilling his demi-tasse with coffee, she made him laugh with a lament for the lack of tea.

"Even after your long absence," he said, "there can be no doubt about your English-ness."

They chatted about Miriam's schooldays while he sipped his coffee and she finished her pot de crème, and then she requested, "Since we are alone, will you say grace aloud?"

Isaac complied, not in Hebrew but in English so that both she and Hannah could understand. His thoughtfulness warmed her, and the ancient blessing she had heard in every corner of Europe gave her a sense of belonging to a great community.

The feeling of contentment had faded by the time they retired to their chambers. Miriam tossed and turned for a long time. The enmity between Isaac and Felix was becoming harder and harder to bear. She liked both of them — and she found both physically attractive.

The soft embrace of the feather bed was a poor substitute for a man's loving arms.

In the morning, Felix ate breakfast in gloomy silence and without consultation climbed up to the berline's box to take the first turn driving. Handing the ladies into the carriage, Isaac grimaced.

" 'Love your neighbour' is a difficult rule to live by," Miriam observed with a sympathetic smile as he joined them.

"Virtually impossible. The sage Hillel had a more practical interpretation: Do not do to others what you would not have them do to you."

"That does sound practical. After all, it's possible to control one's actions but not always one's feelings. You don't have to like

Felix, just not do anything to hurt him. Who was Hillel?"

Fascinated to learn more of her own heritage, Miriam found the time passing quickly. When the berline stopped to change horses she asked teasingly, "Are you not afraid to be spreading heresy by discussing the Torah with a female?"

"Because of the adage Miss Greenbaum quoted yesterday? But you are not my daughter." The gleam in his eye made her blush. "I suppose I must go and dispossess Felix of the reins. I hope he will give them up peacefully, and keep a civil tongue in his head when he joins you."

Felix was subdued, but he politely requested a French lesson. Miriam obliged, and again time sped past. After an hour or so spent on various subjects, he asked her to explain the French monetary system, with its confusion of deniers, centimes, sous, francs, écus, louis, and napoléons. She did her best.

"Trust the French to make it complicated," he said in the end.

"It is, but no more so than the English system. Think of farthings, ha'pennies, pennies, shillings, crowns . . ."

". . . Pounds and sovereigns, which are the same thing, and guineas, which are utterly illogical," he added to the list, grinning. "I never thought of it, but it's just as bad. Money is the root of all evil."

"Love of money is the root of all evil," corrected Miriam, who had, after all, attended a Christian school. "Life would be hard if we had to go back to barter."

"It would indeed." He frowned and said brusquely but with a hint of uncertainty, "Since Isaac is already rich, he must have an excessive love of money to want to earn more by running the Rothschilds' errand."

"Isaac is not rich. He is earning his living. His father was ruined by defaulting debtors."

"Serves him right! He ruined my father."

"Did Mr. Cohen force the earl to accept a loan?"

The question threw Felix off his stride but rallying he ignored it. "If it weren't for him, I would not have had to work for the Government and I would not be here now."

"Why, I thought it was patriotism that persuaded you to escort Wellington's gold," said Miriam with an innocent air.

He looked sheepish. "Well, of course, it's important to the struggle against Bonaparte, though I had rather do my part fighting under Wellington than delivering his army's pay. You surely will not claim that Isaac has any patriotic reason for being here."

"I cannot speak for Isaac, you must ask him for yourself if he is a patriot. But don't dare to say that I am not a loyal English-woman. It's the only reason I accompanied you."

"Rothschild is not paying you?" he asked, surprised.

"He will help us return to England, but we might have managed it without his assistance. In fact, we have friends in Bordeaux who could have arranged to smuggle us across, I daresay. The war cannot stop the wine trade, as I'm sure you are aware. Hannah, we ought to have gone first to Bordeaux, not to Paris."

"We still could ask Monsieur Ségal, Miss Miriam, 'stead of going on to Spain."

"What, after I have been boasting of my patriotism? God forbid."

Felix was honest enough to admit, "Isaac and I would find it difficult to go on without you." He fell silent, but it was a thoughtful silence, not sullen. Miriam dared to hope.

CHAPTER 10

When they stopped for luncheon, Felix asked Miriam to request a private parlour. Suspecting that he wanted to talk to Isaac, as a change from blindly accusing him, she complied, but the inn was too small to afford such a luxury. Disappointed, she failed to appreciate a savoury bowl of cassoulet. By the evening he might have changed his mind again.

The team the ostlers claimed to be their best was bad enough to try anyone's temper. However, Felix chose to regard driving the four ill-matched, balky horses as a challenge to his skill. Despite his care in nursing them along, their uneven paces caused a trace to break. Knotting a makeshift repair with the aid of a spare whip-thong, he drove on, whereupon one of the horses shed a shoe.

The next village they came to had no horses for hire so they had to stop at the smithy to have the horse reshod. Despite a generous tip, the blacksmith worked with excruciating slowness. Miriam could tell Felix's patience, never remarkable, was wearing thin about the edges.

By the time Isaac took over the driving at the next post-house, with a comparatively superb team at his service, she had come up with a plan to restore Felix to good humour: she asked him about curricle races he had driven in. He responded with enthusiasm. Describing his victories he relived his triumph, yet he laughed at the ineptness of his losses with an attractive self-deprecation.

Miriam learned far more than she wanted to know about the team of greys he had raced to Brighton. She also learned a great deal about the carefree life he had led before his father's debts reduced the family to straitened circumstances. The sudden change must have come as a fearful shock.

If Hannah was right about his age, he could not have been more than twenty-one when his splendid future had vanished before his eyes. No wonder he was bitter.

At present, though, he was cheerful and charming. He went on to tell her about the larks he and his friends had got up to at Cambridge. They were all laughing, even Hannah, when the berline rolled into Angoulême.

Because of the delays en route, they barely reached the town before dark. Nonetheless, Miriam managed to procure three bed-chambers and a private parlour. After washing and changing — how she was coming to despise the green silk! — Miriam went down to the parlour with a feeling of mingled optimism and dread. She was certain the evening was going to bring a confrontation between the men. Whether the result would be positive or negative she couldn't guess.

Felix was already in the parlour, standing at the window looking out into the night. In the moment before he noticed her arrival she contemplated the gleam of candlelight on his golden hair, his broad shoulders, the powerful muscles outlined by his clinging knit pantaloons. Obviously his duties at the Treasury left considerable leisure for exercise.

Behind her, Hannah coughed. Felix swung round. Perhaps it was wishful thinking but Miriam thought she saw a gleam of admiration in his blue eyes in the brief pause before he grinned and remarked, "It's a bit Spartan after last night."

His sweeping gesture took in the plain deal table, the wooden chairs that looked as if they belonged in a kitchen, the whitewashed, unornamented walls and the miserly fire in the iron grate.

"Let us hope the cuisine is less Spartan than the décor," she said. "It's amazing how hungry one can get doing nothing but sit in a . . ."

The arrival of a pair of waiters put a stop to the exchange. While they were spreading a white cloth on the table, Isaac came in. He too commented with a grin on the stark bareness of the room, in Yiddish.

Repeating in that language her desire for a good dinner, Miriam noticed that Felix was watching Isaac and herself with a wary look. She felt a sudden rush of sympathy. Not to understand what one's companions were saying must be horridly frustrating. Maybe he thought they were talking about him, even laughing at him.

She took Isaac's arm and tugged him across the room to join Felix by the window. In slow, precise French tailored to his understanding, she said, "Isaac had exactly the same reaction to the room as you did."

To her relief, the gentlemen smiled at each other.

"Very different from last night," said Isaac in equally careful French.

Felix nodded. "Oui," was the only word he could come up with.

The trouble was, a stilted conversation in bad French was bound to make the waiters suspicious. They would expect the travelling companions, all supposedly Swiss and related to each other, to have a language in common. Then Miriam had a stroke of genius.

"While we dine," she said loud enough to ensure the waiters' hearing her, "we shall speak only French. It will be good practice for both of you."

"Bong iday," agreed Felix happily.

"Bonne idée," Isaac echoed with better pronunciation if less enthusiasm.

Inevitably their conversation was laborious, but it was the most relaxed meal they had taken together. Their chief topic was was the good, plain country fare that was set before them, the pièce de résistance being a roast goose stuffed with nothing more exotic than sage and onions. According to Felix, the expert, the wines were also good but ordinary. Laughing, Miriam and Isaac admitted they couldn't tell the difference.

The cognac that arrived with dessert was in another class entirely. After one sip, Felix stared at his glass in awe. "Distilled sunshine," he said in a hushed voice.

"How fortunate that the waiters have left," Miriam said. "You could never have translated that into French. It even looks like distilled sunshine."

"Perfection!" He inhaled the vapours rising from the golden liquid and took another sip.

"I'll try a drop," said Isaac, who usually didn't touch spirits. He reached for the bottle as Felix pushed it across the table towards him. "It must be rare indeed, if you are forced to admit that anything perfect can come out of France."

"I'll give the devil his due." Felix set down his glass, his movements suddenly tensely controlled. "What about you? Do you consider the French enemies? Are you here because you are an Englishman or because Rothschild is paying you?"

Isaac's long, slender hand halted an inch from the bottle, poised there for an instant, then withdrew, his movements as precise and taut as Felix's. "I work for Nathan Rothschild. I am here because he sent me. But I am glad of the chance to help England and I had rather lose my job than do anything to harm her. My family arrived in England half a century before the House of Hanover. Do you consider the Prince Regent an Englishman?"

"Well, of course." Though he could hardly say anything else, Felix sounded vaguely doubtful.

Miriam was about to intervene when she caught Hannah's admonitory eye and subsided.

"Do you suspect your Roman Catholic fellow-countrymen of owing allegiance to the new King of Rome?" Isaac went on with increasing passion. "Or of wanting to fight for his father, whom the Pope crowned as Emperor?"

"I know two or three fellows in the army who are Papists," Felix conceded. "They want to fight Napoleon as badly as I do."

"You do? Then why are you not a soldier?"

Felix flashed a surprised glance at Miriam — he must have supposed she had passed on all he had told her. She was glad she had not. She returned a look of limpid innocence and took a bite of apricot tart, scarcely tasting it. Hannah was right, they must sort it out between them.

"I have not the wherewithal to purchase a commission." His voice was icy. "An officer's pay is less than I can earn as my uncle's assistant at the Treasury, while an officer has higher expenses. And I must earn my living because your father ruined mine."

Miriam closed her eyes in chagrin. She thought she had persuaded him that the earl must have brought his ruin on himself.

She opened her eyes again, astonished, as Isaac answered quite cheerfully, "So your father was one of the few who paid his debts? Congratulations. It was noble spendthrifts who refused to pay what they owed who bankrupted my father. So now we both must work for a living. Do you enjoy your work?"

Felix glared at him. "At the Treasury? I hope I have a spirit above squabbling over pounds and pence!" Jumping up, he flung back his chair. Miriam expected him to stalk from the room without another word, but he turned to her and said stiffly, "If you will excuse me, I'd like to go and see whether the landlord will sell me some bottles of this cognac."

With a smile she gave her permission, trying to read the welter of confused emotions on his face. At least Isaac seemed to have shaken his certitude of his own righteousness.

As the door closed behind him, Isaac remarked, "Somehow the English aristocrat is never too purse-pinched to stock his cellar."

"I hope he has sufficient funds, and sufficient French. It's a pity he doesn't enjoy his work, but your arguments made him think." Impulsively she reached out her hand to him and he took it in a warm clasp. "Thank you for not losing your temper with him."

His grip tightened. "You are fond of him, are you not?"

"Yes. Right from the moment I first saw him he reminded me of the brother of one of my school friends." But it was not as a brother she regarded Felix. An association of ideas sent a tingling rush of sensation up her arm from the hand that lay in Isaac's. Caught by his dark, burning gaze, she knew for a triumphant instant that he was indeed jealous. The tingling penetrated deep within her.

Panicking, she tried to free her hand. He let go without comment.

She picked up her fork and poked at the piece of tart on her plate. Her voice sounded unnatural to her own ears as she asked, "Do you enjoy working for Nathan Rothschild?"

"As a matter of fact, I do. I didn't fully realize it until you started questioning my regret at giving up the scholarly life, but I enjoy being out and about in the world. If I had my choice, I should join the struggle for the full emancipation of English Jews, for the right to vote and to stand for election — and equally for the rights of Catholics and Dissenters."

"And women?"

He laughed. "And women. I had never considered it before, but then I never before knew a woman like you."

Feeling the red tide rising in her cheeks, she concentrated on finishing the apricot tart. "This is delicious," she muttered. She was annoyed with herself for letting him put her out of countenance.

In all her travels, she had never before known a man like Isaac. Nor one like Felix, who returned at that moment, jubilant, with three bottles of cognac gripped by the necks in each hand.

"A real bargain," he announced. "The town of Cognac is quite nearby and Angoulême is the centre for the brandy trade. At least, I think that's what he said. Isaac, you haven't tried it yet? Miriam, you must taste a drop."

He put down his half-dozen on the table, picked up the opened bottle, and poured the amber nectar. Hannah shook her head when he offered her a glass. She frowned at her mistress, but Miriam was too delighted by Felix's good humour to refuse.

He stood at his place and raised his glass in a carefully worded toast. "To France, and may Wellington soon drive out the Corsican usurper."

"L'chayim!" Isaac took a sip of cognac.

"What does that mean?" Felix asked, curious but with a hint of suspicion.

"To Life. L'chayim!" Miriam took a swallow. "Aaargh . . . gh . . . gh . . ." Her throat was on fire. She gasped for breath, choked. Tears started from her eyes and her face flamed.

Isaac put a glass of water into her hand. She gulped from it, spluttering, feeling a fool.

Hannah was at her side, patting and soothing. "Better come upstairs, Miss Miriam. God never meant for females to drink spirits. Distilled sunshine indeed!" She snorted in disgust.

Miriam rose unsteadily to her feet. Blinking the tears away, she saw Isaac and Felix exchange a grin — the wretches were laughing at her! Very much on her dignity, she wished them good night.

As Hannah closed the door behind her, she heard Isaac say, "Like mistress, like maid," and she remembered Hannah choking over a glass of wine at Blois.

Felix guffawed. Her embarrassment appeared to have sealed the peace between the odious pair.

CHAPTER 11

Nursing a headache, Isaac squinted against the brightness of the warm southern sunshine. Ahead, the road from Angoulême to Bordeaux wound between endless vineyards. Diagonal rows of stumpy plants cross-hatched every hillside, hazed with the tender green of new shoots and leaves and tendrils. Between the rows flocks of grey and white geese with orange bills honked and cackled, fattening on weeds and snails.

Isaac winced as the sound of Miriam's gay laughter floated from the open windows of the berline behind him. He wondered how Felix contrived to be so entertaining after the quantity of cognac he had consumed last night.

He had been lively company last night, too, after the women had retired. Once his prejudices were set aside, his pomposity abandoned, he was an agreeable fellow. Isaac was glad the feud between them appeared to be over. It had been an uncomfortable situation, disquieting even — since they were forced to rely on each other in enemy territory, as Miriam had pointed out with her usual good sense.

She laughed again, a bubbling wellspring of mirth. Isaac sternly suppressed a surge of jealousy.

She had rejected him once, when he was a wealthy suitor approved by her parents. Now he was a mere bank employee, while she was still heir to Aaron Jacobson's vast fortune, despite her present shabbiness. He could not help admiring her compassion for the sick, her friendliness, her independent spirit and enquiring mind. To allow himself to dwell on the beauty that shone through the shabbiness must inevitably lead to heartbreak.

Did she know that her touch, her glance, the very sight of her made him burn with desire? He prayed his self-control had hidden his feelings from her. A second rejection would destroy him.

Again the sound of merriment floated to his ears. Felix was amusing, handsome, titled, and she had admitted to being fond of him. Struggling with waves of jealousy, Isaac reminded himself that Felix was also impoverished, and a Gentile. Though he seemed to be overcoming his distrust, he'd never consider marrying a Jewess — but if he did, would Miriam accept? They had only known each other a few days, yet circumstances had brought greater intimacy than weeks of normal social intercourse, time enough to fall in love as Isaac knew all too well.

His mind occupied with gloomy, and futile, speculation, he was taken by surprise when a flock of geese scurried through a gate onto the road a few feet in front of his leaders. He hauled desperately on the reins.

The berline jerked to a halt as the frothy tide engulfed the team's hooves, swirling about their legs. Horses snorted and side-stepped, geese hissed and pecked and flapped their wings, feathers flew.

Isaac hadn't the least idea what to do next. He envisioned the road heaped with squashed poultry, the carriage over-turned . . .

"What the devil?" Felix swung open the door and ran to the horses' heads, kicking aside gabbling geese as he went. He quickly calmed the restive team, then turned a grinning face to Isaac. "I never taught you how to deal with this particular emergency, did I? I once killed a sheep, but all these foul fowl seem to have survived. Well done."

"But how do we get rid of them? Having rushed onto the road as if pursued by demons, they don't appear to want to go any farther. Oh, there is their guardian."

In the gateway, a small, barefoot girl with a dirty face and a shepherd's crook stood thoughtfully sucking her thumb, probably equally dirty. She watched with interest but made no move to gather her charges.

"Faites marcher les oies," Isaac shouted to her. She turned a blank stare on him.

He was about to jump down and attempt to herd the geese aside, trusting Felix to control the horses, when Miriam and Hannah appeared. Flapping their skirts, they advanced on the flock.

"Shoo! Shoo!"

The horses rolled their eyes, but the geese obediently waddled back towards the gate. Isaac tore his gaze from Miriam's slender ankles, only to see Felix admiring the same delectable view.

Miriam turned, pink-cheeked, laughing and slightly breathless, and called, "We'll try to keep them here while you drive past."

Isaac gathered the reins, which he had let lie slack, then dropped them again. After Felix's generous congratulations he no longer felt the need to prove his driving ability. "If the 'foul fowl' escape I'll be in the suds again," he said. "Felix, will you lead the horses?"

"Give me sheep any day," said Felix, starting forward. "At least they don't bite the horses' knees."

One goose dashed under the berline as it passed but emerged unscathed on the other side. Isaac took up the reins again and the others returned to their seats. Looking back, he saw the child shepherd her flock across the road without sparing a glance for the carriage. He shrugged and drove on.

The next posting house was not far ahead. Felix took his place on the box and Isaac joined the ladies.

"You made splendid gooseherds," he told them. "Is it an inborn skill or have you had practice?"

To his delight, Miriam laughed. He hoped Felix heard her. "The only time I've been near a goose before is to eat it," she said. "We thought we'd best take a hand as that little girl made no effort to help."

"She didn't seem to understand when I asked her to move them. Did I say it wrong? *Oie* is goose, is it not?"

"Yes, and you would think she must have understood what you wanted even if it's pronounced differently in the local patois."

"Patois?"

"The peasants of each region of France have their own dialect, as different from standard French and each other as Cockney is from Yorkshire. *Gascon* is even more different, almost a separate language. Unlike the other dialects even the educated people speak it among themselves."

"Do you speak Gascon too?" Isaac asked, impressed by her interest as much as by her knowledge.

"Only a few words. Most of the people we met in Gascony spoke French."

"Where exactly is Gascony?"

"It's more or less the same as Aquitaine, stretching roughly from Bordeaux to the Pyrenees, overlapping the Basque country in the south. There is a great deal of English influence as well."

"English! Why?"

"The kings of England were dukes of Aquitaine for three centuries and the inhabitants of the Bordeaux area, at least, were not pleased when the French kings took it over. They had been exporting wine to England in vast quantities since time immemorial."

"And still do, do they not? Felix was extolling the virtues of claret last night."

"Both growers and merchants would be ruined if they let a minor matter like war between France and England stop the wine trade." Miriam smiled and shook her head. "Think how often we have been enemies throughout history!"

"Don't tell Felix, but for someone who claims to be a true Englishman I know remarkably little about English history," he confessed wryly, "and less about France. So the Gascons favour England? Even against Napoleon?"

"They are decidedly independent-minded. During the Revolution the Royal standard was raised at Bordeaux. They also supplied many members of one of the losing revolutionary parties, the Girondists, most of whom were guillotined. So, though I wouldn't go so far as to say they favour England, they are hardly fervent supporters of Napoleon. That doesn't mean that we can relax our guard. Many people in Bordeaux are Bonapartists and many would recognize English at once if they heard it."

"You had best warn Felix."

"Why do not you, since you are now on friendly terms with him?"

"Because I wish to remain on friendly terms with him."

"And giving him advice would scarce be tactful," she agreed, laughing. "I shall warn him, then. You cannot imagine how glad I am that you no longer hold him in contempt."

Isaac did his best to hide his dismay. He was beginning to fear that if Felix asked Miriam to marry him she just might accept.

Felix was driving again when they reached Bordeaux that evening. Crossing the Garonne, Miriam noted fewer ships than ever anchored in the river or tied up at the docks. Napoleon's Continental System had virtually destroyed the great port's trade.

She had given Felix careful directions to the inn she decided they should stay at, for the city was the largest they had entered since leaving Paris. As the carriage rumbled through the narrow, crooked streets of the old section, she peered anxiously through the window. In the dusk, the ancient, wood-framed buildings all looked alike. She couldn't see the towers of St. André's Cathedral, by which she had told Felix to steer.

They emerged in the new part of town, built in the last century with imposing stone buildings, wide streets and spacious squares. Here it was easier to get her bearings, and she found that Felix had followed her instructions to the letter. A few minutes later the berline pulled up before the Auberge du Prince de Galles.

The shutter clicked back and Felix said, "There's a very narrow archway into the yard. We had best be sure they have rooms to spare before I drive in."

"I'll go and ask," Miriam said. Only yesterday, she thought, he would have driven straight in just to show off his skill.

Isaac handed her down. Turning to smile up at Felix she caught him staring at the inn sign which hung above their heads, creaking as it swung in the breeze off the Garonne River. On it was depicted a man in black armour, resting one hand on his sword, the other holding a shield with a device of three ostrich plumes and the motto "Ich dien."

"Prinny's insignia." Felix started laughing. "That must be the Black Prince, and Prince de Galles means Prince of Wales. A fine welcome indeed. Already I like Bordeaux."

"Remember I warned you," said Miriam severely, and went into the inn.

The Prince de Galles did in fact extend a warm welcome. An ancient inn rebuilt in the seventeenth-century and now on the border between old town and new, it offered small but comfortable chambers and a cosy private parlour. They dined on local delicacies: oysters from Arcachon, pâté de foie

161

gras de Périgueux, confit of duck, and partridge with truffles.

Felix had by now decided that French cuisine was as much to his taste as their wines, but he eyed the Roquefort cheese askance when he learned it was made from goats' and ewes' milk.

"And it's ripened in a cave in a cliff," Miriam said with mock solemnity, "not in some nice, clean dairy. That is why it's mouldy."

"But Stilton has blue mould and it . . . Oh, you are teasing, you wretch." He grinned. "Is it really made in a cave? A clean cave, I trust." He tasted a morsel and came back for more.

"You may be able to inspect the cave for yourself. I believe our best route will take us near Roquefort. I regret to say that we shall narrowly miss the Armagnac region."

"A little detour perhaps?" said Felix hopefully, sipping the Armagnac brandy the waiter had brought with the cheese and coffee. "This is smoother even than the cognac I bought yesterday. Do try some, Isaac."

"No, thank you. What do you mean 'our best route,' Miriam? Shall we not continue by the main road to Spain?"

"We could." She hesitated, unsure whether they would accept her argument. "It is the best road, though not the most direct to

Pamplona. However, it's the way all the French troops and artillery and supplies go, all funnelled through the narrow gap between the mountains and the sea."

"God forbid," muttered Hannah.

"Lord, I wager we'd be stopping to show our papers every hundred yards," Felix exclaimed.

Isaac frowned. "It does sound as if there would be a lot of delays, not to mention the danger. What is the alternative?"

"Hannah, have you got the map?"

Hannah peered at the floor between her and Isaac. Felix reached down on her other side and hauled up her faded tapestry bag. "Is this it?"

"Thank you, my lord. Here you are, Miss Miriam." She loosened the strings and, delving into the depths, pulled out several papers. As she handed them to her mistress, one fell on the table.

Felix picked it up, glanced at it, and broke into howls of laughter. He passed it across the table to Isaac, who studied it with a grin.

"Your work, Miriam? You have a definite talent." He handed her the caricature she had drawn at Jakob Rothschild's house, of Felix and himself as fighting felines. "I particularly like Jakob as a fox."

She covered her crimson face with her

hands. "Oh no! I thought Hannah had disposed of that long since. I do beg your pardon."

"Why? I'd say it was wickedly accurate, would not you, Felix?"

"Superb," he gasped, still laughing as he took the picture for another look. "You rival Gillray, Miriam. It's an honour to be subjected to your pencil. May I keep it?"

"No, you may not." She retrieved the paper and tore it up. "Now you will never take my maps seriously."

"Certainly we shall." Isaac started unfolding the rest of the sheets and spreading them on the table, while Hannah and Felix moved the glasses, bottles and dishes out of the way.

"Every time we went off the main highway I drew maps," Miriam explained, arranging the papers in order. "Uncle Amos often needed to go back to the same place two or three times. They are not at all accurate for distance or direction, but if you follow them you will get where you're going."

"And the little faces?" Felix asked.

Again she felt her face grow hot with embarrassment. "Uncle Amos was always forgetting the names of people and places so I drew one or two of our friends in each village to remind him of who lived there."

"Just like the puff-cheeked winds and the mermaids and sea monsters on old maps," he quizzed her.

"Not at all. These were useful."

"There's Madame Daubigny," Hannah pointed at the sheet she was poring over. "A fine dance that husband of hers led her, and her half blind, poor woman. The doctor gave her an ointment that stopped the itching in her eyes though there weren't nothing he could do for her sight. And there's . . ."

"Thank you for proving my point, Hannah," said Miriam. "Now please, let us get down to business. There are lots of passes across the Pyrenees, but very few are suitable for carriages. The two leading to Pamplona, Maya and Roncevalles . . ."

"Roncevalles?" Felix interrupted. "Where Roland and Oliver died fighting the Moors?"

"Yes, though that will not help us! Maya and Roncevalles are the most direct, but they are therefore the most frequented and the best guarded. We may do better to go farther east and take one of the passes to Jaca. Besides less likelihood of being stopped, I know people in that area. In the mountains inns are few and far between."

"I am willing to trust your judgment," Isaac said gravely. "Better to go the long way round than not to reach Pamplona at all. Felix?"

"Jaca it is. What a disappointment! I should have liked to see the spot where Roland sounded his horn and expired. Show us on your map, Miriam."

She showed them the route, half flattered at their ready acceptance of her advice, half dreading that she had made the wrong decision.

When she and Hannah retired to their chamber and she was brushing her long, heavy hair, she voiced her fear. "I hope I'm right. Suppose it would be better to go by Roncevalles?"

"That's something you'll never know, child, so don't worry your head. If it's fated, it's fated. But it seems to me that now those young fools have stopped snapping the nose off each other's face, if you give them your maps they don't need you along to hold their hands. Monsieur Ségal could get us back to England, God willing."

"Oh no, Hannah, I cannot desert them! They still don't know the country or the people, nor the language once we leave France. Now that they are friends, I daresay we shall have a merry journey. You cannot imagine what a relief it is to me. I could not bear to think that Isaac was so mean-

166

spirited and intolerant as to bear a grudge against Felix. He is everything that is generous, is he not?"

On that happy thought, she tied back her hair with a ribbon and climbed into bed.

"Considering their superb dinners, you'd think the French could produce something other than tartines and coffee for breakfast," Felix complained. "You must admit that an English breakfast is vastly superior."

"Indisputably," Isaac agreed, slathering his fifth slice of bread with apricot jam. "Oh, for an omelette, or some cold beef."

"Ham and eggs, and I wouldn't say no to a kidney or two, or some kedgeree."

"That reminds me," said Miriam. "Once we leave the main road to Toulouse, we may find the inns poorly provisioned. While you two see to the luggage and the horses, I shall ask mine host to pack us a hamper."

The gentlemen applauded, so a few minutes later, when Isaac went to direct the loading and Felix the harnessing, she sent for the innkeeper. The round-bellied, cheerful landlord of the Prince de Galles was happy to oblige. He invited Miriam and Hannah to step down to the kitchens to choose what they would like.

Though it was still early, the day's baking

was done, luncheon preparations not yet under way. The huge, snaggle-toothed chef generously stuffed a large covered basket with sausage and cheeses, preserved goose, half a ham, dried fruits, and a bottle each of claret and Armagnac. Miriam paid with the money Isaac had given her and the innkeeper, himself carrying their supplies, led them by the back way to the stable yard.

The door at the end of the passage stood open. Over the innkeeper's head, Miriam saw a group of eight or ten men in blue uniforms beside the black bulk of the berline.

Isaac and Felix, looking wary, stood with their backs to the carriage. They were watching a short, lean man in a silver-laced bicorne hat and a black coat with a velvet collar and padded shoulders. Miriam could see little but his back and the sheaf of papers in his hands.

"*La police,*" hissed the landlord, stopping short.

She was inclined to go on. Their papers had passed more than one examination already. But at that moment the man in black raised his head and began to speak so she paused to listen.

"*Vous êtes Messieurs Cohen et Rauschberg?* Where is Mademoiselle Cohen?" His voice was high and thin and cold.

"My sister is still in the inn," Isaac replied in his passable French.

"Good. You two go and find the sister," his finger stabbed at two of his men, who turned away. Then he gestured at Felix and Isaac. "Arrest them."

As the gendarmes closed in on their prey, the innkeeper set down the basket and swiftly and silently closed the door. "Come," he said in a low voice. "They will not expect guests to leave through the kitchens."

When Miriam, frozen with shock, did not move, he took her elbow and hustled her and Hannah back the way they had come. Few of the kitchen staff even glanced up from their tartines as they passed but the chef grinned and nodded. Miriam couldn't manage even the faintest smile in return. They hurried on through a scullery, then a well stocked store-room, dodging plaited strings of onions and garlic hung from the ceiling. The innkeeper opened a door. They found themselves stepping out into a narrow, noisome back alley.

He felt in his pocket, produced some coins, and thrust them at Miriam. "Here, you will not be able to take the provisions. I am sorry I can do no more for you."

The door clicked shut behind them and they were alone.

CHAPTER 12

Isaac stumbled after Felix into the dimly lit cell and the door clanged shut behind them. A swift appraisal told him that Bordeaux's splendid rococo police-headquarters building boasted underground dungeons that would not have disgraced a medieval castle.

It stank, one of the stone walls glistened with moisture, and huge iron rings at shoulder height suggested they were lucky to be merely handcuffed and leg-shackled. Feeble daylight filtered down through a metal grille barring a square hole in one corner of the high, rough-hewn ceiling. The only furnishing was mouldy straw.

In the gloomiest corner, an indistinct figure sat up and peered at them.

Felix, his back turned to the apparition, opened his mouth to speak. As Isaac stepped forward to lay a warning hand on his arm, the chain between his boot-clad ankles snapped tight. He staggered, beginning to fall.

Somehow, despite the handcuffs, Felix caught and steadied him. Isaac's expression must have warned him for without a word he swung round to peer into the corner.

Limping closer, the creature revealed itself as a man of indeterminate age, dressed in dirty rags, with several days' growth of stubble on his chin and hollow cheeks. Lank brown hair straggled down to his torn collar.

"Who are you?" he grunted in English.

Again Felix, looking startled, opened his mouth to speak. Again Isaac stopped him. The fellow's English was excellent yet even those three short words held a faint but unmistakable foreign intonation.

In French he said, "I don't understand."

Felix had his wits about him. *"Nous sommes suisses."* Laboriously he repeated the phrases Miriam had taught him. "I speak only a little French. Please speak slowly."

"I am not talking in French." The stranger sounded impatient. "The jailer told me they have seized two English spies and I hoped they will put you here with me. I am English as you. Since three months I am here alone."

His slightly odd use of words confirmed

172

Isaac's suspicion. *"Je regrette. . . ."* He shook his head and shrugged, miming incomprehension.

Felix tugged on his sleeve. Together, chains clinking, they hobbled to the far side of the cell and with some difficulty sat down on the floor, their backs against one of the dry walls. In tense silence they waited.

Twice more the man tried to draw them into conversation. Twice more they met his openings with blank stares. At last he gave up. Abandoning his limp he strode to the door and yelled for the jailer in perfect French.

"How did you guess?" Felix whispered as the heavy door clanged shut again and torchlight receded beyond the small, barred opening.

"I cannot recall anything we have done to give ourselves away since we arrived in Bordeaux. Therefore they must have been told to watch out for us, so it seemed possible they had made preparations."

"That makes sense. Do you . . . do you suppose they arrested Miriam?"

The breath caught in Isaac's throat. He had been trying not to picture Miriam in chains, Miriam locked in a damp, dark cell, alone and frightened, or worse still, Miriam interrogated, surrounded by bullying, threatening men. Silently he cursed Jakob Rothschild.

When he said nothing, Felix went on whispering. "If she had any chance to escape, she'll have taken it. She's pluck to the backbone. You know, I always preferred the sort of girl who looks up to a fellow and lets him take care of her, but Miriam's different. She can look after herself yet she is still feminine, and she's amusing too. I . . . I can't bear to think that they might have caught her."

"If they question you," Isaac said urgently, "try not to mention her. And if they find the gold, say she didn't know about it. Say she just came to interpret, that you would not trust a woman with a secret like that."

"I shall do my best." His grin was mirthless. "But there's little enough on any subject I'll be able to tell them in French!"

Isaac remembered the arrogant lord, so certain of his superiority, with whom he had set out, and he wondered at the change Miriam had wrought.

"That is all to the good," he assured him. "At least you cannot contradict anything I tell them. All the same, we had best try to work out a believable story to explain the gold." They ought to have done so days ago, but cooperation had been impossible then.

He might yet come to regard Felix as a friend, if he could be sure that that was how Felix regarded Miriam.

For the present they were co-conspirators. They plotted in whispers until, no more than a quarter hour later, they heard the tramp of feet in the passage. A face appeared at the opening in their cell door. As a key rattled in the lock they struggled to their feet.

The door slammed open, the fat, heavy-breathing jailer stood aside, and their erstwhile cell companion appeared. He was clean-shaven now and decently dressed, though not in uniform, but he still had a cadaverous look and his hair still straggled untidily over his collar. Several blue-uniformed gendarmes waited behind him in the corridor.

He pointed at Isaac. "You. Come," he snapped.

Isaac almost obeyed before he realized the man spoke in English. Catching himself, he pointed at his own chest and said enquiringly, *"Moi?"*

"Vous. Venez."

He made his clumsy way out to the corridor then as the four gendarmes surrounded him he turned to glance back. Felix, his chin raised defiantly, looked very

175

alone. Between them the door swung shut. The fat jailer turned the key, the metallic click sending a cold shiver down Isaac's spine.

He was sweating by the time they reached the top of the stair from the dungeons to the world above. He spared a thought for those unhappy wretches who made the climb without boots to protect their ankles from the heavy chains. The handcuffs were bad enough, scraping his wrists and straining his shoulders. He prayed he would not later look back on this moment as the last of comparative comfort.

The English-speaking man — one of the gendarmes had addressed him as lieutenant — led the way into a room littered with portmanteaux and boxes and their contents. With a shock, Isaac recognized his own clothes strewn about as if unpacked by a mad valet.

Accustomed to brief forays across the Channel, he had brought nothing incriminating; Miriam had been travelling Napoleon's Europe for years; but what of Felix?

He was given no time to worry as the gendarmes hustled him through to an inner room. Behind a grotesquely overornamented rococo desk sat the dandified little man who had ordered their arrest. A scuffed red leather box bound with brass stood on the desk beside him, its lid hanging open. Miriam's box.

"Le prisonnier Cohen, monsieur le préfet," announced the lieutenant.

Stroking his narrow black mustache, the police chief stared at Isaac, his eyes cold and deadly as a snake's in his impassive face. His thinning hair was elaborately styled to hide his pink scalp but those eyes nullified any hint of absurdity.

One long-nailed finger tapped on the pile of papers lying before him. "Code. You will give me the key."

"Code?" It was not a word Isaac had ever heard in French but it was sufficiently like the English for him to guess the meaning. A startled question flashed through his mind — Miriam an English spy? Impossible! He stepped forward, his chain rattling. "Let me see."

The prefect pushed some of the papers across the desk. The handcuffs made handling them difficult but Isaac picked up the top one and scanned it. The "code" was Yiddish. It took him a moment longer to identify the subject and then he very nearly laughed aloud.

They had worried about the gold. They had prepared a wonderful story for the gold, and here he was trying to account for a box full of medical records!

"Eh bien?"

The sharp query effectively dispelled his amusement. "These are written in Yiddish, monsieur. It is a language, not a code, the language of the Jews of Germany and Poland, but widely spoken wherever there is a community of Jews."

"A Jewish code, put at the service of your English masters." The precise voice was chilly, unbelieving. Without shifting his stare from Isaac's face, he ordered, "Lieutenant, take two men and find me a loyal French Jew, if such an improbable creature exists."

The lieutenant slipped out of the room, leaving the four armed guards ranged against the wall.

"I can translate them for you," Isaac offered, trying to sound unconcerned, "though I doubt they will interest you. They are a doctor's notes on his patients."

The prefect's thin lips curled. "You expect me to believe that? I suppose you can explain why three travellers journeying for pleasure should carry with them a box of medical notes?"

"Naturally, monsieur." Stick as close to the truth as possible, he advised himself. "My uncle was a doctor. He travelled everywhere to investigate different diseases." Isaac hesitated, hampered by his mediocre knowledge of French. He was not sure that he hadn't invented a word or two, but his interrogator seemed to understand.

"Et puis?"

He struggled on. "My sister accompanied him on his last journey. He died in France, so I came here to fetch her. My cousin came with me, and after a period of mourning we decided not to waste the opportunity to see more of your country." An ingenious, credible story at short notice, he congratulated himself.

"An ingenious farrago of lies! We shall wait until Hébert returns." He took a folder from a drawer and opened it. Dipping a quill, he started scribbling, ignoring prisoner and guards alike.

The gendarmes waited in stolid immobility. After a few minutes Isaac grew impatient. A protest was unlikely to do him any good, but not to protest could be considered an admission of guilt.

He thumped with both fists on the desk. "I am a Swiss citizen!" he said sharply. "I object to this treatment. You have no reason to hold us. Release us at once or I shall complain to the Foreign Ministry."

Without raising his eyes from his work,

the police chief asked, "If there is no reason to hold you, why did your sister evade us?"

Isaac took a deep breath, for a moment too relieved to speak. They hadn't caught her! "She was afraid when she saw you take us away. Who can blame her?" Leaning forward across the desk, he added in a hard voice, "If she has come to any harm, I shall consider you responsible."

The man looked up then. Was that a hint of uncertainty in his eyes? His response was noncommittal. "She has only to give herself up and she will be taken care of." He waved at a nearby chair, an elegant gilt and brocade object doubtless meant for important visitors, and returned to his writing.

Taking the gesture to be an invitation, Isaac sat down. The prefect showed signs of being the sort of bully who was quick to capitulate if threatened. However, Isaac was in a weak position when it came to making threats, and in any case he was decidedly uncomfortable with the idea. He suspected any attempt would be less than convincing.

Felix might well be more competent in that direction. But even if Felix were here, his lack of French would disarm him. Unable to come up with a way to capitalize on the prefect's possible weakness, Isaac found his thoughts drifting inevitably to worrying about Miriam and wondering what was in store for himself and Felix.

The quill pen scratched on and a blue-bottle buzzed against the windowpane. Now and then one of the gendarmes shifted his position, the shuffle of feet loud in the still-ness.

Heavy footsteps in the anteroom announced Lieutenant Hébert's return. He brought with him a grey-bearded Jew wearing sidelocks and the traditional gaberdine so much more suited to a Polish winter than a spring day in southern France. The two uniformed men who followed them joined the others standing against the wall.

"Ezekiel ben Joseph, monsieur le préfet. He claims to speak Yiddish and I have told him only that he is to translate some papers for you."

With an air of patient tolerance, Ezekiel took the first sheet and started to read it. " 'In the village of Radovich, two sons of the Mendel family are afflicted with the crippling disease. Their mother reports that both her brother and her aunt had children who died of the same disorder before the age of seven. The symptoms are . . .' "

"Get out! Get out!" the prefect shouted shrilly. Losing his temper, he seemed to Isaac less menacing than when he was calm

181

and dispassionate, but the lieutenant looked alarmed. The bearded Jew departed at a dignified pace.

By the time the door closed behind him, the prefect had recovered his chilling composure. He fixed Isaac with a steely gaze.

"So, it is written in a Yiddish code."

"Not a code. I have explained everything."

"You have explained nothing. You see, Monsieur Pasquier, Prefect of the Paris Police, in requesting that I arrest you has informed me that you arrived in Paris not from Switzerland but from the coast."

Isaac's mind raced. "That was where we met my sister. My uncle died in Calais."

"That can be checked, though it will take several days. By the time I have received an answer, no doubt I shall have found your sister and cracked your code — or persuaded one of you to give me the key. Perhaps we shall find that your uncle, if he existed, also worked for the Emperor's enemies." He turned to Hébert. "Take the English spy back to his cell."

CHAPTER 13

"Come, quickly." Miriam put one hand on Hannah's elbow, the other to her nose.

The alley, blocked at one end by the back of a building, was littered with a stinking refuse of rotting cabbage leaves, onion peelings, and unnameable substances covered with blue and green mould. Down the centre ran a slimy gutter. Picking their way through the filth with all possible speed, they startled a mongrel crouched over something Miriam preferred not to look at. The emaciated cur snarled then loped away, its tail between its legs.

When it reached the alley's entrance, it looked back and bared its teeth again. Miriam raised her arm as if to throw a stone. The dog turned to flee, just as a stout figure in blue uniform appeared around the corner of the inn. Man and dog collided.

The gendarme tripped and fell, dropping a hunk of bread and cheese. The dog snatched it in passing. On his knees, the man scowled after it.

"Sacrebleu! Mon déjeuner!" he wailed. Hoisting himself to his feet he ran a few pointless steps after the thief.

Miriam and Hannah slipped around the opposite corner and hurried down the narrow, twisting street.

At the first crossing Miriam turned right, then left at the next. Hannah was gasping for breath so Miriam slowed her pace. Already their obvious haste had drawn a few curious glances. She was afraid, though, that when the police failed to find her at the Prince de Galles they would search the area.

Hannah recovered her breath as they walked on between the overhanging timbered houses. "May God not forsake them," she groaned. "They're good lads, both of them. Where are we going, child? What shall we do?"

Miriam forced herself to ignore the hollow feeling in the pit of her stomach when she thought of Isaac and Felix in police custody. At present she could do nothing for them. She must concentrate on not joining them.

"We have little choice, we shall go to the Ségals. At worst, Monsieur Ségal will lend us money to escape; at best he may be able

184

to help the others. Do you recognize this street?"

"No, Miss Miriam. It looks just like all the rest to me."

"To me, too. We must be on the west side of the city, I believe. The Ségals live to the north."

Though Miriam felt as if days had passed since she woke that morning, it was still early. Looking up at the strip of blue sky above, she saw that the sun shone on the eaves of the houses on her left. Straight ahead was north, then. Not that anything was straight ahead in that labyrinth, but she feared they might be conspicuous in the wide streets of the new section.

They kept on course by checking the sun's position now and then, and in spite of being one of France's larger towns, Bordeaux in no way compared with London for size. A brisk fifteen-minute walk brought them to streets they recognized. Soon they were gazing across the Rue Médoc, straighter and wider than most, at the Ségals' house. Composed of three of the small, old town houses combined into one, it had an air of prosperity without ostentation.

"The police cannot possibly know we are acquainted with them," said Miriam firmly, and they crossed the road.

185

As she raised her hand to knock on the door, she noticed the carved wooden mezuzah case nailed to the doorpost. Her own home in London had a mezuzah at every entrance, but she had never enquired as to their meaning. A sudden longing for Isaac swept through her.

The smart maid who opened the door regarded them with disfavour. "What do you want?" she asked sharply.

Miriam was suddenly conscious of her shabby appearance. Since Felix had ceased to judge her by them, she had almost forgotten her worn, unfashionable clothes. Still, she had been no more modish last time she was in Bordeaux and the Ségals had welcomed her nonetheless.

"I wish to see Madame Ségal," she told the maid. "Please tell her that Miriam Jacobson is here."

"You are much too early to call on madame. She is not yet come down."

"At least inform her that I am come. We shall wait if need be."

Reluctantly the girl admitted them. She left them in the small but elegant hall and went upstairs, only to return moments later to sulkily invite them to go up.

Madame was in her dressing room, seated before a dressing table laden with porcelain jars of cosmetics. A small, fine-boned woman, her dark hair just touched with grey, she wore a wrap of crimson silk embroidered with vine leaves in gold thread.

"Que je suis ravie de te voir, chérie," she cried, bouncing up and darting across the room to kiss Miriam heartily on both cheeks. "What a delightful surprise. Tell me, shall I dye my hair? This wretched grey, it makes me look old, but even my Lucette cannot find a dye that looks natural! You recall Lucette, Miriam? I see Hannah is with you still. You are pale as ever, chérie, but I suppose you will as always refuse to try a spot of rouge. And how goes *le bon oncle?*"

At last she paused for breath. In the course of her chatter, she had returned to plucking her eyebrows, Miriam had greeted Lucette, and Hannah had moved to help the elderly abigail iron a morning gown of fawn satin, liberally adorned with fine lace.

Seizing her chance, Miriam imparted the news of Uncle Amos's death. Madame jumped up and embraced her again.

"My poor Miriam, *je suis désolée.* Ezra will be greatly afflicted. The doctor was a saint. So, you have not found a husband to keep you on this side of the Channel? Your standards are too high, ma chère. You wish to return to England, without doubt?"

187

"Yes, but . . ."

"Ezra will arrange it. He went to the synagogue for the morning prayer, but he will return for *le petit déjeuner* before he goes to the bank. We shall speak to him then. Have no fear, he will manage it without difficulty. He knows everyone of importance in . . ."

"Suzanne! I am grateful for your offer, but I have a much greater favour to ask. Indeed, it may prove impossible, but I cannot run away and leave my friends in prison without trying to save them."

"Prison!" Suzanne Ségal's attention was well and truly caught. "Tell me all." She moved to a chaise longue and patted the place beside her invitingly.

Miriam was too agitated to sit down. Pacing restlessly, she delivered a much edited version, omitting the destination of the gold, of the events of the last few days. Was it only a few days since the meeting in Jakob Rothschild's house in Paris? It seemed a lifetime.

Characteristically, Suzanne went straight to what she considered the heart of the matter. "You are in love. This is obvious, but I cannot guess of which of the two you are enamoured. Both sound charming."

"Both are charming. I am very fond of

both, but I am not in love with either. They are simply dear friends."

Suzanne gave her a knowing look. "As you will. You have not told me all, I think, and perhaps it is for the best. To rescue prisoners from the police is not so easy as to smuggle fugitives to England, but Ezra will manage it." She cocked her head. "Listen, I believe he is come home."

Miriam wished she had the same faith in Ezra's omnipotence. He was, just as she remembered, no demi-god but a small, neat man with a surprisingly shy smile for so eminent and successful a businessman.

He greeted her kindly as if her arrival were an everyday occurrence, then stepped over to his wife and begged her permission to salute her.

"But of course, chérie. Do I not always delay powdering my face until you come in?" She raised her unpowdered face for his kiss, then took his hand in both hers. "Sit down, my love. Miriam has brought us a grave problem." She took it upon herself to explain the situation, interrupted only by her husband's condolences on the demise of Dr. Bloom. "And I know you can help her, Ezra," she finished, "so pray do not look so solemn."

Turning to Miriam, he lost not one whit

of his solemnity. "I am acquainted with Kalmann and Salomon Rothschild," he revealed. "The Rothschilds have a reputation for honesty in their business dealings. Is Suzanne's exposition accurate, my dear?"

"Near enough, monsieur. I hesitate to request your aid, for the last thing I wish is to endanger anyone else."

He pondered. "I doubt it will come to that, yet for your friends I cannot be sanguine," he admitted. "The only chance is to approach Monsieur Lavardac, but he has little authority over the gendarmerie. Grignol, like all prefects, is appointed in Paris though he is a local man."

"Monsieur Lavardac? The wine merchant?" Miriam asked, puzzled. "How can he help?"

"You know him?"

"If it is the same man, Uncle Amos treated him, for a liver complaint if I am not mistaken."

Ezra Ségal began to look more cheerful. "Very good. Though Lavardac is a republican, he is now mayor of Bordeaux. He owes his health to your uncle and his wealth to me, since my bank financed the smuggling of wine to England which made his fortune. What is more, he has a running feud with Grignol over jurisdictions. We shall pay a little visit to *monsieur le maire*."

"What did I tell you?" cried Suzanne in triumph. "Ezra will save your beloved. He is equal to anything. But you must eat first, my love. Miriam, have you broken your fast?"

She nodded, her throat tight, her eyes filling with tears as she recalled the happy harmony at the breakfast table at the Prince de Galles. How she had looked forward to a future with Isaac and Felix at peace! Would she ever see them again? Inside her, the bubble of fear swelled.

Her friend rushed to embrace her, prattling words of comfort, and tugged her to the chaise longue. "Sit here, chérie, and put your feet up. Lucette shall bring you a cup of tea, and Hannah too, while I feed my starving husband. Well I know how for the English tea solves all problems. A moment, Ezra, I must powder my nose. Heavens, I am not dressed yet! But no one will call so early, I shall dress after you leave to call on Monsieur Lavardac. Unless you would like me to go with you, Miriam? No, very well, Ezra, I can see that you do not approve. Come and eat your petit déjeuner."

The tea, doubtless smuggled from England, was soothing if it didn't actually solve any problems. Miriam and Hannah had time to drink a second cup apiece from the delicate Limoges china before the sulky maidservant came to fetch them.

Suzanne's farewells were punctuated with advice on transforming an admirer into a husband, but her last words were an anxious, "Tell me, Miriam, shall I dye my hair? The grey makes me look like an old woman."

"On the contrary, Suzanne, you look *très distinguée,*" Miriam assured her, stepping into the Ségals' carriage.

Beaming, Suzanne waved good-bye.

As the carriage started off, Miriam said with a sigh, "It is infuriating that our berline is stuffed with gold yet if I need money for bribes I cannot get at it."

"Ma chère, do I not own a bank? Your father's credit is good with me. That is the least of our troubles."

Though the streets were crowded now, they soon reached the new quarter. Monsieur Ségal decided to try the Hôtel de Ville before Lavardac's home or business. They were in luck: the gendarme on guard duty outside the splendid eighteenth-century town hall reported that the mayor was in his office. Miriam did her best not to flinch as they walked past the guard in his blue uniform.

Inside, Monsieur Ségal was recognized at once. Up stairs and down passages, they were rapidly passed from flunkey to flunkey until they reached a large anteroom where a score of people sat or stood about, apparently waiting. A secretary bowed and begged them to be seated while he informed monsieur le maire of their arrival. He vanished into the inner office.

Dismayed, Miriam prepared for a long wait. However, the door to the office opened again at once and Monsieur Lavardac strode out. She recognized the brawny wine merchant although his girth was considerably diminished and his cheeks had lost the sickly yellow tinge she remembered. Uncle Amos's prescribed diet must have succeeded.

The mayor didn't recognize her. "Give me two minutes, mon cher Ségal," he said, shaking his banker's hand vigorously. "A troublesome affair I must clear up — these scoundrelly lawyers! — and then I shall be all yours." He hurried back into his office.

True to his word, he very soon ushered out a tall, lanky individual and invited Ezra Ségal to step in. He looked a trifle taken aback when Miriam and Hannah also rose.

"Mademoiselle is with me," Ségal said quickly. As soon as the office door closed

193

behind them he added, "You have met Mademoiselle Jacobson before, Lavardac. Dr. Bloom was her uncle."

Lavardac expressed his apologies, enquiries, condolences, gratitude for his improved health. "Sit down, sit down, mademoiselle. What can I do for you?"

Miriam turned to Ségal. His version of the story turned out to be as different from his wife's as hers had been from Miriam's original. She realized he was stressing that the prefect's orders came from Paris, that conceivably Grignol was exceeding his authority in arresting foreign visitors to Bordeaux without consulting the mayor.

Suzanne's tale had leaned heavily on the fact that the travellers were transporting gold for the Rothschilds, fellow Jewish bankers. And Miriam, now she came to consider it, had presented to Suzanne an adventure (properly chaperoned!) with two dashing young men, mingled with her longing to go home.

She couldn't help being amused, despite her anxiety.

Lavardac waxed indignant. "That Grignol is a poor excuse for a Gascon! The Paris prefect is not even his superior, merely a colleague. And your passports, mademoiselle, they were indeed signed by the Minister of Finance?"

"And by Savary, the Minister of Police, monsieur. I saw Monsieur Grignol examining them."

"Ha! Then he cannot plead ignorance. Perhaps you are aware, Ségal, that Grignol's family owns a vineyard near Castelnau? You may guess, mademoiselle, that I have a great influence in the wine trade." He winked.

Miriam began to feel more hopeful. Her spirits sank again as the mayor went on.

"However, it is no easy matter to pry prisoners from the dungeons once they have been incarcerated. Legally, you understand, I have no authority over the prefect. I can guarantee nothing." The light of battle entered his eye. "But I shall try! I go at once — there is no one of importance waiting to see me. Do you accompany me, Ségal?"

"That goes without saying."

"My secretary shall make you comfortable here, mademoiselle, unless you prefer to return to Madame Ségal?"

Miriam glanced at Hannah, who looked as resigned as if she knew in advance what the answer would be. "I shall go with you, monsieur."

The mayor stared at her in surprised disapproval. "That is unwise, mademoiselle."

"Please, let me go with you." She couldn't bear to be left biting her nails to the quick, but she didn't think that argument would influence him. "If you succeed in freeing my friends, we may have to leave in a hurry."

"True," he conceded, "but a woman . . ."

"Best let her come, Lavardac. She and her maid can wait in the carriage outside."

"As you wish. You understand, mademoiselle, that if I am unable to free your friends I may also be unable to protect you from arrest?"

"I understand, monsieur, and I thank you." Miriam stood up, impatient of delay. Whatever the danger, she had no intention of waiting meekly in the carriage.

CHAPTER 14

Horrified, Hannah surveyed the anteroom, bestrewn with heaps of clothes. "The vandals!" she exclaimed in Yiddish. "Have they no respect for other people's belongings?"

Dropping to her knees, she started to fold Miriam's green evening gown. The youthful gendarme who had tried to prevent their following the mayor moved towards her, opening his mouth to utter yet another weak protest. She glared at him and he stepped back irresolutely.

The abigail was not likely to come to much harm. Miriam went on alone to the door Monsieur Lavardac had flung open moments earlier. She stopped in the doorway, making no effort to draw attention to herself.

The small, foppish man last seen in the inn yard sat behind an ornate desk, half hidden by Lavardac's stalwart figure. Ezra Ségal stood quietly to one side. Two gendarmes were trying to explain to Grignol that they had requested monsieur le maire to attend only a minute while they enquired whether monsieur le préfet was free to see him. Lavardac's roar drowned their voices.

"One tells me that you have arrested two foreign visitors. I reply, it is not possible that my friend Grignol should make such a stupid mistake."

"It is no mistake, Lavardac." The prefect's face was stony but Miriam caught a flicker of apprehension in his eyes.

"What! You are trying perhaps to ruin the wine trade. Even the Swiss import our wines. Or is it that you wish to destroy the reputation of the Gascons for hospitality?"

"I received orders from Paris to arrest these men."

"From Paris, hein!" Now the mayor sounded sarcastic. "From the Minister of Police, I suppose."

Grignol flushed and his narrow black mustache twitched. "From Monsieur Pasquier, the prefect."

"So, now you take orders from a fellow prefect? You dance to Paris's tune? Where is your pride, Grignol? Are you a Gascon or a goose?"

A hastily suppressed snort of laughter from one of the gendarmes turned the prefect's face purple and brought him to his feet. "If you have nothing better to do, I'll find you something," he snarled at his minions.

As Miriam stepped aside to give them room to flee past her, she spared a quick glance for Hannah. Her maid had finished packing her belongings and moved on to Felix's. Praying that the labour might not be in vain, she turned back to the scene in the office.

She must have missed something, presumably a refusal by Grignol to be intimidated into releasing his prisoners for Lavardac was hauling out the heavy artillery.

"It would be a pity, *mon vieux*," he said with a false air of ponderous bonhomie, "yes, it would be a shocking pity if the harvest of the Grignol vineyard failed to find buyers this year." He appeared not to notice when the prefect blanched and sat down suddenly. "The winemakers are so demanding these days," he continued. "The slightest flaw in the grapes and pouf! they are rejected. I was saying just the other day when I called at the Château Lafite — or was it at the Château Margaux? *N'importe* — I was saying, 'You fellows can ruin a family's livelihood if you decide their grapes are less than perfect.' " He paused.

Grignol rallied. He too had big guns in reserve. "Fortunately, the produce of my family's vineyard is as faultless as my proof that the so-called Swiss travellers are in fact English spies!" He picked up a stack of papers and shook them in his opponent's face. "A whole box of papers written in a secret code."

Lavardac glanced back at Ségal, his confidence obviously shaken. Miriam was aghast. The banker, however, moved forward with imperturbable calm and reached for the papers.

"You permit, monsieur? Ah, as I suspected. Allow me to translate. 'In the village Radovich, two sons of the Mendel family are afflicted with the crippling condition. Their mother states . . .' "

"How did you know?" Grignol howled. "You talked to him! You talked to that hooknose Yid. You're all in collusion but you can't trick me. I'll break the code, I swear it."

"Yiddish," said Ezra Ségal, unmoved. "Dr. Bloom's notes."

"Dr. Bloom's?" Lavardac was delighted. "It is possible that I myself am mentioned?"

Miriam decided the time had come to take a hand. She left the shelter of the doorway. "Of course you are mentioned, monsieur. If my uncle's box is here, and if Monsieur Grignol has not disarranged the papers, I can find your name with ease."

Ségal gestured at a corner and there was the red leather box. No wonder he had not faltered — he must have recognized it for he had often seen Uncle Amos working on his notes in the evenings. The desk had hidden it from Miriam until she entered right into the room.

With the ease of one who had hoisted many a wine barrel in youth, the mayor swung the box up onto the desk. It landed with a clunk. Grignol howled again.

"My desk!"

Obligingly Lavardac moved the box to a chair. The prefect rubbed with a lace-edged handkerchief at the scratches and dents made by the brass studs, while Miriam flipped through the papers. It was sheer chance that when she sorted them in Paris she had noted the wine merchant's name on the back of a page devoted to diabetes among the Sephardim. Otherwise it would have been discarded.

"Here it is. 'Lavardac, Jean-Baptiste, wine merchant of Bordeaux. Jaundice. Prescribed rhubarb, lemon juice, warm baths. Avoid sugar, fat, alcohol.' "

The mayor combined a beaming smile

with a guilty look. "Sugar I avoid," he announced. "Wine and foie gras — I am a Gascon, n'est-ce pas? — I take in moderation. Dr. Bloom was an excellent doctor, and these are indubitably his notes."

The three of them turned to stare at the prefect. His cannon spiked, Grignol seemed to shrink. He took a clean sheet of paper, scribbled on it, and passed it to the mayor.

"I'm a busy man," he said petulantly. "Show this to Lieutenant Hébert." Taking a document from a drawer, he gave it all his attention.

Lavardac scanned the scribbled paper, handed it to Ségal, and picked up Uncle Amos's box. Leading the way out of the office, Miriam glanced back to see the prefect futilely rubbing at his defiled desk with his dainty handkerchief.

In the anteroom, Hannah had finished her packing and in her execrable French was supervising the youthful gendarme as he roped the boxes. Looking sheepish, he sprang to attention and saluted the mayor.

"Find Hébert and bring him here," Lavardac commanded.

"At once, monsieur le maire."

Miriam ran to hug Hannah. "What did Grignol write, monsieur?" she asked over her shoulder.

" 'Cohen and Rauschberg to be released with all their goods,' signed and dated. It suffices. I shall speak to the lieutenant and then I must leave you, mademoiselle. Grignol is not the only busy man, alas."

He bowed over her hand with a courtly grace as she did her best to thank him for his kindness.

A pallid, hollow-cheeked man came in and announced that he was Lieutenant Hébert. Lavardac gave him the release and he read it suspiciously, then started towards the prefect's office.

Lavardac grabbed his arm and bellowed, "The gentlemen you have so grievously wronged are not in there. Fetch them at once, have their luggage loaded on their carriage, and see that good horses are provided."

"At once, monsieur le maire."

Turning to Ségal, Lavardac enveloped the little man's hand in both his huge paws. "I thank you, mon vieux, that was very amusing. If you have further need of me, you know where to find me. Mademoiselle, I am always at your service." He winked at Miriam. "And I shall endeavour to avoid the foie gras. Until we meet again!" With a cheery wave he departed in Hébert's wake.

Suddenly exhausted, Miriam sat down on

Uncle Amos's box. Ezra Ségal patted her shoulder. "Don't worry, my dear. You will soon be on your way."

"With God's help," said Hannah, "blessed be His name."

"And with your help, monsieur." Miriam smiled at the banker. He blushed.

Hannah's young assistant came in with another gendarme and started to carry out portmanteaux and boxes.

"I'd best keep an eye on them," said the abigail. "He's not too bright, that lad." She hurried after them.

They came back for another load, and then for a final few pieces, and still there was no sign of Isaac and Felix. Miriam began to pace restlessly, her hands clasped tight before her. She wished Lavardac had not left. She was tempted to rush into the inner office and demand that the prefect emerge from his sanctum to see his orders carried out. Lieutenant Hébert had a sly air, she recalled. What was he doing?

The banker went to the outer door and looked up and down the hall. "Here come two young men," he said with satisfaction. "I believe they must be your friends."

Miriam rushed to the door. Hébert, and yes, there they were following him, Isaac tall and dark, rueful, limping slightly; Felix tall and fair, an expression of sardonic amusement on his handsome face. She sped to meet them then stopped, horrified, as she realized they both wore handcuffs.

"Why are they still chained?" she demanded passionately.

The lieutenant scowled. Felix grinned and shrugged. Isaac laughed, and the joy in his laughter reassured her.

"We insisted on coming up rather than waiting below for this fellow to find the right key."

Behind them wheezed a corpulent jailer in a bulging striped waistcoat, his red face dripping with sweat. His lips moved as he sorted through one of the two huge iron rings of keys hanging at his waist — well, at his middle. Miriam tried not to giggle hysterically. She felt light-headed with relief.

She was tempted to fling her arms about Isaac and Felix, and had they been alone she might have succumbed to temptation. As it was, she turned back to Ezra Ségal.

"I fear we are keeping you from your business," she said.

He frowned. "I shall stay with you until you depart."

At once her elation fled. She prayed his cautiousness was unjustified, but Hébert's sly eyes disturbed her.

The lieutenant ushered them into a room opposite the prefect's anteroom, furnished with a scratched deal table and several plain wooden chairs. He stayed by the open door while the jailer waddled over to a window and squinted at his jangling keys.

"This is the one," he said triumphantly. "It is too dark below to make it out."

Shuddering at the thought of the gloomy dungeons, Miriam watched the fat man unlock Felix's handcuffs, puffing and grunting as he turned the stiff key. The fetters clanked on the table-top and Felix rubbed his wrists, grimacing. Miriam hurried to examine the damage.

Red indentations and some chafing were the worst of it. "We'll put on some of Hannah's witch hazel," she said, clasping his warm, strong hands and looking up into eyes as blue as southern skies. His gaze caught her, held her in a sudden stillness, burned into her, through her, stopped her breath. Her heart lurched.

And then a second pair of cuffs struck the table. Felix pulled her into a brief, exuberant hug and let her go.

The world started moving again but it seemed unreal. In a daze she checked Isaac's wrists, again prescribed witch hazel, and enquired solicitously about the limp she had noted. When he dismissed it as mere stiffness, she smiled at him in sympathetic gladness. And all the while her whirling mind demanded wildly, Am I in love with Felix?

"The lieutenant is gone!" Monsieur Ségal's sharp words dragged her back to normalcy. "I believe you ought to leave with all speed."

Isaac and Felix swung round to stare at him and Miriam realized they had no idea who he was.

"I shall introduce you later," she said hastily, starting towards the door. The jailer was ahead of her, panting along with the handcuffs under his arm. He squeezed through the doorway and disappeared.

"Where is the carriage?" Felix asked in his painstaking French.

"They brought us here in it," Isaac clarified, "but I don't know how to find it."

They turned to the banker. He shrugged his shoulders, obviously worried. Miriam stepped out into the hall and looked hopefully in each direction. To the left she saw the jailer's back view. Isaac and Felix had appeared from that direction, whereas she and Ségal and the mayor had come the opposite way. Neither seemed promising.

Someone had to decide. She turned left,

leading the others into the unknown. Then they came to a cross corridor and there was Hannah, trotting along followed by her faithful gendarme.

"What has been keeping you?" she asked in Yiddish. "I've waited and waited, may God spare me."

"You know the way to the berline?" Miriam demanded.

"It's a regular maze, but Étienne here knows the way." She patted her youthful companion's arm. "He's a bit slow but he's a good-hearted lad. Just follow us."

Étienne took them to a walled courtyard behind the building. Stepping out into the heat of the midday sun, reflected from the cobbles, Miriam blinked at the brightness. The berline awaited them, with a team already harnessed.

The groom holding their heads announced that he would go with them the first stage so as to bring back the police horses.

"And to report on which road we've taken," Felix muttered.

"They could as easily follow us," Miriam pointed out. She turned to Ségal. "Monsieur, have the goodness to give us directions to the Toulouse road. Oh, Felix, Isaac, this is my friend Monsieur Ségal, who was instrumental in obtaining your release."

The little banker demurred, giving all the credit to his friend the mayor, but the men shook his hand with hearty thanks. He hurriedly explained the way out of Bordeaux.

Felix looked blank. "Did you not understand?" Isaac asked. "I'd better drive first, then." He headed for the box.

"I'll check the harness." Felix followed him.

Miriam kissed Ségal's cheek, making him blush again. "Give Suzanne a kiss from me," she requested. He handed her into the carriage, where Hannah was already ensconced, having bidden her pet gendarme farewell.

Felix returned. As he set his foot on the step, he glanced down with a look of absolute horror.

"Au diable!" he swore. "Those damned chains have ruined my boots!"

Miriam giggled. "I never taught you those words," she chided him.

He sat down opposite her, grinning. "I picked them up myself," he said with becoming modesty, "but I beg your pardon for using them in your presence. All the same, my boots will never recover from this. It's been bad enough having them blacked by inn servants, using soot from the kitchen chimney, I daresay. My valet will never forgive me."

"You must be shaking in your mistreated boots." She smiled at him, glad to return to their previous easy relationship, dismissing her earlier overwrought sensibilities as the effect of the morning's frightening happenings.

She turned to the window to thank Ezra Ségal once more and bid him a final good-by. The berline began to rumble across the cobbled yard. Leaning forward to wave to the banker, she saw standing in a doorway, watching them, the ominous figure of Lieutenant Hébert.

CHAPTER 15

"The groom is leaving us here, but someone is following us." Isaac joined Miriam and Hannah in the carriage, handing each a napkin containing a roll and a piece of cheese.

Miriam spared a mournful thought for the hamper she had left behind at the Prince de Galles. "How do you know?" she asked. "Perhaps he is just travelling the same way."

"There is little enough traffic for me to be certain it's the same man, and even an inexpert horseman on an inferior horse could have passed us. I've had to drive slowly because the road is in a shocking condition."

"So we have noticed, though the berline is well-sprung and a vast improvement over the diligence we travelled in last time we came this way. The Garonne floods every winter, I believe, and washes out the road. Do you think it's Hébert?" She nibbled distastefully at the hard, dry cheese.

"Following us? It could be. Yes, quite likely. Felix told me just now you saw him watching us when we left. He speaks English, you know, so he would be an obvious choice to follow and try yet again to trap us."

"Felix said he was waiting in the cell when you arrived. They were all prepared for us, were they not? Do you think the Paris prefect has arrested Jakob Rothschild?"

"The Minister of Finance is a powerful man. He should be able to protect him."

"I daresay he will talk himself out of danger as easily as he talked me into it." She shivered, though the afternoon was still warm. "I wish we were safely hidden among the foothills of the Pyrenees! I had hoped to disappear as soon as we turn off the main road at Langon, but now they will know which way we have taken."

"We have escaped them once, we'll do it again. Tell me how you found Monsieur Ségal, and how he persuaded the mayor to aid us."

Isaac's obvious attempt to distract her succeeded for a while. She even laughed when she described Grignol's discomfiture.

"So your uncle Amos saved our skins again. I'm sorry I never knew him."

Miriam flushed as she recalled how she had used Uncle Amos as an excuse for rejecting Isaac. He might have forgiven, but she could never forget her unconscionable unkindness.

"Amos Bloom was a saint," Hannah declared. "Now eat your nuncheon, child, before you faint from hunger. And then Mr. Isaac will excuse you if you take a nap, as I mean to, for if ever there was a wearying day this was it."

Of course, the overwrought sensibility that brought the past so vividly to mind was due to hunger and exhaustion. Obediently Miriam gnawed on the cheese, then gave up and tore off a piece of the roll, scarcely less hard.

"I'm sorry," Isaac said with a wry look, "it was the best I could get in a hurry. You did warn us that the country inns cannot be relied upon."

"What I wouldn't give for a cup of tea to wash it down! Suzanne Ségal gave us tea. That reminds me, I wanted to ask you what is the purpose of a mezuzah?"

He explained, and she listened while she chewed away at the roll. At last the last crumb disappeared. She did feel better with food, however unsatisfactory, in her stomach. Hannah was nodding in her corner and Miriam was ready to join her. She leaned

213

back against the squabs.

"Sweet dreams," said Isaac. His voice and his dark eyes were filled with — was it tenderness?

She smiled at him, too sleepy to wonder. Her eyelids drifted down . . .

. . . And flew open as she sat up with a start. She had been sound asleep. It took her a moment to realize that she had been roused by the rattle of the shutter above Isaac's head.

"I thought you ought to know," said Felix, sounding worried, "that rider is still following us."

Though Hannah continued to doze, the news drove sleep beyond Miriam's reach. She was the one who knew the country; it was up to her to devise a way to elude their pursuer. Should they drive on beyond Langon, hoping he might lose interest before they turned south? That would take them out of their way and they had already lost half a day in Bordeaux. Could they evade him in the maze of country roads, even if he knew which direction they were heading? They would need to get far enough ahead to be out of his sight for long enough to disappear.

As she gazed out unseeing at the wide, blue river and the vineyard-covered hills beyond, an idea came to her. A plan began to form.

"Can Felix drive in the dark?" she asked Isaac. He looked surprised. "I mean, we have always stopped at dusk, but I don't know if that was because we happened to reach a good place to stay, or because you were both tired? The diligence continues day and night."

"I don't know. I'll ask him." He turned his head and reached up to open the shutter. Catching herself admiring his long-fingered, elegant hand and wide-browed profile, she hastily glanced away. "Felix, Miriam wants to know whether you can drive the carriage in the dark."

A snort answered him. "Of course I can drive in the dark."

"Along country lanes?" asked Miriam.

"Along country lanes?" Isaac transmitted.

There was a pause redolent of caution. "Narrow country lanes? With ditches?"

"Narrow, yes," said Miriam. "Ditches, I cannot be sure."

"Narrow and winding with deep ditches," Isaac informed him, grinning. "And hills, and streams to ford."

"If we can get hold of good lanterns, and you aren't planning to break any speed records, then yes."

"Then if you are rested, Isaac, I think you had better take the reins as far as Langon. Felix will be driving half the night."

"He will?"

"Unless you feel able to drive in the dark?"

"Not me!" He shuddered.

"As I guessed. Just a minute." Miriam gently disengaged the strings of Hannah's reticule from the maid's wrist and delved into it. Taking out a handful of small brown glass vials, she read the labels then held one up to the light. "Good, there's plenty left. Tell Felix to stop and I'll explain."

"I'm glad to hear it. Felix, Miriam wants us to change places."

"Far be it from a lowly coachman to question madam's orders," came Felix's response and the berline drew to a halt at the side of the road.

The cessation of swaying and jolting woke Hannah. As Isaac opened the door, Miriam said to her, "Can you pretend to have the headache? Or I shall and you must support me."

Hannah blinked at her. "The headache? But I feel very well, thank God. All I needed was forty winks."

"Pretend! Our follower must suppose that you are travel sick, to give us a reason for stopping."

"Sick of travelling I am, right enough," she grumbled.

"Come, let me help you to step down."

With Isaac lending a solicitous hand, Hannah descended to the dusty road. She stood hunched, holding her head and her stomach and groaning artistically. Felix had climbed down from the box. Holding the reins, he looked back along the highway.

"You can cut out the wailing and gnashing of teeth," he announced. "Our man has stopped a good furlong back. That proves he's after us, though. Is someone going to tell me what is going on?"

Hannah stopped groaning but kept her hand to her head. Miriam put an arm around her waist and walked her slowly towards Felix, with Isaac following. "Has either of you a proposal for losing that fellow?" she asked.

Isaac shook his head.

"Hit him on the head and run," suggested Felix.

"May God spare us!" Hannah moaned.

"I have a notion how we may contrive." Strolling up and down supporting Hannah, she outlined her plan.

"I'd rather hit him on the head," Felix complained. "Must you use my brandy? I wish I spoke better French."

"So do I." Isaac was doubtful. "I daresay I can manage it, but I'd rather not. On the other hand, I cannot possibly do the driving."

"If we do it at all," said Miriam impatiently, "there is no choice about who does what. The only question is, have you come up with a stratagem more likely to succeed?"

"No."

"Not yet."

"Well, we have until later this evening to decide. But I do think Isaac had best drive now, in case."

Passing the reins to Isaac, Felix handed the women into the carriage and joined them.

"Put your feet up, my lord, and try to sleep," Hannah advised in the motherly voice she used when she called Miriam "child". A few days more, Miriam was ready to wager, and she would be addressing his lordship as "lad".

Felix smiled at the abigail. "Yes, ma'am, if Miriam will excuse me?"

"Of course." She couldn't help contrasting his response with his haughty disapproval the first time Hannah had joined them at the dinner table. Now that he had come down off his high horse, he really was as charming as she had told Suzanne.

He turned sideways, leaning back against the squabs, and raised his legs onto the seat. The movement brought his battered boots into his sight. "Desecration!" he lamented.

"Better your boots than your skin," Miriam pointed out with a chuckle.

"Certainly not. Under your knowledgeable care my skin would heal. Even my valet and the best champagne blacking could not render my boots presentable, alas."

"Champagne! You are bamming me."

"Not I. Oh, I gave it up some years since, but Beau Brummel claims to use champagne in his blacking and I once was one of the many aspiring young dandies who ape him. I believe he made it up, along with the story that it takes three men to make his gloves."

Miriam laughed. "How absurd! Why should anyone want to copy him?"

"For the most part it's all to the good. He made elegant simplicity fashionable, and clean linen, at which one can hardly quibble. He's a good fellow, though he does give himself airs. I'd hate to be the butt of one of his witty remarks."

"I've heard of him. Is he the gentleman who spends an entire morning tying his cravat?"

"If it takes an entire morning to perfect it. He believes that like a butterfly a gentleman should emerge perfect from the cocoon and then give no more thought to his appearance. You never see the Beau primping before a mirror in public."

"That an odd mixture of sense and nonsense." As a schoolgirl she had yearned to be a part of that Polite World in which Felix never doubted his place. He made it sound attractive and amusing, whetting her appetite.

"All nonsense I call it," snorted Hannah. "If you have any sense, my lord, you'll stop worrying about your boots and try to sleep."

Felix grinned and obediently closed his eyes. Careful not to dirty the cushions, he had left his booted feet, white with road dust, sticking out over the edge of the seat. Miriam thought he'd be much more comfortable if he took the boots off altogether, but somehow it was impossible to suggest such a thing. Boots first, then coat, then neckcloth . . .

Hastily she tore her gaze from his powerful body, emanating masculine vigour even in repose. Outside, a grey mist was rising from the river, blotting out the far bank and hiding the westering sun. Miriam shivered.

On the box, Isaac shivered. Even so far

south, the spring evenings were chilly and he had packed away his greatcoat. One more foolish mistake.

Why had he admitted his uncertainty over his ability to play his rôle in Miriam's plan? Given a decent command of French, Felix would have done the deed without blinking. Felix was competent and sure of himself, torn by no doubts as to the rightness of his actions. In normal circumstances Isaac considered himself competent, but he couldn't pretend he was cut out to be a hero — and a hero was what he wanted to appear in Miriam's eyes.

She made him think of Miriam the sister of Moses, in the Book of the Exodus — Miriam whose ingenuity had saved her baby brother; who had led the women in celebrating the escape from Egypt; who had supported Moses throughout the wandering in the wilderness, yet had not hesitated to reproach him when she disapproved of his actions.

Isaac smiled to himself. Yes, his Miriam was well named — if only she was his Miriam and not Felix's. His smile faded.

It didn't help that he had heard her laughing just now. The sound still rang in his ears. And before him floated a vision of her gazing up into Felix's face, clasped, however briefly, in his arms.

He was not going to find it easy to continue to treat Felix with complaisance.

The mist from the Garonne was blowing across the road by the time he drove into the village of Langon. If it grew any thicker it would hinder their pursuer, but it would also make Felix's task more difficult. Unfortunately, Isaac was denied the consolation of wishing his rival to fail.

He looked back over his shoulder. The rider was closer now and Isaac was almost certain he was Hébert. That would make his job easier, he hoped. At least he had some idea of what to expect from the lieutenant.

The inn he stopped at, though large, looked as if it had seen more prosperous days. Whitewash flaked from the walls and the faded sign was indecipherable. Doubtless Bordeaux's loss of trade had reduced traffic from the interior. Isaac drew up before the door.

At once an obsequious couple rushed out, bowing and curtsying and begging the travellers to step in. Felix emerged from the carriage, his hand raised to cover a yawn. He helped Miriam and Hannah down. A couple of servants appeared and the landlord began to direct them to carry in the luggage.

"We do not need everything," Miriam said, "but if we leave it with the carriage will it be safe? Is there an ostler on duty all night to watch for thieves?"

"But assuredly, madame. Always there are two men alert to provide horses for the diligence. Your bags will be perfectly safe."

"Good. We shall need three chambers and a private parlour."

"At once, madame," said the landlord's wife. "If madame will be so good as to step this way, out of the cold."

Miriam disappeared into the inn. Hannah showed the servants which bags were needed, and Felix strolled forward to look up at Isaac.

"Our man is still there?" he asked softly in French.

"He was a moment ago." Isaac glanced back. "I expect he'll wait until we have gone in before he comes any closer."

Felix nodded. "I hope this . . ." not knowing the word he waved his hand at the mist, ". . . goes away soon."

"It is probably clearer away from the river. Are you rested?"

"I slept a little, but Hannah insists that I must go to bed right after dinner. She treats me just as my old nurse does."

Isaac grinned at his indignant tone. There was something innately likeable about the dashing young gentleman allowing his old nurse to bully him.

Hannah went into the inn with the servants carrying bags and boxes. Felix followed them, and Isaac drove the berline to the end of the extensive stable yard farthest from the building.

A few minutes later he stepped into the warmth of the inn. Lingering by the doorway, he watched as a rider wrapped in a greatcoat rode into the yard and dismounted. By the light of a lantern now lit against the dusk, he caught a glimpse of the man's face.

Hébert.

CHAPTER 16

Isaac was hungry enough to eat a horse. Nonetheless he recoiled when the waiter started removing covers from the dishes, releasing a veritable miasma of garlic. He had thought himself inured to the all-pervasive odour, and he had come to tolerate, almost to enjoy, the unavoidable flavour, but this was overwhelming.

Felix turned greenish and even Miriam wrinkled her nose.

The food looked delicious: a tureen of thick soup, some roast fowl, a couple of ragoûts, a variety of vegetables, and crusty golden loaves.

"Which dish is it that contains garlic?" Miriam asked the waiter.

He stared at her in surprise. "But everything, mam'selle. How is it possible to cook without garlic?"

"The soup is the strongest," said Hannah. The steam from the earthenware tureen before her wafted straight towards her quivering nostrils.

"Pray remove the soup," Miriam requested.

The waiter shrugged his shoulders and obeyed. There might have been a slight diminution of the smell as the door closed behind him, but Isaac wouldn't have taken his oath on it. He started to carve a duck and discovered that it was stuffed with whole cloves of garlic.

Naturally the meat of the bird was impregnated with the stuff. He and Miriam and Hannah managed to eat a reasonable meal, but Felix, though he bravely tasted several dishes, ended up with bread. He swore that it, too, tasted of garlic, as did the wine.

So did the cheese, when the second course arrived, and Miriam pushed away a sugar-glazed pastry after one bite.

"Even that," she said with a shudder. "I don't dare try the coffee."

"Nor I," Isaac agreed. "That settles it, Felix, we shall have to use your cognac. Garlic-flavoured brandy doesn't bear thinking about."

Felix sighed. "Come up to my chamber and I shall give you the flask."

"I'd best make sure Hébert is actually in the coffee room or the tap room," Isaac said. "If he has retired already we'll have to change our plan."

He and Felix went together to peer through the open doors of the powerfully garlicky coffee room — no sign of their quarry — and then the tap room, which smelled more of alcohol and tobacco. The lieutenant slouched on a settle in a corner, a nearly empty wine bottle on the table before him.

"It looks as if your job is half done," said Felix, grinning, as they turned away.

"He doesn't look as if he's happy with his job. Poor chap, I'd hate to have to face Grignol and tell him I had failed."

"Don't feel too sorry for him. His failure is what we're hoping for, remember."

"I'm not likely to forget. We'd best pay the reckoning now. I shall tell them we want to leave early."

"Good idea. If we don't have to find someone to pay later, we might be able to slip away without rousing anyone but the ostler."

Isaac settled with the landlord, rejecting his offer to send someone to wake them at first light. "I have an alarum-watch," he explained.

The landlord nodded wisely. "Of course, Swiss watches are famous. In case you depart before I myself am about, I wish you bon voyage, messieurs."

"Well done," said Felix in a low voice as the innkeeper hurried off about his business. "With luck he will never realize that we left at midnight rather than five in the morning."

Returning to the private parlour, they found that Miriam and Hannah had left, presumably retired to their shared chamber. Isaac couldn't blame them, for though the table had been cleared the aroma lingered.

"Thank heaven we'll be gone before breakfast," Felix muttered. "I'll be damned if I could face it first thing in the morning."

They went up to his chamber. From his portmanteau he took one of the precious bottles of cognac and a chased silver pocket flask. Careful not to spill a drop of the nectar, he filled the flask and screwed on the top.

"What a devilish waste," he mourned, passing the flask to Isaac and drinking a mouthful from the bottle. "Ah, that will help me sleep. Good luck, old fellow." He shook Isaac's hand and clapped him on the back.

Reflecting on the change in Felix's attitude since they had left London together, Isaac crossed the corridor and raised his hand to tap on Miriam's door. He caught himself just before his knuckles struck the wood. Miriam's door. Miriam's bedchamber. A wave of heat flooded his body.

Was she expecting him, or had she returned to the parlour? Worse, was she in her chamber but expecting him to meet her in the parlour? If he knocked would she be embarrassed? Angry?

Somewhere in the village a church clock struck nine. There was no time for hesitation. He glanced up and down the corridor and then knocked.

The door opened at once. By the light of a pair of candles he saw that Miriam's usually pale face was flushed, her smile tentative, with a hint of uncertainty in her wide eyes. However she reached out to take his arm and tug him into the room, closing the door behind him.

Hannah stood guard, her face disapproving.

"I was afraid someone might interrupt us in the parlour and see what we were doing," Miriam said a trifle breathlessly. "Did Felix give you the flask?"

He passed it to her. Their hands touched, sending a flash of lightning up his arm. For a moment she stared at him, her soft lips parted, then she swung round and set the flask on the dressing table.

"Hannah, you have the vials and the court plaster?"

"Right here, Miss Miriam."

"We decided that if we put the laudanum into the flask, Hébert might taste it and be suspicious, or he might take a dangerous amount, or you might accidentally swallow some. So we have put just enough into this little vial to send him to sleep for twelve hours, or more since he will take it with alcohol. I'll stick the vial to the flask with the plaster, like this. Be sure to keep the other side turned to him until you reckon he is drunk enough not to notice the taste, then pull out the stopper of the vial before you pour the cognac into his glass. You see?"

Isaac moved closer to look. "You are ingenious . . ." and beautiful. He struggled to resist the desire to take her in his arms.

Hannah spoke. "I made sure the stopper's in firm, sir, so as it won't fall out before you want it out. It'll come out easy if you give it a bit of a twist."

"I see. I'm off then, and if all goes well I shall wake you as soon as the inn quiets down."

"I shall try to sleep, but Hannah will stay awake, just in case you are forced to drink more than you mean to. She can go down to the tap room to see what has happened without arousing suspicion." Miriam gave him a quizzing look. "If she finds you under the table, she will fetch Felix to rescue you and carry you out to the carriage."

"I'll do my best to avoid that fate, even if it means pouring the stuff down my sleeve. Wish me luck?"

"I wish you luck, but I know very well you will be successful even without it."

He put the flask in his pocket, raised her hand to his lips, and departed.

Lieutenant Hébert was slouched a little lower in his corner of the tap room. The bottle in front of him was empty. As Isaac paused in the doorway, a buxom barmaid went over to him, picked up the bottle, and said something.

Hébert took a handful of coins from his pocket. Counting them, he scowled. He waved the girl away. She grabbed his glass and flounced off, disappointed.

Isaac sauntered across the room. He felt silly and conspicuous, for his usual gait was a stride or a pace. No one took any particular notice of him though — except the lieutenant, who regarded him with a sour grin.

"So, the Englishman." His consonants were slightly slurred.

"Swiss. No hard feelings, eh? I'll treat you

to a drop." Signalling to the waitress, Isaac sat down.

"Where's your cousin?"

"He and my sister have retired already, exhausted from our contretemps with Monsieur Grignol this morning." The waitress arrived and he ordered a bottle of red wine, then continued, "He sent you after us, I take it?"

"Monsieur le préfet never gives up. I'm to follow until I find proof you're English spies. He'll have my head if I don't bring you back, and monsieur le maire will have it if I do," he added gloomily.

"You'll have a hard time proving we are English spies, since we are Swiss tourists."

The girl returned with the wine and two glasses. Isaac paid her while Hébert filled the glasses.

"*Salut!*" He downed his wine.

"*Santé!*" Isaac sipped his and grimaced. The stuff was harsh to a palate Felix was beginning to educate. He refilled Hébert's glass.

"If you're jus' Swiss tourists, you won't min' saving me some trouble by telling me where you're going."

"Not at all. Toulouse first, then Carcassonne. My cousin wants to go to Marseille but my sister doesn't, so I cannot be sure

232

after that."

"Rough place, Marseille."

"So I've heard. We shall probably just go to Avignon and then homeward up the Rhône valley."

"No side trip to view the Pyr . . . Pyrenees?"

"We are Swiss. We live among the Alps."

"Hunh. Drink up, drink up, you're not drinking," said the lieutenant irritably, pouring his fourth glassful. He was leaning with both arms on the moisture-ringed table, his long, lank hair dangling about his face.

Isaac manfully swallowed his wine and filled his own glass again. The bottle was nearly empty. "To tell the truth, this is not much to my taste. I've got some good brandy here if you'd like to try a nip." He took the flask from his pocket, careful to keep it the right way round.

"You're a goo' fellow even if y'are English. Waste of my time following you 'roun' if y'ask me. Waste not, want not." Hébert poured the last drop of wine, swilled it, and held out his glass.

It was sacrilege to put the cognac in a dirty glass, but Isaac was afraid the barmaid might object to his bringing a full flask into the tap room. He poured half an inch of the amber liquid. Hébert sniffed, tasted, and a dreamy look came over his face. He warmed the glass in his hands, breathing deep of the heady vapours before he sipped again.

Isaac eyed his own glass with distaste. He'd have to empty it before he could drink any cognac, but he knew his own limits. If he drank the wine he'd be in no fit state to start on the spirits, yet the notion of dumping it in his sleeve did not appeal. Philosophically returning the flask to his pocket, he raised the glass to his lips and took a small sip. After all, he consoled himself, superior brandy was a newly acquired taste and Felix still had several bottles.

Hébert's eyelids were drooping. Isaac wondered if he had drunk two bottles before the one they shared. He didn't want the man to pass out before he dosed him with laudanum; there was too much risk that he would wake too soon.

"Spare a drop more?" Hébert unsteadily pushed his glass across the table.

As Hannah had promised, the vial's glass stopper came out with a quick twist. It proved less easy to tilt the flask in such a way that all the laudanum flowed out without a flood of cognac overfilling the glass. Isaac managed to pour no more than half a glassful. He pushed it back across the table.

"Too full." The lieutenant squinted at it

with bleary-eyed reproach. "No room for bouquet. Too bad, English don' unnerstan' wine." He raised the glass for a toast. Isaac winced as a little brandy slopped over the side. "Vive Napoléon!"

It seemed wise to second the toast. "Napoléon," Isaac murmured, and finished his wine.

Hébert took a hefty swallow of cognac, perhaps with the laudable aim of leaving room in the glass for the bouquet. He grimaced, staring at his drink with a puzzled air. "Same stuff? Tas' differen'."

"Same stuff." Isaac poured himself a little and sipped, barely wetting his tongue. "The best."

"Mus' be 'cos you filled it too full," he complained. He rolled another swig around his mouth, pulled a face, swallowed, and toppled face down on the table.

Too late Isaac grabbed for the glass. An ounce of superb cognac and half a dose of laudanum sloshed onto the floor.

Isaac groaned. Left to himself the man would probably sleep through the night, but here in the busy tap room he was not likely to be undisturbed. He had only taken half the drug. A good shaking might well rouse him.

The barmaid stalked over, scowling.

"Dead drunk, hein? Your friend can't stay here. This is a respectable house."

"He's just overcome by fatigue. I shall help him up to his chamber, if you can find out for me which it is."

"Jean-Paul!" she called to the tapster, "which room is this citizen in?"

"He didn't take a chamber. Said he had to keep watch all night or his patron would hang him."

"Watch what?"

The tapster shrugged. "Who knows?" He turned away to serve a customer.

Zut alors! The girl turned back to Isaac. "Our *patron* will chuck him out. He won't stand for drunks littering the place. You want to share your room with him?"

"God forbid!" That was the last thing he wanted to do, for more than one reason. He eyed the snoring man with distaste. Yet he couldn't let Hébert be thrown out. The chill night air was bound to revive him. "I'll hire another chamber for him," he decided.

"Don't blame you. He's going to be sick as a dog by the looks of him. I'll tell the pa-tronne. She'll send someone to show you the way."

The landlady came herself. "If monsieur will be so good — payment in advance? With such a one as your friend, you under-

236

stand, and my husband says you mean to depart early tomorrow . . ."

"Of course." Isaac paid her, adding a sizable tip. "My friend does not travel with us, however. You will permit him to sleep as late as he wishes in the morning, I trust."

"But naturally, monsieur. He can have the second room to the right on the third floor. Here is the key. You will want someone to help you, without doubt?"

He looked at Hébert. The lieutenant was not a particularly large man. There was always a chance he might start talking when he was moved. "Thank you, madame, I can manage him."

She shrugged. "As you will."

Taking Hébert by the shoulders, he leaned him back on the settle. The landlady helpfully pulled out the table as she left. Isaac bent down and draped one of Hébert's arms across his back, put his arm around the man's waist, and awkwardly raised him to his feet. He was not accustomed to assisting drunkards. No doubt this was something else Felix would do better.

As they started across the tap room, Hébert's feet moved automatically in step and he began to mutter. Only a couple of words were comprehensible, but those were ". . . English spies. . . ." Cold all over, Isaac raised a prayer of thanks that he had rejected assistance.

A few heads turned to glance at them as they passed, but no one was interested in so commonplace a sight. They reached the bottom of the stairs without incident and began the climb.

If he had dared leave the lieutenant unattended, Isaac would have gone to wake Felix. The staircase might as well have been the Matterhorn, so difficult was the ascent. In the end, he hoisted Hébert right up onto his shoulders, head hanging down one side, feet the other. This brought Hébert's face into close proximity with his own. He reeled as a blast of alcohol-laden breath struck him.

Labouring up the stairs, he cursed the landlady for sending him to the top of the house.

When he reached the chamber, he guessed the reason. The room was little more than a garret, the straw mattress covered with a sheet that had seen better days, and by the look of it more than one use since it was last laundered. He couldn't blame the woman. It was all too likely that the lieutenant would cast up his accounts when he awoke, if not before.

With that in mind, Isaac loosened his

neckcloth and laid him on his front, with his head turned sideways. On impulse he took off Hébert's riding boots. Another impulse suggested removing them, to slow the pursuit, but that would serve to confirm the man's suspicions. Besides, the unfortunate fellow was going to be in hot water enough if he returned to Bordeaux without prisoners. No need to make his life any more miserable.

Leaving the room key on the night table, Isaac thankfully repaired to his own chamber.

He took up a volume of Maimonides, but he couldn't concentrate. As the sounds of activity in the inn gradually diminished, he found himself wondering whether he ought to have put the laudanum in the first glass of brandy. Lacking experience of drunkenness, he had misjudged the man's condition. If Hébert woke too soon and picked up their trail, it would be his fault.

CHAPTER 17

The river mist was no more than a faint haze veiling the waxing moon, and even that they soon left behind. The rumble of wheels, clink of harness, and regular thud of hooves sounded loud in the stillness. An owl hooted close by; somewhere in the distance another answered.

Hannah drowsed in her corner. Miriam had slept for an hour or two at the inn. She was tired, but now she felt taut as a bow-string, unable to relax. Besides, it seemed unfair to doze while out on the box Felix steered them through the night.

"Are you sleepy, Isaac?"

"Not really. I keep thinking perhaps I ought to have stolen Hébert's boots."

"His boots! Good heavens, what happened back there? Tell me all about it. How did you manage to persuade him to drink with you in the first place?"

"He was somewhat disgruntled to have

been sent after us, quite willing to let bygones be bygones and the future take care of itself. In fact, he was drunker than I realized when I joined him. He passed out sooner than I expected. I made a mull of it, waiting too long and then the laudanum was diluted with too much brandy."

"Oh dear, I wondered about that after you'd gone. Hannah pointed out that the vial would only empty if the flask was tipped completely upside down. Next time I drug someone's drink I shall try another method!"

"It would have worked admirably if I had not poured most of a bottle of wine into the lieutenant first." Isaac sounded cheered. Miriam hoped he had stopped blaming himself.

"I cannot imagine how you contrived not to join him under the table. I quite expected that Felix would have to carry you out. So Hébert didn't actually take all of the laudanum?"

"Only about half. Will that be sufficient?"

She frowned in thought. "Probably, in combination with a lake of alcohol, as long as no one makes a deliberate effort to wake him."

"I made sure of that. I hired a chamber for him and carried him to it."

"What a stroke of genius! I daresay he will sleep till noon. You tucked him up in bed?"

"Well, not quite, but I made him as comfortable as I could. That's why I took his boots off, and why I was wondering whether I ought to have run off with them."

"No. It would only have convinced him that we were trying to escape him. As it is, he is more likely to be grateful to you for arranging for his comfort. You have carried it off admirably."

"It was nothing, compared to your delivering us from durance vile yesterday."

"All I did was call on friends, and they would have accomplished nothing if you had not held out against Hébert's wiles and Grignol's intimidation."

"I find it in my heart to pity Hébert." Isaac stifled a huge yawn: a long indrawn breath and a white glint of teeth as the carriage rounded a bend and moonlight fell on his face.

"I must not keep you talking," said Miriam remorsefully. "I shall be able to rest all day, but as soon as it grows light you will have to drive. Put your feet up and try to sleep. You can take off your boots — I promise not to steal them."

"I own my toes would be delighted. They have been imprisoned far longer than I was.

If you are sure you don't mind?"

"Not at all." She couldn't see him, hidden once more in the impenetrable dark of moon-shadow. There was nothing for her wayward imagination to seize upon.

Or so she tried to persuade herself as his boots thudded to the floor. Nonetheless, she was glad of the distraction when he clicked opened the little shutter and called softly to Felix.

"How goes it?"

"Well enough, but tediously slow. I dare not speed up. If we land in the ditch, we'll really be in the suds."

"It's a far cry from a curricle race to Brighton," Isaac sympathized.

"And of somewhat more importance than winning a wager," said Felix dryly. "Go to sleep. We're coming to a ford and I have to concentrate."

Isaac shut the hatch and stretched out on the seat with a low laugh. "I thought I was inventing the streams to be forded," he said. "We are fortunate to have a competent driver. Good night, Miriam."

"Good night." Listening to hooves and wheels splashing through the stream, Miriam smiled dreamily. It was hard to believe that less than a week ago Felix and Isaac had been at daggers drawn.

The next thing she knew was the familiar jangle of bits and chains as the team was changed. She opened her eyes just enough to see that the half-moon was now low in the western sky before she drifted back into sleep. When she woke again, the sky was dawn pale and Isaac, moving stiffly, was climbing out of the carriage.

She felt as stiff as he looked. Hannah groaned as she straightened.

"Where are we?" she asked.

"In the middle of nowhere, as far as I can see. Felix must have stopped because it's light enough for Isaac to take over the reins. I'm going to get out and stretch my limbs."

"I'll come too."

Miriam stepped down and helped Hannah after her. Isaac was stretching and bending. Felix stood holding the reins, looking pale and weary.

He summoned up a smile. "Sorry to disturb you, but I've been driving with my eyes closed for the past half hour. I hope I haven't taken any wrong turnings."

Miriam consulted the sky. "I'd say we are on course. We are still heading south, and on a reasonably respectable road."

"A respectable road!"

"Most of the lanes are too narrow for two carriages to pass."

"Well, there would certainly have been some paint scraped had I met another vehicle in the dark." He handed Isaac the reins. "It's some way since I changed horses. Posting houses are few and far between so you had better stop at the next. Good luck. Just don't try to hurry. If Hébert is behind us on horseback, he can catch up however fast we go."

He was so sound asleep when they reached Roquefort that Miriam didn't wake him for a breakfast of rolls and coffee. She bought bread and some of the famous local cheese for him, then insisted that Isaac carry the smelly stuff outside until Felix wanted it. As they crawled southwards, he slept on, waking at last when Isaac stopped for luncheon. They had an unsatisfactory meal in a small village, then Felix drove on.

They reached Pau as the sun set, having covered a good hundred miles since leaving Langon in the middle of the night. To the south, the twilit river valley roared with melted snow-waters; across the horizon stretched the ridge of the Pyrenees, a formidable barrier of peaks and saddles, stained with a rosy glow. Felix, once more at the reins, pulled up at the first respectable inn in the little town.

The innkeeper was less than delighted to

see them. He didn't expect travellers at this time of year, he grumbled. But, yes, he could provide three chambers and a private parlour . . . and dinner? Of course, dinner, he agreed doubtfully.

Too tired to search for more congenial lodgings, they went up to their rooms.

Miriam and Hannah's chamber was comfortable enough, and reasonably clean. Hannah declared that the sheets were damp and sent the chambermaid off to procure a warming pan.

"And tell her to air and warm the gentlemen's beds too," she instructed Miriam. "Laying weary bones in a damp bed is a recipe for sickness, and I for one am wearied to death just with sitting. I'm not as young as you children, to be burning the candle at both ends. I've half a mind to skip my dinner and go straight to bed soon as the sheets are dry."

"My poor Hannah." Miriam hugged her. "You sit down here right this minute, with your feet on this footstool. I'm perfectly able to unpack what we need, and the gentlemen will not mind if I don't change my gown for once." She looked down with disfavour at the high-necked brown cambric travelling dress. "They are too exhausted and hungry to notice, I believe! I shall have your dinner sent up on a tray."

"I own I'll be glad of a bite to eat, child. But I ought to go with you."

"Fustian! I shall survive one evening without a chaperon. I don't mean to stay up late, I promise you."

Miriam went down and ordered a meal for Hannah. She found Felix in their private parlour, filling a glass from a carafe of wine.

"Will you have some?" he asked in a low voice. "It's surprisingly good for a local vintage. Jurançon, they call it."

Miriam accepted a glass. "Why are we whispering?"

"The coffee room is just the other side of this wall and the window gives onto the street, so Isaac thought we ought not to speak loudly in English. He has gone to reconnoitre. He wants to be quite sure the lieutenant has not succeeded in following us."

"Neither of you saw anything of him on the road since we left Langon, did you?"

"No, though it would not have been as easy to spot him as on the main highway. But I doubt he's still after us. I believe your clever stratagem was utterly successful." He toasted her and refilled his glass.

Isaac came in. "No sign of Hébert so far. There is a local gendarme playing dominoes in the coffee room, though, so we had best keep quiet. The landlord is suspicious; he wanted to know what brings a party of Swiss to this out-of-the-way corner of the world."

"What did you tell him?" Felix asked, handing him a glass of wine.

"That we are homesick for mountains."

They were all laughing when a pair of waiters came in with trays. Felix sniffed the air suspiciously, but there was only the faintest hint of garlic.

"You must be dying of hunger," Miriam said in French as he seated her. "You have eaten next to nothing in two days."

The meal set before them turned out to be scarcely calculated to assuage the pangs of hunger. The soup was pale and flavourless; the fish had spent too many days out of the river; the neck of mutton, from a sheep who had spent too many years in the mountains, was mostly bone and gristle; the whites of the leeks were missing, the greens smothered in a lumpy sauce and too tough to chew.

Even the bread was stale. As Felix washed down several dry slices with copious draughts of Jurançon, Miriam rang the bell and complained to the waiter.

He shrugged. "What will you, mademoiselle? The patron is not prepared for unexpected visitors and you are dining late. The best has gone to the coffee room already. Tomorrow you may order in advance and things will be better."

Miriam gave up and asked for more bread and cheese. Felix ordered a fresh carafe of wine.

"It's the only thing worth consuming," he pointed out gloomily.

As the level of wine in the second carafe sank, Felix's spirits rose. Miriam began to feel a trifle concerned, but he remembered to keep his voice low even as he made her and Isaac laugh with tales of youthful pranks. A dinner of dry bread, he explained, had been a frequent nursery punishment.

"I'm glad Hannah is not here," said Miriam at last, "or she would be shaming me with recounting all my nursery peccadilloes."

"Were you a naughty child?" Isaac asked. "I cannot imagine it."

"The words that come to mind are 'pert', 'forward', and 'saucy'."

"Now that I can imagine," said Felix, grinning.

Isaac pushed back his chair. "I'll just go and check once more to see if Hébert has caught up with us. If he is here, we shall have to do some quick thinking. We are so close to the border, there isn't much room for maneuver."

He left, and an awkward silence fell between Miriam and Felix. Alone with him, suddenly she was ill at ease. She went over to the window, parted the curtains, and peered out into the street.

Nothing moved except a dog trotting purposefully about its own business. Moonlight illuminated the castle on its height overlooking the valley of the Gave de Pau. The little town seemed to be sleeping.

That assumption was belied by a burst of argument from the coffee room next door, doubtless the domino players. In the quiet that followed, Miriam heard footsteps crossing the parlour, approaching her. Reflected in the window glass, Felix stopped close behind her. His breath stirred the tiny hairs on the nape of her neck.

"Do you know how beautiful you are?" His expression was unreadable in the image on the glass.

There was no mistaking the meaning of the hands at her slender waist, smoothing the brown cambric over the curve of her hips, rising to cup her breasts. Even as she turned to protest a shiver of excitement raced through her.

"Felix . . ."

He caught her to him. One hand in the small of her back crushed her to the hardness of his body, the other tilted her face up to his. His eyes burned like blue flames and candlelight sheened golden on his hair. His lips were warm and firm, urgent, entreating. The tip of his tongue touched the corner of her mouth, traced the shape of it.

With a little moan, Miriam melted against him, her arms of their own accord rising to encircle his neck, to pull him down to her. His hands moved to caress her hips again.

Behind him the door opened and closed. "Still not a sign of the lieutenant, but there are now three gendarmes in the coff . . ." Isaac's voice broke off abruptly. Fists clenched he strode across the room.

Felix released Miriam and turned to face him, his shoulders tense. Miriam wanted to faint, wanted to die, wanted to pick up her skirts and run away, but she dared not leave them. If they came to blows, if they even raised their voices, they would bring danger crashing down on all their heads.

"How dare you!" Isaac spat out in an undertone.

"I'll be damned if it's any of your business!" Felix hissed.

"When you start making indecent advances to a woman travelling in my company . . ."

"Indecent advances, the devil! All I did was . . ."

They had both reverted to whispers as if afraid that anything else might too easily rise to a shout. Miriam began to feel hysterical.

"I saw what you were doing, you drunken libertine!"

"Bourgeois prude!"

She decided it was time to intervene, before insults led to a challenge. The only ploy she could think of was to burst into tears, so she did. It was easy.

Felix flung from the room. Isaac took her gently in his arms and stroked her back, murmuring soothing words.

"Don't cry. Please don't cry. I'll see that devil never has another chance to touch you. Hush now, hush."

She raised tear-drenched eyes to his sympathetic face and saw the sympathy become tenderness, the tenderness passion. His arms tightened around her. She felt the pounding of his heart — and her own.

"Miriam." His voice was low and husky.

He kissed the tears from her eyes, ran a trail of kisses down to the lobe of her ear. Strange sensations shook her. Her arm went around his waist, clinging to the lean strength of him. Her fingers played with crisp, dark hair that smelled faintly of sandalwood. The smooth, olive skin over one high cheekbone was irresistibly close to her mouth. She kissed him.

He buried his face in the crook of her neck. "Miriam," he murmured again. "Miriam."

Through the thin cambric his breath was hot on her throat. His mouth found the pulse there. She began to dissolve — or was she going to explode?

Horrified, panic-stricken, she jerked away from him.

"How could you! Oh, how could you take advantage of me when I was distraught? Is this your revenge for nine years ago? I had thought better of you."

His shattered look pierced her to the quick. She spun away and ran from the room.

Guilt kept pace with her up the stairs. Isaac was not to blame — Felix was not to blame — if they had interpreted her reactions as encouragement. She had encouraged them, both of them.

Filled with wretchedness, she hurried to her only refuge.

"Hannah!"

Her abigail, her nurse, her dearest friend, was still seated by the window. She half rose in alarm as Miriam rushed into the chamber. "What is it, child? What ever is the matter?"

Miriam dropped to the footstool. "They had a blazing row. At least, I can hardly call it that since it was carried on in whispers." Her smile trembled.

Hannah gave her a shrewd look. "And what was it they come to cuffs about?"

She gazed down at her hands. "They both kissed me. I wanted to . . . I would have . . . Oh, Hannah, I think I'm in love with both of them."

"That's not love, child," said Hannah dryly, stroking her bowed head. "That's lust. I've said it before and I'll say it again, what you need is a husband." She folded her unhappy nurseling to her breast and rocked her.

Miriam knew she was right. She should never have embarked upon this adventure. She should have found a way to go home quickly and had her family find her a husband. Like a ripe plum, she was ready to fall into the hands of any determined seducer.

She pressed her fist to her mouth to stifle a sob. Her fingers smelled of sandalwood.

CHAPTER 18

When Miriam and Hannah went down next morning, rather later than usual, Felix was in the parlour attacking a vast omelette. As Miriam entered he sprang to his feet and came towards her, looking shamefaced.

"I must humbly beg your pardon," he said. "My behaviour last night was utterly disgraceful. I can only say I had too little to eat and too much to drink. Dare I hope that you will forgive me?"

Just so must he have gazed at his nurse in pleading repentance when he was a mischievous little boy. He was irresistible, and Miriam was all too aware of her own share of blame. She held out her hand to him and he took it in both his. At breakfast-time, in broad daylight, his touch failed to stir her.

"You are forgiven. I should have thought of ordering omelettes last night, and the night before, then you would have had no excuse."

"Last night we were all too tired to think, not to mention the uncooperative waiter, who is not on duty this morning, I'm glad to say. As for the inn at Langon, no doubt any omelette from that kitchen would have been stuffed with garlic. This one is excellent. Not last night's cook, I suspect. Shall I order the same for you?" He led her to the table and seated her.

"Yes, please, but not quite so enormous."

"Hannah?"

The maid also accepted, and urged him to eat his breakfast while it was hot. She appeared to regard him with indulgent reproof, no doubt precisely the way his nurse had. He obeyed, after pouring coffee for them. While he ate and they waited for their omelettes, they discussed the day's route.

"We have to decide which of two passes to cross," Miriam explained. "One involves something of a detour in France, the other in Spain."

"The sooner we leave France, the happier I shall be."

"The Col du Pourtalet, then. It is higher and less likely to be well guarded, too. I wish I knew whether it has been fortified since last I came this way."

"We shall reconnoitre before we attempt the crossing. After my experience of a

French jail, I've no intention of ever letting you see the inside of one," he said seriously. "If it looks dangerous we will find another way, or Isaac and I will just have to manage without you. After all, I must uphold the chivalrous reputation of an English gentleman."

She smiled at that, but she was far from certain that he was really joking. It might well rankle that she had not only rescued him from prison but also devised the plan that had foiled pursuit. Given the circumstances, she could not have acted otherwise, yet once again she had failed to conduct herself like a well-bred English lady.

"No need to decide now. We cannot expect to cross today. The road is difficult from here, climbing into the foothills, and we are starting late. For tonight we can stay at the inn at Laruns, or I have friends in a village at the foot of the pass. They would certainly put us up, though not in anything approaching luxury."

"The closer to the pass the better," Felix suggested.

He was taking his last bite when the accommodating waiter came in with two covered plates and fresh coffee. Isaac followed close behind.

Felix nodded to him noncommittally. "I

shall go and choose our horses," he said and departed.

While the waiter bustled about, Isaac remained standing by the door. He looked out of spirits, disheartened.

"An omelette for monsieur?" the waiter enquired on his way out. Isaac did not answer.

"If you please," Miriam said distractedly. Flustered, she rose and went across to Isaac. "I owe you an apology. I did not mean what I said last night."

"It is I who owe an apology." His response was reserved. "You were correct in saying that I took advantage of your agitation and I most deeply regret it. However, I beg you to believe that no thought of revenge entered my mind."

"I do believe it." She held out her hand. He bowed stiffly and her heart sank.

"Miss Miriam, come and eat your breakfast, do. Good morning, Mr. Isaac. Still no sign of that horrid lieutenant, I hope?"

"Good morning, Hannah. I have already checked this morning and there's no sign that I can see. I suspect he would have arrested us by now had he arrived."

He spoke cheerfully to Hannah, but when Miriam engaged him in a discussion of the route his manner remained reserved, though she thought he was making an effort to appear natural. She was painfully conscious of every change of tone, every shade of expression, every motion of his strong, slender hands.

He agreed that they should try to reach the village of St.-Jean-d'Ossau by nightfall and attempt to cross the Col du Pourtalet the next day. "Will there still be snow in the pass?" he asked.

"I'm not sure. It never melts on the high peaks."

"I own that, being merely a counterfeit Swiss, I am looking forward to a closer view of the mountains. They are impressive even from here."

She smiled at him. "The sight is as awe-inspiring as one's first view of the sea."

"Miriam!" Felix was back. "Does *escarpé* mean steep? I thought so, from the fellow's gestures. And I take it *précipice* is the same as the English? It's a dashed good thing their horses are better than their food. I have picked a prime team." He turned to Isaac and said with polite formality, "Since the berline is heavy, when we descend steep hills one of us will have to be ready to brake with the skid pan while the other drives. As we have not needed it so far, perhaps you would like me to demonstrate its use?"

Isaac's mouth tightened momentarily. "It seems advisable," he conceded.

They went out, together yet further apart than they had been for three days. Miriam sighed.

She saw little of either of them as the road climbed into the foothills of the Pyrenees. After crossing a ridge, they followed the course of the Gave d'Arrau — a deep gorge with rushing streams tumbling down its sides to join the torrent. Forested slopes of beech and chestnut were just beginning to turn a dozen different shades of green and always the snow-capped, cloud-wrapped peaks barricaded the horizon. Though she had seen it before, the spectacular scenery distracted her from her despondent reflections, but the unhappiness lingered.

South of Laruns, the road was little more than a cart track. One mountain grew ahead until its precipices, snow-fields and slopes of scree seemed close enough to touch. When there seemed to be nowhere to go but straight up, they swung eastward across the flank of the Pic du Midi d'Arrau, and a mile or two farther on they came to the tiny hamlet of St.-Jean-d'Arrau.

In the dusk, smoke rose into the thin, frosty air from the chimneys of slate-roofed stone cottages. A score of the humble dwellings clustered around a whitewashed church, with perhaps half a score more scattered across the slopes. Long-fleeced sheep with curved horns grazed in the meadows all around, new lambs skipping about their mothers.

Miriam opened the hatch and directed Felix along the narrow, stony street to a group of three cottages standing slightly apart from the others.

"Are you sure?" he said dubiously. "None of those houses looks large enough to take in guests."

"There are three Jewish families. Between them they will find room for us."

"And the rest of the village?" he asked, driving on. A group of children paused in their singing game to watch the carriage pass.

"Basques. They do not consider themselves French, though most of them will speak French with strangers. Many are equally fluent in Spanish and they take little notice of the border. We ought to consider hiring a Basque to guide us to Pamplona."

"An excellent notion." Chickens fled squawking and a dog barked a warning as he stopped the berline beside a neat picket fence. "Will this do?"

"Yes. I shall go to the Abravanels first."

Isaac sprang to the ground from his post at the rear to hand her down. Followed by Hannah, Miriam picked her way between beds of winter vegetables towards the door of the center cottage, noting the mezuzah on the doorpost.

A boy of ten or so in a woollen coat and a beret dashed around the corner of the building, skidded to a halt when he saw the visitor, then ran into the house shouting.

A moment later he rushed out again, his seven-year-old sister after him. *"Bon soir, Tante Miriam,"* he said importantly. "We are very happy to see you."

"Bon soir, Aaron; bon soir, Sara." She hugged the little girl, a pretty child with her black hair in a long plait who hurried on to hang on Hannah's arm, prattling in French.

"Maman says please to come in at once, out of the cold," Aaron went on. "I have to close the shutters because Papa is away."

Miriam explained that she had two friends with her. In no time the horses had been turned loose in a meadow and the travellers were warmly welcomed into the kitchen that formed the greater part of the cottage. From the low ceiling hung strings of onions, garlic, and dried peppers, and a pot bubbling over a blazing fire filled the room with savoury aromas. Esther Abravanel, a wiry, grey-haired woman, begged her guests to take a seat on the benches at the long, scrubbed-pine table.

Felix and Isaac looked around with somewhat uneasy interest. Miriam realized that neither had ever visited a peasant home before. A week ago she would have quailed at the prospect of exposing the Abravanels to their contempt. Now, though they were once more at odds with each other, she trusted both to conduct themselves with gentlemanly courtesy.

Esther sent Sara and her still smaller sister out to chase the chickens into their coop for the night. The oldest girl, in her mid-teens, was stirring the pot hanging over the fire. Her cheeks were pink, whether from the flames or from bashfulness, and she kept stealing peeks at the two handsome gentlemen. At one corner of the table Simeon, a lanky boy a year or two older than Aaron, was studying an ancient, well-thumbed Hebrew text, by the light of the only candle. Isaac, sitting beside him, was soon involved in clarifying some obscure phrase.

Miriam and Esther exchanged news. After shedding a few tears for Amos Bloom, Esther explained her husband's absence. Isidore Abravanel had taken a mule-train laden with the entire village's winter produc-

tion of sheepskins down to the tanner in
Pau. With the proceeds he would purchase
such staples as flour and salt, and if his
bargaining was successful perhaps some
sugar and coffee. He was expected back in
three or four days.

Felix looked aghast at the idea of coffee
and sugar as dispensable luxuries, Miriam
noted with amusement.

She had just begun to disclose that she
and her companions were on their way into
Spain when emissaries from the other two
Jewish households arrived. The young wife,
baby on her hip, and the old widow at once
offered the hospitality of their cottages.
Isaac and Felix gratefully accepted.

However, Esther insisted that they must
stay to supper. Soon a stewed chicken arrived from one neighbour and three loaves
of coarse brown bread from the other, to go
with the thick vegetable soup cooking over
the fire.

"Will they go hungry?" Felix asked Miriam in a low voice, in English. "I'd rather
do without . . ."

"You cannot refuse what is offered without
insulting them."

Isaac had overheard. "Hospitality is a
religious duty," he said, "but there is no
duty to deprive oneself or one's family. You

can eat with a clear conscience."

"And you must eat well, to show you appreciate the food," Miriam added.

"Good. I am still making up for two days of starvation."

Isaac seemed surprised and approving of Felix's concern, while the idea of hospitality being a religious duty appeared to intrigue Felix. Miriam hoped that the breach she had inadvertently caused was beginning to heal.

Isaac was invited to say the blessings at supper, but he gracefully deferred to Simeon, to the lad's grave pleasure. Felix pleased Esther and her eldest daughter, Rachel, with his compliments on the soup, especially when he returned for a second helping. Aaron wanted to know about the horses; Sara and little Naomi, round-cheeked and curly-haired, chattered about the doll Papa had promised to bring from Pau.

After a few minutes, the children started addressing the men as Uncle Isaac and Uncle Felix. Amid the cheerful family atmosphere, Miriam felt her heavy heart begin to lighten.

To sit up late, wasting candles and firewood, was unthinkable. As soon as the meal was over, Hannah and Rachel washed the earthenware dishes while Aaron and Simeon escorted Isaac and Felix to their respective lodgings. Returning, the brothers spread straw pallets on the kitchen floor, for Miriam and Hannah were to share their bed in the tiny chamber above.

The boys regarded it as a great treat. Sara and Naomi had to be forcibly restrained from joining them.

After retiring so early, Miriam found it no hardship to rise at dawn with the rest of the household. She had breakfasted and was affixing a piece of court plaster to a sore finger presented for her inspection by Naomi, when Felix and Isaac arrived together.

Naomi slipped down from Miriam's lap and went to show her plaster to the gentlemen. Then, after a moment's contemplation, she climbed onto Isaac's lap and settled there. Though he looked a trifle disconcerted, Isaac's arm went round her automatically. With perfect trust, she leaned back against his chest. Miriam decided he would make an admirable father.

Felix got down to business. "We have both asked our families about the pass, and no one knows how many guards there are, or if there is snow on the ground."

"They never go in that direction," Miriam said, "as Jews are not welcome in Spain."

"So I understand. However, they also said that the village Basques, though they often cross the border, use sheep and mule paths through the mountains so they also are unlikely to know. Isaac and I are agreed that we shall reconnoitre this morning."

She swallowed her protest. Reconnoitring was a waste of time, but they were trying to protect her and she would give them that satisfaction. If they decided the guard post presented threat enough to want to leave her and Hannah behind, then she could summon up the arguments to change their minds.

"Very well." She hid a smile when they both looked surprised and relieved at her easy acquiescence. "I shall go and ask Joshua Cresques whether he has any patients he'd like me to examine."

"Cresques?" Felix was astonished now. "My host last night? But he is a carpenter."

"And bonesetter, and the nearest thing to a doctor this side of the apothecary in Laruns. Uncle Amos taught him as much as he could when we stayed here before, but I may be able to help."

Felix and Isaac strode off up the track leading south to the pass. Miriam spent a busy morning, for in the way of small villages news of her arrival spread and several people came to consult the late Dr. Bloom's assistant. She invited Joshua Cresques to join her and Hannah in dispensing advice and what few medicines she had with her.

She was too busy to notice the passage of time until they had to clear the table so that Sara and Naomi could set it for the noon meal. Then she realized that the men had been gone for over five hours. The border was no more than two or three miles away.

Leaving Hannah to finish clearing up, she went out and gazed up the road. Though she had to shade her eyes against the sun, a few hundred feet away a mist was creeping across the track.

"How long has it been misty?" she asked Simeon, who was digging in the vegetable garden.

He joined her. "Not long. Sometimes it blows down very fast. If you like, I'll walk up that way and call to them."

"Will you? Thank you."

He set off and she went back into the house, worried.

Not five minutes later, she heard him calling breathlessly, "Aunt Miriam! Aunt Miriam!"

She went to the door. He bounded down the track towards her, his face a mixture of horror and excitement.

"What is it? What has happened?"

"They're coming. Uncle Isaac is carrying Uncle Felix, and Uncle Felix is all bloody!"

Isaac staggered out of the mist.

CHAPTER 19

"He's dislocated his right shoulder." Miriam was amazed at how steady her voice was. She looked over at Isaac, slumped white-faced and exhausted by the fire, a mug of hot soup cradled in his hands. "There would have been much more damage if you had not thought to bind his arm to his side."

"But then I had nothing to bind his head." She turned back to Felix. They had laid his unconscious body on a pile of quilts on the kitchen table. If Isaac's face was white, his was grey, now that Hannah had cleaned off the blood.

"The head wound is not serious, they always bleed a great deal. But he has concussion. Has he come round at all since he fell?"

"I don't think so. He was a dead weight all the way down."

"I cannot imagine how you managed to

carry him, but that is probably a good sign. Uncle Amos said the worst cases seem to be those where the patient rouses and then loses consciousness again. Joshua, you had best try to reduce the dislocation before he wakes."

His calloused thumb remarkably gentle, the sturdy carpenter pulled back one of Felix's eyelids. "He's out good and proper," he grunted, "but be ready to hold him down. It's a painful business."

Miriam knew it, and also that the manipulation was bound to further injure torn and bruised tissue, but it had to be done.

"God willing, the poor lad won't feel it," said Hannah. "May God grant him health."

Felix did not stir while Joshua forced his arm back into its socket. Miriam and Hannah annointed with arnica and witch hazel the frightful swelling and bruising of his shoulder and the many other bruises and scrapes he had sustained in his slide down a scree slope. Then Isaac and Joshua carried him up the narrow stairs, his arm immobilized, his head bandaged, and put him to bed in the boys' tiny chamber.

When the men came down to the kitchen Hannah went up to sit with Felix. Joshua trudged off home to tell the Abravanels their kitchen was once more their own. Isaac took

Miriam's hands in his.

"Will he recover?"

"I cannot like it that he has been so long insensible, but all I can do is keep him still and warm. I hate it when there is nothing to be done but wait. And his arm . . . I'm afraid . . . Sometimes the shoulder never heals fully, never regains its strength, and Felix is so. . . ." The words caught in her throat.

Isaac enfolded her in his arms. She leaned her head against his chest and took comfort from his quiet strength.

They heard the children's voices outside and stepped apart. For a moment Miriam felt chilled and bereft. Then Sara appeared in the doorway and asked, wide-eyed, "Is Uncle Felix dead?"

"No, silly." Aaron arrived behind her and gave her a push. "Uncle Joshua would have told us."

"Hush, children." Esther came in and embraced Miriam. "How is the poor young man? My dear, remember that my house is your house."

Miriam hugged her. "I fear we shall need to take advantage of your kindness. I must go up and see that he is as comfortable as possible."

She had scarcely set foot on the bottom

stair when Hannah called.

"Miss Miriam, he's waking up."

She reached the bedside as he opened his eyes, hazy and unfocussed. He attempted to change his position and a groan rose to his lips. Miriam leaned over the bed and laid one gentle but firm hand on his left shoulder.

"Keep still, Felix. You are hurt."

A travesty of a grin twisted his mouth. "I guessed as much," he mumbled. "What happened?"

"You fell on the mountain. Isaac carried you back to the village. You have a dislocated shoulder and concussion, and I dare not give you enough laudanum to make you sleep, though you can have a few drops to dull the pain."

"Not yet. Must discuss . . . Where is Isaac?"

"Tomorrow will be time enough for discussions."

"Today. Wellington's gold. . . ." He closed his eyes, a tiny wrinkle of pain between his fair brows, but when she began to move he gripped her hand. "Today."

"Hannah, ask Isaac to come up, please."

Meeting Isaac at the door, she said in a low voice, "He will not rest easy until we have made plans. Do not argue with him now, I beg of you."

He nodded, frowning, and stepped forward to stand by the bed. Felix opened his eyes, clearer now.

"I'm sick as a dog, old fellow. You'll have to go on without me. Good people here . . . take care of me."

"I fear you are right, we cannot afford to waste any more time. We ought to leave tomorrow. You will be safe here until we return."

"Never thought . . . trust you with all that gold. Now . . . trust you with my life." He raised his left hand and Isaac grasped it. "No good way to say thank you, is there?"

"We'll take it as said. You must rest now."

Felix's arm dropped back onto the quilt and his eyes closed again, his face turning slightly green. "Gad, . . . feel devilish."

"Isaac, tell Hannah to bring the sal volatile and the laudanum," Miriam ordered. "Felix, are you going to cast up your accounts?"

"Don't think so. Touch and go for a moment."

"Well, for pity's sake don't be too bashful to give us warning."

He managed a crooked smile. "Never been called bashful before."

Like a docile child he swallowed his medicine. Hannah stayed with him, and

Miriam went down to talk to Isaac. There was one thing she had to make perfectly clear and she wasn't sure how he was going to take it. She didn't want an audience, so she suggested stepping outside for a breath of fresh air.

They stood side by side, leaning on a gate, watching the carriage horses grazing among a half dozen sheep and a long-eared mule. The sun was warm; above a belt of dark green pines on the far side of the meadow, the snow gleamed blinding white on the rampart of peaks ranging east and west into the distance. Overhead a vulture circled lazily, black against the pale blue sky.

Miriam laced her fingers together. She was not wearing gloves, and despite the sun her hands were cold. Or was the cold internal?

"Isaac, I cannot go with you. I must stay to nurse Felix."

He stiffened and for a moment was perfectly still. Then he said in a voice of calm deliberation, "Esther, Joshua, the others will look after him."

"He needs more expert care than they can give. If his shoulder is not treated correctly, it could develop permanent stiffness. Nor can I be sure as yet how serious the head injury is. I cannot leave him."

"But I. . . ."

"We shall find a Basque guide. You would have to have someone to help you drive in any case. Isaac, you are perfectly capable of reaching Pamplona on your own, even of finding General Wellington, wherever he may be. Felix was forced on you by the British Government; I was forced on you by Jakob Rothschild. You never really needed either of us."

"No!" The word could have been agreement, but it sounded more like a cry of despair.

Miriam continued quickly, before her voice broke. "Nathan Rothschild entrusted this mission to you, and it is vital to England. You must go on. I must stay."

The two French border guards, huddled in their stone hut atop the Col du Pourtalet, were quite satisfied with Petye Uriarte's tale, backed as it was by two bottles of Felix's cognac. It was none of their business if some mad Spanish grandee wanted to purchase a rather shabby berline in France and hire a couple of men to drive it home for him. They shrugged, raised the bottles in salute, and waved the driver on before hurrying back to the comparative comfort of their meagre fire.

Isaac had little leisure to contemplate the

success of his ploy. Whether he was driving or perched behind wielding the skid pan and safety chain, the road demanded all his attention. He was glad of the occupation — it kept his mind from Miriam.

The track zigzagged down the mountain, usually with a precipice on one side, sometimes on both sides, falling sheer to ravening torrents hundreds of feet below. In places the track itself turned into a stream; in others, rock falls necessitated terrifying detours. Fortunately Petye, though he had never before driven anything but a donkey cart, took to the reins like a scion of the English nobility.

A small, dark, round-faced Basque in his early twenties, who sang as he drove, he had been suggested as a guide by Aaron Abravanel.

"The grown-ups won't talk about it," the boy told Isaac, "but everyone knows Petye's a smuggler, and he wants to join the guerrilleros in Spain."

"Guerilleros?"

"They are bands of men fighting the emperor's army, not proper soldiers with uniforms just people who hate Bonaparte. He tries to make the Basques obey his laws when they have perfectly good laws of their own, like us Jews. Can I come with you too?"

Aaron, disappointed, was left behind, but Petye had eagerly agreed to guide Isaac to Pamplona. Though his native language was Basque, he claimed to speak Spanish almost as well as he did French. And when Isaac refused to explain why he insisted on taking an apparently empty carriage rather than a much faster mule, instead of asking awkward questions Petye slyly winked. Isaac was glad to have him.

They came down safely out of the high mountains, spent the second night at Sabiñánigo, and in the morning turned westward. Though the road was still bad enough to require the driver's concentration, the brakes were only needed occasionally. Isaac's thoughts flew back across the Pyrenees to the village of St.-Jean-d'Ossau.

Miriam believed in his competence; her faith in him was a flame that burned steadily in his heart. He clung to the memory of her slender figure beside him in the sunshine, the warm suppleness in his arms . . . no, he must not think of that. She had chosen to stay with Felix.

How would she have finished that sentence: "Felix is so. . . ."? So vigorous, so full of life? So handsome? So — virile?

278

The possibility tortured him. For all her unfeminine decisiveness, Miriam was utterly female, and women had their physical needs as much as men. Under Jewish law, a husband was expected to provide his wife with sexual gratification. He had never supposed that Miriam's response to his embrace, and to Felix's, meant that she was a shameless slut, but that she needed a husband. That was, after all, one reason why early marriage was a Jewish custom.

Her family had proposed an early marriage for her. She had rejected it — rejected him — out of hand. Did she now want Felix? He could not forget that she had torn herself angrily from his kisses whereas only his interruption had ended Felix's caress.

And now she had chosen to stay with Felix. She loved Felix.

Isaac wondered whether she realized how unlikely it was that the heir to an earldom should take for his bride the daughter of a Jewish Cit, however wealthy, even if he loved her. If he offered for her hand, his family would fight the marriage tooth and nail. Apart from other considerations, the Roworths blamed a Jew for their ruin, though Felix seemed to have overcome his prejudice to some extent.

To the extent that he would propose to

Miriam? And if he did not, and Isaac proposed, would she accept him despite loving Felix? Or would she once again reject him?

He shuddered at the thought.

By the time he and Petye reached Pamplona, Isaac had almost succeeded in convincing himself that as a rational person he could not possibly have fallen in love in a week.

They drove through the gate into the ancient city on the ninth of April, the first night of Passover. Petye wouldn't have cared if he had known, but Isaac regretted being unable to celebrate the festival. The best he could do was to avoid leavened bread when he treated Petye to a superb meal at the inn where they stopped. He had come to like and respect the cheerful, willing Basque.

Petye had family and friends in Pamplona but he agreed to stay with Isaac until he had made contact with Kalmann Rothschild. If Kalmann failed to turn up, Isaac hoped Petye's guerrillero contacts might help him smuggle the gold to Lord Wellington, always supposing they knew where Lord Wellington was to be found. One way or another he had to deliver the gold. Miriam expected no less.

Next day he walked to the cathedral square well before noon, anxiously scanning the faces of the passers-by though he knew he would recognize Kalmann from a distance.

The chimes of the cathedral clock rang out over the city, and there was the young Rothschild crossing the square, his high-crowned, narrow-brimmed silk hat conspicuous among the Basque berets. As he caught sight of Isaac striding towards him, his plump, face took on an expression of surprise and — embarrassment? However, he shook Isaac's hand heartily.

"You made good time," he said in Yiddish. "You had no trouble on the way?"

They strolled on through the town as Isaac gave a brief description of the various trials and tribulations of the journey. Kalmann seemed relieved when he learned that Felix and Miriam had been left behind. Isaac began to be puzzled.

"When did you arrive in Pamplona?" he asked. "Have you already made arrangements for transporting the gold from here onward? I assume it will have to be transferred from the berline to a mule train."

"The situation is somewhat complicated," Kalmann evaded.

"But we cannot drive the berline across the French lines!"

"No, no, the berline has served its purpose. To tell the truth, Jakob was far from sure that you would reach Pamplona."

Isaac halted, grasping Kalmann's arm. Something was definitely amiss. "What do you mean? You expected to lose the gold?"

Kalmann glanced around. A row of ancient houses faced the city walls across a narrow cobbled street. No one else was in sight, or in earshot. "The only gold in the berline is there to deceive the English lord," he revealed. "Most of the weight is lead. It is best if you do not tell the English lord. His government does not need to know our methods."

Staring at his bland face, Isaac felt his neck muscles tense in the effort not to shout. "You Rothschilds stole the gold?" he demanded through gritted teeth. "You used Miriam and me to keep Felix happy while you covered your tracks?"

"God forbid! Trust is our greatest asset; why would we steal from the British Government? No, Jakob took the gold from Nathan to banks in Paris and exchanged it for notes on banks in Barcelona and Zaragoza. I brought the notes to Spain and exchanged them for gold. Both cities resisted the French invaders and the people hate them, so it was not difficult to persuade even the suspicious to cooperate in transporting the gold to Pamplona."

"Then what . . . We were decoys." As the realization struck, Isaac began to shake with anger, his voice rising. "You intended the French to follow us, to arrest us even, to divert suspicion from what was really going on!"

"We had every expectation of being able to buy your freedom if you were caught."

"And in the meantime? That you should endanger Miriam for nothing, risk her being confined to prison — and worse — merely to distract attention from your trail!"

"Hush." The street was no longer empty. Kalmann jerked his head towards an interested old man and a pair of giggling girls who had stopped to watch the altercation. "We had best move on before someone wonders what language we are speaking."

He started walking and Isaac perforce fell in beside him. Fury seethed within him, remembering the lascivious army captain at Blois, the dungeons of Bordeaux, the cold, cruel eyes of the prefect. He had hated Miriam's involvement even when he thought it was in a good cause.

"I would not have sent a woman," Kalmann said. "Jakob hoped it would lessen the danger, both by making your travels appear more natural and because of Miss Jacobson's languages and experience. Was she not of assistance to you?"

Isaac's laugh was harsh. "As I told you, without her we'd still be imprisoned in Bordeaux. She saved our skins, at grave risk of her own! And that was not the only time. We'd not have gone far without her," he admitted grudgingly.

As if his admission closed the subject, Kalmann turned to business. He had discovered, roughly, Wellington's whereabouts, hired mules, and arranged for an escort of Basque guerrilleros. Assuming that the guerrilleros hated the French more than they loved gold, another fortnight or so should see the mission completed.

They rode out of Pamplona before dawn the next day. Travelling mostly by tortuous goat tracks, often invisible to anyone but their guide, they rode southwest through bare, bleak, stony mountains towards the Portuguese border. Sometimes they saw clouds of dust on the plateau far below, where the road from the French border carried troops to the French army headquarters at Salamanca. Sometimes they detoured around towns or fortresses held by the French. Always either Isaac or Kalmann was on guard at night, keeping watch over Wellington's gold.

During Isaac's brief hours of restless sleep, wrapped in a blanket on the hard, cold ground, he dreamed of Miriam — or of Miriam and Felix. Waking, he had to acknowledge it was just as well she was not on this leg of the journey. Once again his anger at Jakob for involving her flared.

One day a scout returned to announce that he had met with a band of Spanish guerrilleros. Wellington's army was encamped at the village of Fuentes de Oñoro, right on the Portuguese border, some fifteen miles west of the French stronghold at Ciudad Rodrigo. But *El Aguila,* the Eagle as the Spanish called Wellington, had ridden south to inspect General Beresford's army at Badajoz.

Masséna was expected to try at any moment to relieve the starving French garrison at Almeida, the last outpost on Portuguese ground. A battle was imminent and General Lord Wellington was elsewhere.

A battle! Kalmann decided discretion was the better part of valour: no sense risking the gold falling into French hands after bringing it all this way. Isaac argued that in the confusion after a battle handing over the gold to the British might prove difficult, dangerous, or impossible.

The matter was settled by the guerrilleros.

Honour demanded that they seize the chance to come to blows with the French. The mule train picked its way down from the Sierra de Gata and plodded towards Fuentes de Oñoro.

The sentry gaped when a rumpled, grimy, unshaven Englishman stepped forward to answer his challenge. He'd heard Nosey had just ridden in from Badajoz, a rumour that was confirmed as Isaac and his ruffianly crew were passed from hand to hand. At last a young lieutenant led Isaac and Kalmann across a boulder-strewn stream and into the hillside village, a tiered labyrinth of one-story stone cottages, walled vegetable patches, and narrow, twisting alleys.

"The Beau's quartered near the top," he said. "His lookout post is up there by those slabs of rock, near the church. He's a busy man so I hope you have something of importance to tell him."

"I am quite certain his lordship will be pleased to hear my news," Isaac assured him dryly.

Arthur Wellesley, Viscount Wellington of Talavera and Wellington, and Baron Douro of Welleslie, radiated energy. His light blue eyes, brown hair, and hooked nose were unremarkable but his presence filled the tiny room. He scanned the letters from the

Treasury and from Nathan Rothschild and tossed them on the battered table that served him as a desk.

"Mr. Cohen, Herr Rothschild, you have brought the gold? Splendid." He fired some rapid orders at his staff then turned back to the visitors and shook their hands. "You have my most sincere thanks, gentlemen. Ned here will see you get your receipts all right and tight. Now if you will excuse me, I have a battle to prepare for."

The two things Isaac wanted most in the world at that moment were a bath and a bed. Ned Pakenham, the general's adjutant and brother-in-law, found him both. He also provided receipts — three copies, for Jakob, Nathan, and the Treasury, — horses, and a guide.

Neither Isaac nor Kalmann had any desire to linger. The next morning they started back towards the Pyrenees. Towards Miriam — and Felix.

CHAPTER 20

As Miriam watched the berline climbing through a golden dawn towards the pass, she felt as if she were being torn in two. Felix needed her, Isaac didn't, but how she wished she had not been forced to choose between them.

The carriage disappeared around a bend. "Fare well," she whispered. No mere conventional phrase, it was a fervent prayer for Isaac's success and, above all, his safety and his return.

She went back into the house. Hannah had spent the night at the Cresques' and would soon arrive to take over in the sick room. Felix had slept, albeit restlessly with pain and laudanum fighting for supremacy. When Miriam had left him to see Isaac on his way, he had been showing signs of rousing. She was anxious to determine the extent of his concussion.

Esther and the children were at the table,

breakfasting on weak, milky coffee and bread with berry jam.

"Sit down and eat," Esther invited. "How goes Monsieur Felix this morning?"

"He was still sleeping when I came down. I must go and see if he is awake now. If it will not inconvenience you, please leave my breakfast on the table and I shall eat shortly."

"I'll put some coffee by the fire to keep hot," Rachel volunteered. "Monsieur Felix will need some too."

"I'll carry Uncle Felix's breakfast up the stairs," Aaron cried.

"Wait until he is awake," said his mother.

Miriam smiled at the eager boy. "I'll tell you when he's ready," she promised, and went up.

Felix turned his head on the pillow as she entered the little room under the eaves. His blue eyes were bright beneath the white bandage, though his face was still very pale under the tan he had acquired in the past week.

"Good morning."

She was relieved to note that his voice was crisp and clear, no longer slurred. "Good morning. How do you feel this morning?"

"Much better. My arm hurts like the very blazes, but I'm past that devilish feeling I'm about to shoot the cat. Has . . . has Isaac left?" He sounded diffident and apprehensive.

"A few minutes ago." Her brow wrinkled in puzzlement as he closed his eyes with a look of relief. "I would not let him wake you to say good-bye. Did you have something to say to him?"

"Not exactly, or rather, nothing helpful. I was not sure . . . I could not recall whether you really said yesterday that you were going to stay here or whether I had imagined it. I was afraid you'd leave me here . . . I'm sorry, Miriam. If I had been more careful this would never have happened and we'd all be on our way together."

She took the hand stretched pleadingly towards her and pressed it. "Hush, now, you did not injure yourself on purpose. It's . . . disappointing that we have to split up, but Isaac will get the gold to Wellington without us."

"Yes, he'll do the trick." He paused, visibly steeling himself. "My shoulder, tell me the truth, is it permanently damaged?"

"Oh dear, I had hoped to avoid that question for a while." Pulling a wry face, Miriam sat down on the side of the solid wooden bed, built by Joshua Cresques in his woodworking rôle. She kept Felix's hand in hers. "Though I cannot be sure as yet, there is a very good chance that it will heal completely. The chief reason I stayed is that I know how to help stop it stiffening. For the present it must be kept completely still, but in a few days we shall begin to exercise it gently. I warn you, it will hurt abominably."

"I shall do anything you tell me to." His gaze held hers. "Anything."

Heavy footsteps on the stairs. Miriam hastily stood up and smoothed her skirts, a futile effort since she had spent the night fully dressed. Joshua came in.

"Mam'selle Hannah sent me to give monsieur a hand," he announced. "She said as you're to go down and young Simeon will help if need be."

"You will be very careful not to move his shoulder?"

"I knows what I'm about, mam'selle. Off with you now. This here is man's work."

Blushing, Miriam fled.

Below, Hannah made her sit down and eat. The Abravanels were off about their chores, except for Simeon who was at his books awaiting a summons from above. Aaron kept dashing in to see if it was time to take Uncle Felix's breakfast upstairs.

Joshua came down without having needed

Simeon's assistance, to the boy's disappointment.

"I'll just go and see that Felix is comfortable," Miriam said, finishing her coffee, "and remind him to keep his arm still."

"That you won't, child. You look like you haven't slept in a month of Sundays. Off you go with m'sieur Joshua, for his wife's a-waiting on you with a nice warm bed. I'll make the lad as comfortable as may be, and I daresay I can control him just as well as you can."

Suddenly irresistibly sleepy, Miriam obeyed. Trudging to the next cottage at Joshua's side, she recalled with a smile a time not much more than a week since when Hannah shrank from presuming to sit down to dinner with his lordship.

When she returned, much refreshed, to the Abravanels' cottage in the middle of the afternoon, she found a hive of activity similar to that she had left at the Cresques'. Preparations for the Sabbath were underway, with cooking and cleaning and heating of water for bathing. After asking Esther if there was anything she could do to help, she escaped to Felix's room. The bustle below was audible, and Hannah was explaining it to Felix as she mended a frayed seam.

She put the sewing into Miriam's hands. "I promised to teach Rachel how to make those German honey-cakes your uncle used to like," she said, and departed.

"I'll be all right on my own," said Felix as Miriam sat down by the window, "if you have things to do elsewhere."

He was half-sitting, leaning back against a pile of pillows. Miriam was glad to see some colour in his cheeks.

"I must finish this seam if I don't want a scolding." She re-threaded the needle. "I hope Hannah was not boring you with her chatter."

"Not at all, it was interesting. She mentioned that your Passover festival is next week. Would it be possible for me to attend, do you think? Not if it's a private matter, of course, or secret."

"Secret! Oh no. It is a celebration of the escape from slavery in Egypt, and a reminder not to oppress others as we Jews were oppressed there. I'm sure you will be welcome at the seder, if you are well enough."

"I shall be. I mean to get up tomorrow."

"You will do nothing of the sort! No, really, Felix, if you will not lie still for at least another couple of days, I shall wash my hands of you."

"But it is so devilish tedious being confined to my bed," he complained.

Fortunately the tedium was relieved next day by the Abravanel children. Esther had with difficulty restrained them from visiting the fascinating stranger for a whole day, but on the Sabbath, with no chores to be done, it was impossible. Felix was delighted.

The first to arrive was Naomi, who had to show him her "writing". As he studied the squiggles, she climbed up onto the bed and settled beside him. "It says 'God send you good health,' " she explained, her chubby face serious.

"No, it doesn't." Sara had arrived. "You're just learning your letters."

"Well, that's what it means."

"The meaning is what matters," Felix assured her.

"I'll write some more for you. I'll write 'Shalom'."

"Anyway, you are not supposed to write on the Sabbath," said Sara virtuously. "Only to read."

"I can't read yet," Naomi pointed out.

Miriam began to feel the familiar irritation with the petty restrictions, though in deference to her hostess she would observe them. She would have liked to sew, or draw, but she sat with idle hands gazing out of the window. Somewhere beyond the mountains Isaac was driving towards Pamplona, his mission too urgent to let Sabbath observance delay him.

"Is it all right if I tell you a story?" Felix asked.

"Yes, please, Uncle Felix," the girls chorussed.

Felix's idiosyncratic version of Cinderella fascinated them, though Sara couldn't refrain from correcting his stumbling French occasionally. Miriam listened with amusement, until her thoughts wandered back to Isaac. He had not argued when she said she must stay with Felix, but his look of betrayal haunted her. She was very much afraid he saw it as another rejection. But Felix needed her!

He didn't appear to need her at the moment. His face animated, he described Cinders' glass slipper to children who had never worn anything but wooden sabots.

He seemed equally at home with the boys when they came up. He couldn't help them with their Hebrew studies, but he racked his brains to tell them about the Greek and Roman classics he had studied at school. They peppered him with questions. In the end, Miriam had to send them away when Felix began to look somewhat haggard.

"Time to rest," she said. Her arm supporting him, she removed several pillows and gently helped him to lie down. Despite her care, he caught his breath in pain. He did need her. "Do you want a drop of laudanum?"

"No, I believe I shall sleep if you will stay and talk to me for a while to distract me from this deuced shoulder of mine. Tell me about the Abravanels. Their poverty makes me ashamed of my complaints of penury, yet they are obviously well-educated. I had not thought French peasants so learned."

"As far as I know, these three families are the only literate people in the village, apart from the priest. Jews have always valued learning, if only as a means to studying their religion. Of course it helps in other ways too."

"In this out-of-the-way corner of the world?"

"Esther's husband earns his living buying and selling for the whole village because he can read and write. The Basque farmers reckon he's less likely to be cheated. After the sheep-shearing he'll be off to Tarbes to the wool merchants with the fleeces, and when they have cheeses to spare, he takes them to Roquefort."

"Is it Basque the Abravanels speak among

themselves? It sounds quite different from the Yiddish you and Hannah and Isaac speak."

"It's Ladino, the language of the Jews of Spain. It's very close to Spanish, with Hebrew influence. In fact, when I told Jakob Rothschild I speak Spanish I was fudging a trifle. I can get by in Ladino."

Felix laughed drowsily. "That's better than Isaac or I could do," he murmured. "I hope he's managing in Spain."

Miriam thought how lonely Isaac must be, able to communicate only with his youthful Basque guide, forced to rely on him for everything.

When she was sure Felix was asleep, she went out for a walk in meadows starred with wild flowers. She hardly saw them. Again and again her gaze was drawn to the snow-fields and rocky precipices that separated her from Isaac. Was he thinking of her? When would he return?

Isidore Abravanel returned home on Monday, a short, kindly man driving mules laden with purchases. On Tuesday evening, Felix escaped from his bed to join the Passover seder. Quietly respectful, he listened to the age-old four questions, asked by Naomi, and the answers explaining the meaning of the symbols, the prayers, the story of the Flight from Egypt. Miriam had never liked him better.

On Wednesday she started to exercise his shoulder. The strain left them both exhausted, Felix white-faced and more than ready to return to his bed.

"I don't know which is more difficult," he said with a shaky grin, "trying to keep the muscles relaxed while you torture me, or not screaming my head off."

"If it were not for the children, I'd say go ahead and scream." Her smile was not much steadier. "I hate doing this, but I'd hate it worse if I did not and you lost full use of your shoulder." She wiped his damp forehead with her herb-scented handkerchief.

He caught her hand and kissed it. "You are very good to me, Miriam."

Blushing, she hastily disclaimed. "It would be bird-witted not to use what medical knowledge I possess."

As Felix regained his strength he grew restless. He helped with chores as much as he could with one arm in a sling, and advised Isidore on the care of a sick mule. He played with the children, who adored him. He also flirted with Rachel, paying her extravagant compliments in his ever-improving French until she blushed and hid her face whenever he appeared.

Miriam saw that Esther was concerned and decided it was her duty to remonstrate with him.

"I wish you will not tease Rachel so," she said one day when the others were about their chores. "You put her quite out of countenance."

"It's all in fun," he protested. "I say nothing that I would not whisper in a pretty ear in a London ballroom. Just an amusing flirtation, nothing serious."

"But Rachel has never been in a London ballroom. She is not at all up to snuff, as you know very well. What is mere amusement to you is quite likely to hurt her, or at least to make her dissatisfied with the sort of youth who is likely to court her seriously."

He grinned. "What trust you have in my fatal charm."

"Fustian," she snorted. "It's mistrust of your dangerous wiles. Leave her alone, Felix."

"Your wish is my command."

Days passed. Miriam walked often in the woods and meadows, sometimes with Felix and the children, sometimes alone as Hannah was not much of a walker. Weeks passed. The shearing was finished; shepherds headed for the high pastures with their flocks, Isidore for Tarbes with the wool. More and more frequently Miriam's eyes turned to the mountains: where was Isaac?

She dreamed of him. Occasionally she was safe in his arms. More often she saw him lying broken at the foot of a cliff, or surrounded by grim-faced French soldiers, and she woke shivering with horror.

She knew Felix was worried about Isaac too, but they never discussed him though they talked for hours about every subject under the sun.

One golden-green afternoon in May, they returned from a walk with Sara and Naomi. The girls ran ahead to the cottage. Felix put his hand on Miriam's arm.

"Let's not go back just yet."

They strolled up the track towards the pass and stopped at a favourite spot where a boulder offered a seat with an endless panoramic view over the foothills. Miriam sat down. Felix stood, one foot on the rock beside her, gazing into the distance where enemy France faded into a blue haze.

He no longer wore a sling. Though he was still careful how he used his right arm, to all appearances he was once more the strong, vigorous, handsome gentleman who at first sight had embodied her schoolgirl dreams.

She flushed and turned her head as she realized she was staring, but he had not noticed.

"Miriam." His voice was slightly hoarse. He cleared his throat. "Miriam, will you marry me?"

Startled, she looked up at him. "M-marry you?" she stammered stupidly.

"Is it so unexpected?" His smile was wry. "I cannot believe you are unaware that I love you. I have little enough to offer you, to be sure: an empty title and empty coffers, someday a mortgaged estate. I cannot give you life of luxury, only my heart."

"What does money matter! My father is a wealthy man and I am his only child. But . . ."

"You are an heiress?" Felix was shocked. "I did not know! How could I guess?"

"You could not."

"You do not think me a fortune hunter?"

"Of course not." She gestured impatiently. "That does not matter. Rich or poor, I cannot marry you, Felix. It would never work."

He sat down beside her and took her hand. "Is it religion? You are too charitable to hold my ignorant prejudices against me. I have been learning to admire your people. You could bring up our children as Jews, even my heir. I should be proud to be the father of the first Jew in the House of Lords."

"Oh Felix, how generous, how noble you are." She felt a rush of love for him, though it crossed her mind that he knew far too little about Judaism to make a serious decision affecting his children's future. "But my dear, your family would never approve. I could not bear to cause a breach between you, and besides . . ."

Suddenly he was no longer listening, his attention turned to the road beyond her. She swung round. Down the slope plodded four tired horses, pulling a shabby black berline.

"Isaac!" Joy overflowing, she jumped up and ran towards the carriage. She wanted to hold him, to be sure he was real, alive, well. "Isaac!"

The berline stopped and he descended — slowly. He held out his hand and smiled — stiffly.

"Miriam, Felix, it's good to see you again. You look to be in prime twig, Felix."

"Nearly as good as new. And you, you reached Wellington safely?"

"I did. I'll tell you about it later. It's been a long journey, I'd best drive on down to the village." He turned and climbed back up to the box. The berline passed them and

302

continued down the hill.

When Felix took her hand, Miriam knew he had seen her joy, had watched it fade from her face.

". . . And besides," softly he finished her sentence, "your heart is not yours to give in exchange for mine. He's tired, Miriam, let him rest. But if you ever change your mind, I'll be waiting."

CHAPTER 21

Isaac was wearied to the bone. The flood of energy that lifted him at the sight of Miriam sitting by the roadside had drained away when he saw that Felix was holding her hand.

So they had reached an understanding during his long absence. Against great odds she had won the man she loved and he ought to be happy for her. If that was beyond him, at least he wished her happy. He had never intended to hurt her as he knew she was hurt by his stiff greeting. Her gladness at his return was unmistakable. Though he could never be her husband, she counted him a dear friend and it was up to him to play that unwanted part to the best of his ability.

But he was so tired. After riding swiftly back through the arid Spanish mountains, he had driven most of the way from Pamplona. While Kalmann had boundless energy and considerable endurance, he had not the sustained strength necessary to control a team of four horses over long distances. And now, sitting at the table in the Abravanels' kitchen, Kalmann insisted that they must leave St.-Jean-d'Arrau on the morrow.

"I am needed elsewhere," he said in his gutteral French, "and I must first arrange your passage from Bordeaux to England."

"Isaac needs a rest," said Miriam militantly.

"I can handle the ribbons," Felix put in. "My shoulder scarcely aches at all."

"Because you avoid using it! Do you want to undo all my good work?"

"I'll be careful. I'll take the easy parts." He grinned at Isaac. "That's the advantage of being a nonpareil teacher, you can leave the difficult bits to your nonpareil pupil."

"Even a nonpareil needs a rest," Miriam maintained.

With an effort, Isaac summoned up a smile. "A good night's sleep will put me to rights," he assured her, grateful that her concern embraced him as well as Felix.

And though he had not truly believed his own words, he did awake much refreshed. Nor did he find it as difficult as he expected to resume the old companionship with both Miriam and Felix, since they kept their warmer feelings for each other discreetly concealed.

The Abravanel children made no attempt to conceal their feelings. They didn't want Aunt Miriam and Uncle Felix to leave. Even Simeon's twelve-year-old dignity was sorely tried, and only Kalmann's impatience finally put an end to the little girls' hugs and kisses. At last the berline rumbled down the village street with Miriam hanging out of the window waving good-bye to the three hospitable households.

After Felix's first brief stint at the reins, Miriam made him start wearing a sling again when he was not driving. To her relief he admitted that using the skid pan to brake on steep hills was beyond his present abilities. As a result she saw little of Isaac as they retraced their route towards Bordeaux. However, during one of his brief rests inside the carriage he told her about his travels in Spain and his meeting with Lord Wellington.

"You mean that is all he said to you?" she asked indignantly. "After all your trouble and danger!"

"Sir Edward Pakenham said the general tends to be abrupt in his speech, and after all he was preparing for a battle."

"A battle! Thank heaven you didn't arrive

in the middle of it. I wonder what happened."

"At least his soldiers went into the fight with gold in their pockets."

"Thanks to you. It's odd to think that the berline is no longer laden with gold." She knocked on a side panel. It gave forth a hollow sound. "If we were arrested again, at least we'd not have to worry about that."

The look of anger that crossed Isaac's face startled her, but after a moment's hesitation he said only, "It is easier to drive without the extra weight."

She knew he was concealing something from her, though she could not imagine what. She did not venture to ask. His first coldness had not lasted long, but she was constantly conscious of a hint of wariness in his manner. Always kind and courteous and outwardly friendly, he was holding her at a distance.

It hurt, yet she could not blame him for it. Though she had only done what seemed to her necessary, in Isaac's eyes she had chosen to stay with Felix rather than to go with him.

Her only consolation was that Felix's shoulder was rapidly healing. She kept a solicitous watch to ensure that he did not overexert himself.

"Fussing like a mother hen," observed Hannah. Hannah had regretfully agreed that Miriam was right to refuse Felix, though she thought the better of him for asking. "Now, if it had been Mr. Isaac as offered . . ."

"I cannot even be sure that he cares for me. Sometimes I wonder whether I truly know him at all."

"Perhaps he doesn't know himself what he wants. All men are fools. But it's my belief he thinks you've fallen for his lordship."

"If he is willing to yield to Felix without trying, he does not love me," Miriam said unhappily. "There is nothing I can do."

At Langon they rejoined the main road to Bordeaux, with its memories of Hébert's sinister figure on their trail. Miriam suddenly began to wonder whether sailing from Bordeaux was such a good idea after all.

"We are known to the gendarmerie," she reminded Kalmann. "Both the prefect and his lieutenant have good reason to bear grudges against us. Could we not go to some other port?"

"The sooner you leave France the better," he grunted. "I shall not stay more than one night in Bordeaux, but my contacts there will give you shelter until they can smuggle you out. You won't have to stay at an inn."

She didn't argue. Though the quiet young man was so different from his lively brother Jakob, he gave the same impression of being an irresistible force. Nonetheless, she insisted on his driving into the city, after sunset, while the rest of them hid inside the carriage with the blinds down. Surely a black berline was common enough not to be recognized in the dusk.

Kalmann took them straight to the Ségals. Suzanne welcomed Miriam with open arms and inspected Isaac and Felix with undisguised curiosity.

"So these are the charming young men you told me of," she whispered slyly. "Which do you mean to have?"

"What makes you think I have a choice?"

"Chérie, it is plain to see they are both in love *à la folie.* But I shall not tease you now." She raised her voice. "You are all tired from travelling, *sans doute.* My husband will be home shortly. If you will be so good as to follow my servant, messieurs, your chambers are already prepared."

"You were expecting us?" Miriam asked, surprised.

"I did not know precisely who or when, but Ezra told me to expect guests."

"I remember now, Monsieur Ségal mentioned that he was acquainted with Kalmann Rothschild. I should have guessed Kalmann would bring us to you."

"I am delighted that he did."

"So am I," said Miriam fervently.

After that, she was not at all surprised when Ezra revealed that they were to be smuggled to England on a ship owned by the mayor of Bordeaux himself — along with a cargo of fine wine, naturally. Next day, after Kalmann's departure and when Suzanne was out visiting, Monsieur Lavardac came to make final arrangements over a glass of wine in the Ségals' elegant salon. His chasse-marée, he promised, could show a clean pair of heels to any ship of war or customs cutter.

"You've come at just the right moment," he said. "*L'Alouette* returned from a voyage a week ago. We shall load her tonight and she'll sail with the tide at midnight tomorrow night. By dawn you'll be well out into the Gironde estuary and ten days will see you set ashore on the Cornish coast. So Grignol was right about you after all!" He laughed heartily. "We'll drink a toast: to the Republic of France, and confusion to the Corsican usurper!"

Felix raised his glass. "To the vineyards of

France, and long may their products find their way to England, in defiance of tyrants and taxes!"

The mayor roared with laughter and clapped Felix on the back. "A man after my own heart," he exclaimed.

"Have you heard any recent news from Spain?" Felix asked. "Isaac, what was the name of the village where . . ."

Isaac frowned at him. ". . . Where I heard Wellington was encamped? Fuentes de Oñoro."

"That's the place. Your lord general beat Masséna, with the aid of a regiment of French émigrés, I've heard. The Chasseurs Britanniques, they're called. Masséna retreated to Ciudad Rodrigo, and then claimed victory because the garrison of Almeida blew up the fortifications and escaped."

Miriam looked at Isaac, but he seemed as unsure as she was whether the news was worthy of celebration.

Monsieur Lavardac left soon after, taking with him as much of their luggage as they could manage without overnight. He promised to send a carriage the following night to pick them up an hour before midnight and take them to the ship.

Ezra saw him out. As soon as they left the

room, Felix turned to Isaac and said with some indignation, "He knows who we are. I cannot see that it matters if he knows where you went."

"It is unfortunate that he had to be told we are English. The less information he has, the less he can disclose inadvertently, and I doubt this is the last time the Rothschilds will be sending gold to Wellington."

"I daresay you are in the right of it," Felix acknowledged. "And I daresay we ought to stay closeted in the house until tomorrow night. Deuced dull!"

He soon found a way to relieve the tedium. When Ezra went off to his bank and Suzanne returned from her unavoidable engagement, Felix embarked upon a flirtation with his hostess.

Compared to Rachel Abravanel, Suzanne was a sophisticated woman and a practiced coquette. Miriam found their sparring amusing, even instructive. Isaac, however, seemed uncomfortable. After a light luncheon, when they returned to the salon, he begged permission to investigate Ezra's library.

Though Miriam would have liked to go with him, she felt uneasy about leaving Felix and Suzanne alone together. Not that she thought anything would happen — after all Felix was a gentleman and Suzanne a married woman. But then, that was really the problem. Surely Felix ought not to address those rather warm compliments to a married woman, or indeed to any respectable female, especially as, just a few days since, he had claimed to be in love with Miriam.

She was beginning to be disturbed, almost embarrassed, when Suzanne was called out of the room to deal with some domestic emergency.

"Your friend is a charming lady," said Felix, in high good-humour. "I'm glad my French is now sufficient to entertain her."

"How can you flirt with her like that!" Miriam couldn't help reproaching him. "You are her husband's guest."

"It's all a game," he said with a careless gesture. "She's no peasant girl; she understands that it doesn't mean anything. After all, there can be no question of marriage. It is you I love and want to marry, Miriam."

His ardent look made her blush, but it did not change her distaste for his behaviour. Suzanne came back with a gay complaint about servants and Miriam made an excuse to go and join Isaac.

When she entered the small, book-lined study, he rose politely to his feet, one finger marking his place in the volume he was reading. After one glance at her face, he at once asked, "What is wrong, Miriam?"

"Nothing, really," she said uncertainly. He raised his eyebrows. "Oh, I daresay I am being over-nice. It is just that I cannot be quite comfortable with the way Felix flirts with Suzanne, though of course I know it means nothing, as he has explained."

"I am sure he is simply amusing himself to pass the time." Isaac hesitated. "Do not forget that he is a member of London Society, even if he does work for a living. I believe such games are commonplace in the Polite World, as they like to call themselves."

Miriam smiled. "Yes, you are right. I should have recalled the stories I heard at school. I suppose flirtation is a reasonable way to treat females if you consider females to be unreasonable creatures."

"As I do not. Did you come looking for something to read? Monsieur Ségal has a choice collection encompassing everything from religion and philosophy to poetry and novels."

"If you don't mind, tell me about what you are reading."

"As a matter of fact," he admitted sheepishly, "it is a novel I should hesitate to discuss with even the most reasonable of females."

She went off into peals of laughter. "I was quite certain it was some weighty philosophical tome. Show me where Ezra keeps his novels and I shall choose one for myself."

They settled in the comfortable leather chairs but, despite her mirth, Miriam found it most distracting to know that Isaac was reading a naughty French novel. She kept peeking across at him, only to find him peeking at her. In the end, she thought he was as relieved as she was when Suzanne came in.

"It is a beautiful afternoon. Come and walk in the garden. It is walled so you will be quite safe there."

Miriam had almost forgotten their dangerous situation. Just one more day and they would be aboard the *Alouette*, as safe as they could be until they set foot on English soil.

The next evening, shortly before eleven, the travelers gathered in the dimly lit entrance hall with the Ségals. In hushed voices they exchanged thanks and best wishes.

Suzanne embraced Miriam. "It is a difficult choice," she whispered, "but I believe Monsieur Cohen is the one for you."

"So do I," Miriam whispered back.

"Chérie, I wish you luck and bon voyage. But you have said nothing of my hair. You do not like it?"

"You dyed it? It is so natural I did not even notice." With an affectionate smile, Miriam kissed her good-bye.

Somewhere a clock began to strike. There was a tapping on the front door. Dousing the single candle, Ezra opened the door. A boy stood silhouetted against the lamp-lit cobbles, and behind him waited a small closed carriage with a pair of horses. The coachman on the box had his hat pulled low, his collar turned up — at night, even in May, a chill breeze blew off the estuary.

"Ready, monsieur?" whispered the boy.

A last flurry of good-byes and they set off through the dark, eerily silent streets. No one spoke, and even the wheels and the horses' hooves, muffled with rags, made little sound.

Miriam was surprised when, rather than heading for the docks, they soon left the town behind. Now and then a gibbous moon appeared between racing clouds to show a gleam of water on their right. They were driving north along the Garonne.

A mile or so beyond the town, the carriage stopped in the shelter of a clump of trees close to the river. The boy jumped

316

down from the box and opened the door.

"Get out now, *s'vous plaît, messieurs, 'dames,*" he said in a low voice, "and wait here. I got to make sure the boat's come."

Felix stepped out and helped Miriam and Hannah down. Isaac followed with their few bags. He closed the door behind him and immediately the carriage started off again. It was pitch dark under the trees, but Miriam made out the boy a dozen yards off, kneeling on the edge of the grassy bank, apparently speaking to someone below. She glanced back. The carriage had pulled out from the trees to turn, and as it turned the moon conspired with its own reflection in the river to cast a pale light on the driver's face.

"Hébert!"

In her shock she cried the name aloud. The driver whipped up his horses, thundered towards and past them, and disappeared into the night.

CHAPTER 22

"Come on, let's go." Isaac didn't pause to confirm that Miriam had seen the lieutenant. He grabbed their bags and they all dashed across the grass.

The boy had stood up and was staring after the carriage. *"Que diable a-t-il?"*

"Gendarme," said Isaac curtly. "Hurry."

A boat rocked gently on the water a few feet below the bank, with two men at the oars. Isaac picked up Miriam in an undignified flurry of skirts and lowered her into an oarsman's arms. Hannah squawked with alarm as he dispatched her after her mistress. The boy dropped the bags over then slid down the bank to join them, and Felix and Isaac followed suit. Seizing the boathook, the boy pushed off. The boat glided out from the bank.

The men bent to the oars and for a few minutes the only sounds were the rhythmic creak of the rowlocks and the lapping of ripples against the boat's sides. Then, somewhere in the darkness, a chain clanked.

"There actually is a ship out there," said Miriam softly, with a sigh of relief.

Isaac peered ahead. The moon shone hazily behind a thin veil of cloud at present but he saw a black shadow that might be a small vessel at anchor in the middle of the wide river. "Yes, I think I see it. The way the moonlight comes and goes, it's difficult be sure of anything."

"Impossible," Felix agreed. "Miriam, are you sure you recognized the lieutenant? You didn't imagine it?"

"The coachman looked just like Hébert." She sounded uncertain.

"Judging by the way the carriage departed, I'd guess he really was our dear friend," said Isaac. "I wonder how far off his friends are?"

"We'll hear them before we see them," Felix pointed out.

They fell silent, straining their ears. Clear across the water came the distant drumming of hooves. The boatmen heaved on the oars with renewed vigour.

"Sound carries," said one in a low voice. "Keep silent."

The hoofbeats drew nearer, then someone called an order and they stopped. At that moment the moon sailed out from behind her veil. In the boat, white faces turned towards the bank, where a confused mass of men and horses milled about. Shouts and shots rang out as the gendarmes spotted the fugitives. A bullet whined overhead.

And again they were plunged into pitch-darkness. Behind them gunfire crackled but the marksmen were shooting blind. Nothing came near them.

Isaac sensed rather than saw the ship as they approached, until a dark lantern was slung over the side, its single beam illuminating a dangling rope ladder. The boy caught a hawser with the boathook and pulled the boat in close to the grey-painted wooden side as the rowers shipped their oars. Isaac grasped the bottom of the ladder.

"You first, Hannah," said Miriam. "I shall be close behind."

"Oh, miss . . ." The lantern showed the maid's fearful face, but she bravely started upwards.

Isaac did his best to stop the ladder swinging as Miriam followed. From above came a murmur of voices and the steady clanking of chains. The *Alouette* was already weighing anchor.

Sporadic shots sounded, presumably aimed at the lantern's glow, but the ship was beyond their range. Grignol had arrived too late.

The boy swarmed up after Miriam, and then Felix steadied the ladder for Isaac. Isaac was near the top and reaching for the rail when a jerk told him Felix was coming after him. The heavy-laden ladder swung free. He glanced down and saw Felix's upturned face. Below him was nothing but swirling water, once more gleaming in fickle moonlight. Arm over arm along the looped hawsers, the boatmen were pulling the boat back along the side of the ship towards the stern.

Isaac looked up again. Miriam stood at the rail, smiling at him. Then she glanced down and her expression changed to horror. A sudden jerk on the ladder was followed by a splash.

"Felix!" came Miriam's anguished cry.

Felix floundered in the water, reaching desperately with one arm for the end of the ladder. Isaac half climbed, half slid back down. His feet on the lowest rung, he hung on with one hand and stretched the other toward his friend, his rival.

Too far. His arms taking his weight, he lowered himself with a gasp into the river's startlingly cold embrace. He hooked his left arm around the bottom rung, reached out with the right.

Hands met. The ladder swung wildly as he pulled Felix towards him against the drag of the river. The *Alouette* was under way. Isaac's muscles protested at the brutal usage, but Felix moved closer, closer, until at last they both grasped the ropes and clung there.

Before Isaac could call for help, a second ladder and a rope with a canvas sling snaked down. Two sailors followed. Isaac and Felix were hauled up and deposited on the deck, shivering and streaming with water.

"Your shoulder, Felix?" Miriam's voice was steady, but Isaac saw tears glinting on her cheeks and knew that Felix's flirtation with Suzanne had not altered her feelings for him. "I'll have to bind it again. But first, both of you go below at once and get out of those wet clothes! You are fortunate that the crew are expert at retrieving barrels from the water."

Felix grinned wryly. "My good fortune is that Isaac has developed a habit of rescuing me from the results of my folly. I should have known I couldn't make it up that ladder."

"So should I," she whispered.

"I don't suppose we was any of us thinking too clearly just then," said Hannah briskly. "But we've seen the last of the lieutenant and that nasty prefect. Now off with you and get dried off."

Isaac was turning to obey when Miriam laid her hand on his arm. For a dreadful moment he was afraid she was going to thank him for saving her beloved's life.

"You won't let Nathan Rothschild send you to Bordeaux again, will you?" she beseeched him, her eyes searching his face in the moonlight. "Hébert and Grignol will not forget."

Warmed by her concern, he nearly revealed then that their journey to Bordeaux and beyond had been a ruse. But he couldn't ask her not to tell Felix, as Kalmann had insisted. He put his hand over hers. "Nathan is no ogre. He will not expect me to go."

She nodded and gave him a little push towards the cabin boy, who was waiting to show the way below.

His and Felix's quarters proved to be not a cabin but a corner of the space between decks, screened off by sailcloth hangings and furnished with a pair of hammocks. The only cabin, the captain's, was reserved for the ladies. Thither, after binding Felix's arm, Miriam and Hannah retired. Isaac helped Felix into his hammock and climbed cautiously into his own. He scarcely had time to wonder at how comfortable it was before he fell asleep.

As Lavardac had promised, by morning they were far out in the Gironde, the banks a hazy line on each side. The *Alouette* darted down the estuary like the bird she was named for, not, as the captain explained, the soaring *alouette des champs,* the lark, but the sandpiper, the *alouette de mer.*

The captain, a barrel-shaped, black-bearded man, considered it a huge joke to have been shot at by Monsieur Grignol. He spoke English of a sort, his accent a curious mixture of French and Cornish so thick that Isaac found his French easier to understand. He welcomed his passengers on deck, but sent them below whenever another vessel approached.

Felix, pale after his ordeal and his arm once more in a sling, found the companionway difficult to ascend and descend. Though he made light of it, that afternoon when Miriam ordered him to his hammock, he made no protest.

Isaac helped him into the hammock and went up again to find that Hannah had also retired to her quarters. He and Miriam found a sheltered spot to sit looking out over the ruffled blue estuary, dotted with white sails. Herring gulls screamed overhead, timbers creaked, and every now and then a shouted order was followed by the rattle of pulleys and snap of canvas as the *Alouette* came around on a new tack.

"Can you conceive of anything more peaceful?" Miriam murmured with a sigh. "It's impossible to imagine storms and sea battles and shipwrecks."

"Don't try to imagine them," Isaac advised, laughing. "At least, not until we are put ashore."

She smiled at him, her brown eyes sparkling. The breeze played tantalizingly with wisps of glossy red hair. " 'Gather ye rosebuds while ye may,' " she quoted.

"Who said that?"

"Some poet we read at school. Our teacher was at pains to point out the deficiencies of such a philosophy."

"It has its attractions, though, on a day like this." Isaac decided to dismiss the future and enjoy the few uninterrupted hours he had with Miriam.

That night under cover of darkness, the *Alouette* slipped through the narrow opening of the Gironde, past the Cordouan lighthouse, and out into the Bay of Biscay. She skipped and frolicked across the rolling

Atlantic waves. When Isaac helped Felix out of his hammock in the morning, Felix stood quite still for a moment, turned green, and grabbed at the nearest bulkhead for support. Isaac grabbed the nearest container, an empty tankard, and handed it to Felix just in time.

At last Felix looked up, pallid and sweating. "I didn't think I had drunk so much brandy last night," he groaned.

"I don't believe it's a hangover. You are just seasick."

"Just! I'm dying!"

"You might feel better in your hammock. To some extent it counteracts the roll of the ship."

So Felix returned to his hammock, and admitted that he now merely wanted to die. Isaac soon found out that Hannah, too, was incapacitated. He and Miriam were unaffected.

In fact, he had never felt better. "Gather ye rosebuds while ye may," he told himself. Once they were back in London he might never see her again. A banker's courier was not likely to be a welcome guest in the home of the wealthy furrier, nor, if Felix's parents blessed his marriage, at the home of the Earl of Westwood. But Isaac had a week of her company ahead of him. Except for her visits to the sufferers, for whom she admitted she could do little, and the jovial captain's occasional intrusions, he had her to himself.

Ignoring twinges of guilt for profiting from Felix's illness, he took advantage of every minute. They talked endlessly, strolled around the deck, stood at the rail watching the rocky cliffs of Brittany slide past or the red-gold setting sun quench its fires in the limitless western seas. Together they marvelled at dolphins and flying fish, and fed the squawking gulls on scraps. And then she would worry over Felix's health, or go down to sit with him for a while, sometimes to coax him into eating dry biscuits to keep up his strength, sometimes just to cheer him, and Isaac would be devoured by jealousy.

That she fussed over Hannah, too, was no consolation. He knew her deep devotion to the faithful servant, so he was prepared to believe her equally devoted to Felix.

The days slipped away. Fair winds carried the *Alouette* around the tip of Brittany and sped her across the Channel. Then one afternoon the captain announced that as soon as it grew dark they would be blindfolded and transferred, along with his cargo, to an English lugger.

The news threw Miriam into a flutter of apprehension. Whatever happened, the longed-for return to her native land was going to change her life completely. One way or another she was bound to lose the freedom she was accustomed to. Would she also lose Isaac? She was more than ever certain that she loved him, but she still could not decipher his feelings.

How she regretted that night in Pau when she had responded to Felix's kiss and rejected Isaac's. If only he would kiss her again!

She threw herself into preparing her patients for the move. The last day or two they had both recovered enough to take a little exercise and food, but they were both sadly pulled. At least Felix's shoulder had benefited from the prolonged rest.

The transfer from ship to ship as a blind, helpless bundle was terrifying, but for once all went smoothly. The smugglers' slings and tackle worked as well for people as for barrels. Aboard the lugger they were left blindfolded and warned not to speak. Miriam gained the impression that they put in to shore somewhere to unload the barrels. At last the blindfolds were removed and the small ship sailed openly into Plymouth.

Shortly after daybreak the next morning, the travelers sat down to breakfast in the coffee room at the Drake's Arms.

"Dry land at last," Hannah sighed thankfully.

"Everyone speaking English at last," said Felix, laughing, "and not a whiff of garlic in the food. I'm famished."

"Home at last," Miriam murmured, but it did not feel like a homecoming. What did it matter where she was if Isaac didn't love her?

CHAPTER 23

Soon after arriving in London, Isaac and Felix walked through the City to St. Swithin's Lane and turned into New Court. Nathan Rothschild's clerks recognized Isaac. After a few minutes wait, they were ushered into Mr. Rothschild's private office.

"Good afternoon, gentlemen." Despite fourteen years in England, seven as a naturalized citizen, his accent was still that of the Frankfurt ghetto. A stocky man in his mid-thirties, beginning to bald, his full lips had a faintly amused expression belied by the piercing quality of his dark eyes. Isaac had seen him at the Royal Exchange, leaning against his favourite pillar near the Cornhill entrance, his face stony and his eyes blank. There, no one could guess his thoughts or intentions. Those who tried were often mistaken, and Nathan Rothschild had built a fortune on their mistakes.

Isaac gave him two copies of Wellington's

receipt, and a letter from his brother Kalmann, wrapped in the oilcloth that had preserved the papers from the waters of the Garonne. Nathan waved them to chairs, opened the package, and perused the contents.

"Very good," he grunted, and pushed one copy toward Felix. "Here is a receipt for the Treasury, my lord. Mr. Cohen will go with you to present it to ensure that all is in order, but first I must have a private word with him, if you will be so good as to wait."

Somewhat surprised at his summary dismissal, Felix stood up and took the receipt.

"We can go to the Treasury tomorrow if you prefer," Isaac suggested.

"No, I'll wait. Good day, Mr. Rothschild."

"Good day, my lord." As the door closed behind the outsider, Nathan leaned back in his chair and nodded at Isaac. "A good job, Cohen."

"Did you know we were to be used as decoys, sir?" His anger stirred anew.

"No, that was Jakob's notion, I gather, as was involving this Miss Jacobson. He is young yet. I am acquainted with Aaron Jacobson and I doubt he'll be pleased to hear his daughter was used so."

"Miss Jacobson will tell him of the journey, of course, but neither she nor Felix —

Lord Roworth — knows we were escorting a load of lead."

"Your discretion is admirable." Nathan stared consideringly at Isaac. "Kalmann says that he and Jakob expected to write off as expenses the gold used to disguise the lead. He suggests that, for your efforts in preserving it, you should receive half its value. I shall have an account opened in your name in the amount of three thousand pounds."

"Three thousand . . . !" He stiffened. "You do not need to buy my silence, sir."

"I am aware of that. Permit me to reward a capable and trusted employee. They are not so easy to find."

"Thank you, sir. I am not such a fool as to refuse," he said ruefully. An idea struck him. "Do you think . . . I don't suppose you would consider hiring Lord Roworth? I doubt he earns much at the Treasury and I know he dislikes his position. He's a good fellow."

Nathan's eyes narrowed and he tapped his lower lip thoughtfully. "Lord Roworth. Viscount, and heir to an earldom. His title and connections could prove useful to me, I daresay. Do you think he would be willing to work for a Jew?"

"I cannot say, but at least he won't be horrified at the notion as he would have been two months ago."

"Ach, so? You have changed his mind about us?"

"I believe so, sir, I and Miss Jacobson. He might even support Jewish emancipation when he takes his seat in the House of Lords."

"I shall offer him a position," said Nathan decisively. "Ask him to step back in."

So Isaac went out and sent Felix in. Tactfully he stayed in the outer office, presided over by Mr. Rothschild's chief clerk. Pacing about the room, he at once began to wonder what had possessed him to propose Felix as a Rothschild employee.

If he accepted Nathan's offer, would it make him more or less likely to wed Miriam? Isaac was not even sure whether he wanted Felix to wed Miriam, for the sake of her happiness, or to give in to family pressure and cry off, thus giving Isaac some hope of winning her.

With three thousand pounds in the bank, he no longer felt himself utterly ineligible. But nine years ago he had been wealthy and she had rejected him anyway. He suppressed a groan.

Felix came out a few minutes later, his step jaunty, his face jubilant. He shook

Isaac's hand and slapped him on the shoulder.

"I have you to thank for this, old fellow," he said.

"You have accepted?"

"At double the salary, how could I refuse? You know my family's situation. Let's go to the Treasury right away, get the business over and hand in my resignation."

They walked to Lombard Street and found a hackney to take them to Whitehall. Isaac lent no more than half an ear to his companion's wry remarks. As the somewhat smelly vehicle carried them down Cheapside and past St. Paul's, he came to the conclusion that Felix was not talking like a man about to tie the knot with an heiress.

"Are you going to marry Miriam?" he interrupted.

"What? Me? Given half a chance I'd marry her like a shot, but she won't have me."

"Won't have you?" Isaac's heart gave a cautious hop.

"I asked her in St.-Jean and she turned me down," said Felix simply. "I told her I'd be waiting if she changed her mind, but I don't have much hope."

The world whirled about his head. "Are you sure?"

"Believe me, when the woman you love turns you down you know it."

"Yes . . . yes, of course." The moment had come when he could no longer hide behind a painful memory. He ached to hold Miriam in his arms, to keep her at his side for ever, and to win all, he must risk all. He reached for the hackney's door handle. "I have to find the matchmaker, but I can't remember her name."

Felix grabbed his arm. "Getting out in the middle of Fleet Street won't help. Deuced if I can see what you want with a matchmaker, but if that's the way of it, I daresay it can wait till after we have been to Whitehall."

"Weiss, that's it! Mrs. Weiss. Somewhere in Whitechapel. My landlady might know how to get in touch."

"She's bound to, old fellow. Stands to reason. Landladies know everything," said Felix soothingly. "And if she doesn't, you can always just go and throw yourself at Miriam's feet."

Isaac laughed. "To be sure. I'd rather do the thing properly, but if it's impossible, I'll just go and throw myself at Miriam's feet."

Miriam allowed her parents several hours of unalloyed rejoicing over the return of their long-lost only child. She waited until they

met before dinner in the drawing room —
refurbished in the same shades of red — to
inform them that she had come to her
senses and intended to marry the man they
had found for her nine years ago.

"I have come to realize," she said de-
murely, "that you knew what was best for
me all along, Mama."

Seated beside her on the crimson-
brocaded love seat, her mother patted her
hand. "It would have saved a great deal of
heartache if you had come to your senses
sooner, my dear," she said. "However, better late than never. Of course, Isaac Cohen
is no longer eligible, but your father will
find someone equally suitable."

"Only the best for my dear girl." Mr. Jacobson, standing by the fireplace with his
hands linked behind his back, nodded and
beamed. His side-whiskers had greyed during Miriam's long absence, she noted with
a pang, and new lines in his face suggested
sadness. She feared she was responsible.

Impulsively she jumped up and ran to
embrace him. "Dearest Papa, you need not
go to any trouble to find me a husband.
Isaac Cohen will suit me very well."

"Out of the question," her mother said.
"If it was only a matter of his losing his
fortune — but he has taken some quite

menial employ and abandoned his Talmudic studies. Indeed, I have heard that he is become almost a free thinker! Your Papa wants a man of learning for you, Miriam."

She turned to face her mother, her arm about her father's waist. He put his arm around her shoulders and gave her a gentle squeeze. His love comforted her though she felt no need of his support.

"You mean a religious scholar, Mama, but you are not religious, so why should I be? Isaac is no less learned for having abandoned a strict interpretation of the law. I respect and admire his views and I want to marry him."

"And how do you know so much about Mr. Cohen's views, miss?"

Miriam smiled. "As yet I have told you little of how I found my way home. For the past two months I have been traveling with Mr. Cohen, and another gentleman. And Hannah, of course," she added as Mrs. Jacobson's face froze in an expression of horror.

"Ah, Hannah, bless her. She has been a faithful servant. Nonetheless, you must be married, and quickly. But not to Isaac Cohen."

"Then I shall run off with the other gentleman who traveled with us."

"Since you talk of running off, I assume he is equally ineligible."

"That is a matter of opinion. He is Felix, Viscount Roworth, heir to the Earl of Westwood."

Her mother gasped, and she felt her father take a sudden breath. "You have been moving in exalted company, my love," he said.

"He asked me to marry him, Papa." She looked up at him and he kissed her forehead.

"No!" said Mrs. Jacobson sharply. "Better a poor, nonobservant Jew than a wealthy, titled Goy. If you must have Isaac Cohen, then you shall have him. Has he, too, asked for your hand without consulting your father?"

Miriam turned her face to her father's shoulder. "No."

"Well, you need not fear he will spurn the match, penniless as he is."

She swung round and cried out, "Isaac has too much integrity to marry for money!" Then in a low voice she continued, "And I do not know whether he loves me."

Mr. Jacobson took charge. Hugging his daughter to him, he spoke over her shoulder to his wife: "My dear, you had best send for the matchmaker at once."

■ ■ ■ ■

"But I do so want to marry him!" Miriam gazed apprehensively at the gilt-framed mirror, where dark red ringlets were taking shape under Hannah's skillful hands. "And soon. After all, I'm seven and twenty — most people would say I am on the shelf. I want children."

"God willing, I'll be taking charge of your nursery yet, Miss Miriam."

"Oh Hannah, do you think he has really forgiven me? I could not bear it if he turned and walked out, or sent the matchmaker to say he has changed his mind."

"Hold still now, child. How can you think such a thing of Mr. Isaac? You know him better than that. He's not the sort to cry off after raising expectations."

"No, of course not. I do love him so."

"You should be thanking God for the chance to change your mind. There now." With a last twirl of the hairbrush, Hannah stepped back to admire her handiwork.

"Thank you, Hannah dear." Miriam stood up and smoothed the skirts of her new morning gown. Of moss-green cambric, it was plainly trimmed with a lighter green ribbon around the high waist, tied in a bow beneath her bosom, and rosettes of the same ribbon around the hem. She knew Isaac did not care about her fortune, but she wanted to avoid any appearance of trying to dazzle him with riches. Her mother had tried to dress her in the finest silks money could buy. Inevitably Miriam won, and now her elegant simplicity gave her confidence.

"And no need to carry a shawl to hide any worn spots," the abigail observed with satisfaction. "To think we spent nine years scrimping and saving! Just the jade earrings, now, and you'd best be off to show the mistress."

Miriam had deliberately chosen to wear the same delicately carved jade as on that long-ago day. Not that Isaac would recognize the earrings. She regarded them as a symbol of how much everything had changed, though outwardly the situation seemed so much the same.

As she crossed the hall to her mother's dressing room, she wondered what would have happened if she had accepted her parents' choice then. Would the naïve, expectant girl she had been ever have found happiness with the dedicated religious scholar? Had she wasted nine years, or saved herself from a life of regret and discontent? She could never know.

She knocked on her mother's door and entered. "I am ready, Mama."

Mrs. Jacobson, seated at her dressing table in a rose silk wrap, turned to inspect her daughter.

"Well enough. At least you have preserved your figure, my dear, and your face is unlined, only you are a trifle pale. You had best pinch your cheeks."

"No, Mama."

"Perhaps the tiniest dab of rouge — you are of an age where it may be considered permissible."

"My complexion is naturally pale, Mama, and Isaac is well aware of it. I will not paint for him."

"I hope you mean to behave with dignity, Miriam," said her mother sharply. "Your disgraceful behaviour last time is still talked of. There is no need for anyone to discover that you have been on intimate terms with Mr. Cohen in such improper circumstances."

Miriam shuddered at the possiblility her relatives might suppose that Isaac had been coerced to wed her. "I have no intention of telling anyone, you may be sure."

"I am relieved to hear it. The rest of the family will arrive shortly. I must dress."

Miriam went downstairs and wandered

into the library. Uncle Amos's battered box stood in a corner. Suddenly she missed him desperately, overwhelmed with longing for his support. What would Isaac say when they met again? What was she going to say to him, in front of parents, uncles, aunts, and cousins to whom the last such occasion was a never-to-be forgotten family scandal?

She went through into the hatefully red drawing room, crossed to one of the tall windows, and gazed out at the early roses blooming in the garden. If only she could meet Isaac out there, the two of them alone together.

Her father came in. Joining her by the window, he patted her shoulder. "Beautiful as your mother," he said awkwardly. "Isaac Cohen is a lucky young man."

"Oh Papa, I hope he thinks so."

He smiled at her. "Mind you, I don't say you are not lucky too, my love. I have talked to him this week, and to Rothschild also. Young Cohen is a fine fellow, with a future ahead of him in politics, we hope."

"I don't care what he does, Papa, as long as he is happy and he wants me to share his life."

"You need have no fear of that," he assured her.

Her nervousness began to abate, but it

turned to irritation when, a few minutes after her mother's arrival, the butler ushered in a dozen relatives. Her unmarried female cousins flocked about her, giggling and offering congratulations just like last time. Only this time they were all considerably younger than Miriam and their glances were not envious but sly. Their sparrowlike twittering almost drowned the butler's next announcement.

"Mrs. Weiss and Mr. Cohen."

The matchmaker's buttercup-yellow pelisse and the fruitbowl of lemons and oranges on her extraordinary bonnet eclipsed the man who entered behind her. As she started to speak, sounding excited but somewhat anxious, Isaac stepped to one side and looked at Miriam.

The uncertainty in his face was more than she could bear. She sped across the red Turkey carpet into his arms. He caught her to him and she flung her arms about his neck, raising her face to him with a little sigh of content. He kissed her with all the love and longing and passion so long pent up.

Her mother, her aunts, and all the cousins, not to mention the matchmaker, exclaimed in scandalized horror. Miriam did not hear a word.

We hope you have enjoyed this Large Print book. Other Thorndike, Wheeler, Kennebec, and Chivers Press Large Print books are available at your library or directly from the publishers.

For information about current and upcoming titles, please call or write, without obligation, to:

Publisher
Thorndike Press
295 Kennedy Memorial Drive
Waterville, ME 04901
Tel. (800) 223-1244

or visit our Web site at:

http://gale.cengage.com/thorndike

OR

Chivers Large Print
published by BBC Audiobooks Ltd
St James House, The Square
Lower Bristol Road
Bath BA2 3SB
England
Tel. +44(0) 800 136919
email: bbcaudiobooks@bbc.co.uk
www.bbcaudiobooks.co.uk

All our Large Print titles are designed for easy reading, and all our books are made to last.